SPANISH HEART

Praise for Rachel Spangler

Learning Curve

"Spangler's title, *Learning Curve*, refers to the growth both of these women make, as they deal with attraction and avoidance. They share a mutual lust, but can lust alone surpass their differences? The answer to that question is told with humor, adventure, and heat."
—*Just About Write*

"[Spangler's] potential shines through, particularly her ability to tap into the angst that accompanies any attempt to alter the perceptions of others…Your homework assignment, read on."—*Curve* magazine

Trails Merge

"The meeting of these two women produces sparks that could melt the snow on the mountain. They are drawn to each other, even as their pasts warn of future pain. The characters are beautifully drawn. Spangler has done her homework and she does a great job describing the day to day workings of a small ski resort. She tells her story with wonderful humor, and gives an accurate voice to each of her characters. Parker Riley's best friend Alexis is as true to the sophisticated 'City' girl as Campbell's father is to the country. *Trails Merge* is a great read that may have you driving to the nearest mountain resort."—*Just About Write*

"Sparks fly and denial runs deep in this excellent second novel by Spangler. The author's love of the subject shines through as skiing, family values and romance fill the pages of this heartwarming story. The setting is stunning, making this reviewer nostalgic for her childhood days spent skiing the bunny hills of Wisconsin."
—*Curve* magazine

The Long Way Home

"Well written and very thought out, *The Long Way Home* accurately paints the picture of a woman struggling to move beyond her past in order to look forward to her future. Spangler's characters are dynamic yet realistic, giving the reader a chance to see aspects of herself, her family, friends, colleagues, and community members within each persona. Their troubles, hopes, fears, and doubts are the same as the rest of us."—www.Cherrygrrl.com

"Rachel Spangler's third book, *The Long Way Home*, explores how we remake ourselves and the consequence of not being true to our real selves. In the case of Raine, her perceived notions of small-town life may have been tainted by being 17. The reality of what she finds when she returns as an adult surprises her and has her wondering if she'd been wrong about her home town, her parents, and her friends. Spangler's story will have you staying up very late as you near the end of the book."—*Lambda Literary Review*.

By the Author

Learning Curve

Trails Merge

The Long Way Home

LoveLife

Spanish Heart

Visit us at www.boldstrokesbooks.com

SPANISH HEART

by

Rachel Spangler

2012

ISBN 13: 978-1-60282-748-6

This Trade Paperback Original Is Published By
Bold Strokes Books, Inc.
P.O. Box 249
Valley Falls, NY 12185

First Edition: October 2012

CREDITS

Editors: Lynda Sandoval and Stacia Seaman
Production Design: Stacia Seaman
Cover Design by Sheri (graphicartist2020@hotmail.com)

Acknowledgments

At seventeen, I had the opportunity to spend two weeks traveling through Spain with my high school Spanish teacher, her daughter, and a few classmates. We'd been in Barcelona only a few hours before my teacher was hospitalized. We went on without her, which forced me out of my comfort zone and into a foreign country and culture. I learned more about myself in those two weeks than at almost any other time in my life. Spain opened my eyes to the stunning diversity of a world I'd only suspected existed, and her people offered me a beautiful model of openness and generosity that I still marvel at. Though I haven't been back in ten years, my experiences there so shaped my worldview that I feel as though I've carried a piece of Spain with me on every adventure I've taken since. While Ren and Lina's story is their own, it's my most sincere hope that through their journey you'll be able to share some of the love I still carry for Spain and her people.

I was inspired to write *Spanish Heart* at the 2009 Golden Crown Literary Society conference. I'll be forever grateful to the women of the organization who encouraged me to grow as a writer, but if I'd known the book wouldn't be published for over three years, I might have told them to write it themselves. This one put me through the wringer, emotionally and professionally, to the point that I almost trashed it. At one point, the only person who believed this story could become a great book was Lynda Sandoval. She almost single-handedly resurrected the characters, then breathed new life into both them and me. She was editor extraordinaire, therapist, and devoted friend all at once. I can't possibly thank her enough, but I know she's as proud of the final product as I am, and I hope that serves as a just reward for all her faith.

I've also had the help of a long line of beta readers throughout this process, and each one helped me inch closer to a story worthy of these characters. Toni Whitaker and Barb Dallinger got first crack and gave me invaluable questions to consider and gentle comments on tone. Will Banks told me bluntly that there was still work to do. Later, he said he liked it, which I took as high praise even though it made me wonder what he'd say about a book he didn't like. Finally, I handed it over to two women charged with keeping me honest about their homeland. Towanda Press and Maite De Tapia Escribano did an amazing job protecting the authenticity of Lina's voice. May the Lord bless them for their patience in deciphering my attempts to speak Spanish and their attention down to the finest details of dialect.

Speaking of attention to detail, everyone involved in the project worked extremely hard to balance one character who is fluent in Spanish and another who is just learning. Stacia Seaman took what felt like a full morning out of her busy schedule to chat with me about ways to manage an American speaking Spanish, and how to format and punctuate those bits of dialogue. Between two top-notch editors and two native speakers, the bits of Spanish throughout the story should accurately reflect the character's voices and circumstances. Any remaining slips are mine alone.

Sheri, my cover artist, somehow managed to look into my heart and create a picture of one moment that sums up so much of this story. I don't know how she did it, but I'm so thrilled she did.

My family is my foundation, from my grandparents who taught me how to travel, to my parents, who trusted me enough to let me travel to Spain without them (I hope none of them regret that after reading this book). Thank you to my son, who inspires me every day to keep growing. I hope to someday share the country I love with you, Jackie. And, Susie, thank you for always supporting my dreams, even when they involve three years of whining, second-guessing, and over-processing everything out loud. I think the only thing I didn't doubt during this process was that you'd stand by me come what may.

Lastly, thank you, dear reader, for opening your heart and your mind to these women I've poured so much of myself into over the last few years. They are yours now.

Solo Deo Gloria

For Susie—this one is your fault because through all the drama, you never let me just give up on it.

Day One

A rush of new sights, sounds, and smells overwhelmed my senses. My heart hammered in my chest, competing with the shrill hum of a pack of motor scooters rushing by the busy intersection in front of me. My lungs expanded to take in the Mediterranean air, thick with the smell of salt and fresh-cut flowers. A wash of vivid colors spilled from the vendors and down wide walkways, from street performers painted silver and gold to fruit stands displaying oranges, apples, and grapes. Around me, people spoke in a multitude of languages, Spanish, French, English, and some sounded like a mix of all three. Nothing about the first twenty years of my life prepared me for my first taste of Spain.

"This is Las Ramblas." Our tour guide, Lina, spoke above the noise. "It's a major street in Barcelona, and you can follow it all the way down to the Mediterranean Sea."

I stood rooted to the top step of the Metro station, too shocked to move yet. Earlier this morning, my friends and I had awakened in our sleepy little Midwestern town. Now we stood a continent away from everything familiar, at the heart of one of Europe's crown jewels. None of us had ever seen anything like this back home. Señora Wallace, our Spanish teacher and trip organizer, started walking, and we all followed her through the maze of open markets, past restaurants and art houses. She wasn't always easy to see amid the rush of bodies, weaving in and out of shops and restaurants. I'm not very tall but she was even smaller, and she had dark hair like most of the locals. Her only stand-out feature was her china-doll complexion and her rosy cheeks. Thankfully her twelve-year-old daughter, Hannah, was like her mini-me and never strayed from her side, so I knew if I could see one of them the other was probably nearby.

I tried to stay close to my group, but everything around me presented a possible distraction. The open stalls of a market offered exotic fruit, and new aromas wafted out of every open door. One place smelled like fish, another like cinnamon, yet another something altogether foreign. Music spilled into the streets from drummers and guitar players, their cases open to collect change.

I only stopped to tap my toe to the beat for a second, but that was long enough to lose sight of my classmates. Panic engulfed me as I scanned the faces of strangers. The rush of Spanish roared through my ears in a jumble of sounds I couldn't decipher. I'd been on this adventure for a matter of hours, but I'd already messed up. The uncertainty that pulsed through my brain was the antithesis of everything I'd hoped to find here. So much for coming to Spain to find myself, or to build confidence, or learn to trust my instincts. Amid all the strange new sights and sounds, I was flooded with the same sensation I'd been drowning in for years: I was lost.

Then as quickly as the fear spiked, it dissolved when my eyes met Lina's.

She stood a few feet away, watching me with a soft, genuine smile. I'd kind of expected a tour guide to be like an outdoorsy version of a librarian, not like a college student, but she looked young and not at all teacherish. She wasn't model good-looking, but cute, with long dark hair and hot-chocolate-colored eyes—

the girl-next-door type, if the girl next door were raised on the Mediterranean Sea.

"You like Spanish music?" she asked.

I shrugged. I'd never heard any before, but I liked it so far.

She stood beside me, her steady gaze unnerving, and I looked away to study our feet. She wore tennis shoes, which struck me as odd because sneakers didn't seem very European. Then again, what did I know about Europe? That morning everything had seemed so clear, but now I didn't even know what I was doing there.

"What brought you to Spain, Ren?"

"Huh?"

"We're going to travel together for the next ten days. What do you want to get out of your time here?"

I want to figure out who I am.

I want to stop feeling so inept all the time.

I want to get laid.

She smiled at me broadly, sparking a little twinge in the pit of my stomach. She seemed so calm and secure in this place and in herself. How could she understand what it felt like to be stranded with your life on hold while you floundered in nothingness? Surely I couldn't tell her what I really wanted. Or more accurately, what I didn't want. She'd think I was a loser if I said I didn't want to be confused anymore, that I didn't want my life to be on pause, but that I had no idea how to push play on my own existence. And what would she say if I told her the whole truth—that the only thing outstanding about me was my sexual orientation, but I was even a poor example of a lesbian, one destined to start college still a virgin?

I couldn't tell anybody why I really came to Spain, especially a stranger, so I said, "You know, culture and stuff."

She nodded. Her dark brown eyes stared into mine like she was searching for a real answer behind my defenses. It made me uncomfortable, like she might see the truth, so I turned back to the street musicians, trying to ignore the feel of her gaze.

"You should find plenty of 'culture and stuff' around here if you keep your eyes open."

She went on ahead of me. I followed closely this time while I thought about what she had said. My eyes were open. I glanced down every side street and into every store, but I still wasn't sure what I was watching for. I only hoped I'd know it when I saw it.

❖

We'd strolled to the end of Las Ramblas, exploring the little shops and merchant stands along the way. I caught up with my classmates Andi and Caroline as we walked. We'd known each other since kindergarten, and they'd both graduated with me first from high school, then from the local community college. Inseparable since childhood, they shared a lot of the same features and interests. Both were sandy-headed, brown-eyed, and giggly. They liked boys, shopping, boys, dancing, boys, celebrity gossip, and boys. Their biggest differences? Andi was a lot taller than Caroline, and Caroline had a boyfriend back home who she liked to talk about…a lot. I usually ended up feeling like a third wheel. It wasn't their fault. They always tried to include me, and they couldn't have been more awesome when I came out. If anything, my being gay seemed to make them like me more. I was the only lesbian they knew, which gave me some sort of a claim to fame. They thought I was a little exotic and a total rebel, which I liked, but it also put a lot of pressure on me to live up to those standards.

Caroline raised her eyebrows at me. "So what's with you and Lina, Jackass?"

"What?" I asked, not because she called me jackass. She's done that forever. I'm not sure why, but it's irreverent and goes along with my cocky image, so I don't complain. I'd rather them see me as reckless than clueless.

"I saw you two talking. Is she one of your people?"

I rolled my eyes, pretending to find her juvenile while wondering why I hadn't asked myself that question.

Was Lina gay? I glanced back at our tour guide, this time searching her for any hint of a community connection. Almost exactly my height, she had her dark hair pulled back in a ponytail that curled loosely at the end. She wore khaki shorts and a white, scooped-neck T-shirt, the light colors of her clothes setting off the olive tone of her skin. Nothing about her appearance screamed lesbian. I didn't want to stereotype, but quite frankly that's all I had to go on. My palms were sweating. I didn't have any idea how to tell if someone was a lesbian. When you live in a town with no lesbians, you don't get any practice finding them, another reminder of how much I had to learn in such a short time.

"Why would it matter if she was gay?" I asked defiantly. "It doesn't affect her ability as a tour guide."

"Chill," Caroline said. "I just wondered how you can tell."

"When it's important, you know. It's like a sixth sense," I said with as much confidence as I could muster, then silently added, *Or at least I hope that's how it works.*

❖

As we approached the end of the street, we all snapped pictures of the giant Christopher Columbus monument. The statue perched atop an ornate column several stories tall to overlook the harbor. Below it, four massive stone lions guarded the base of the tower.

"This is the spot where Columbus returned from his famous trip to the Americas," Señora said while we scrambled onto the huge lion sculptures around the base and posed for pictures. "If not for him, we might not be here right now."

I didn't even try to pay attention to her lecture or the logic behind it. I wasn't interested in academics now. Two years of classes at the community college hadn't given me any more direction than I'd graduated from high school with. I needed more practical life lessons. I'd actually wanted to spend the summer between community college and university backpacking through Europe, but my parents weren't ready to let their only kid go that quickly. They worried enough about my lack of direction, and couldn't handle anymore aimless wandering, so as a compromise, they'd offered to pay for a ten-day school-sponsored trip through Spain. I wasn't dumb enough to turn down a free trip to Europe, and to be completely honest, even I doubted my ability to go it alone, no matter how much I wanted to be self-sufficient. I resented the idea of a chaperone, but if I had to pick a favorite teacher, it'd be Señora, and she spoke the language in case I had any questions. Not that I had the courage to ask her how to say "dyke bar" in Spanish yet, but maybe I would eventually.

I lounged leisurely on the sculpture, enjoying the sea breeze rustling my shaggy brown hair until something caught my eye. My breath caught at the sight of a little patch of rainbow cloth flapping in and out of view. I stood on the back of my stone lion to see better and could just make out the swatch of cloth, several blocks away down a narrow side street, but it was certainly a rainbow flag. It was a miracle I'd spotted it. Maybe I wasn't as lost as I thought. Perhaps I did have some sort of gay sixth sense or a bit of the intuition I'd always hoped to develop.

I slid down the back of the lion, jumped off the monument, and walked toward the side street. I couldn't see the rainbow flag from where I stood, but it was there. The international symbol for gay and lesbians practically called to me. I was on the right track. If I could find other lesbians, I could get some of the experience and hopefully some of the self-confidence I was searching for.

"Ren," Caroline called.

Crap. I stopped, but I didn't turn around. I didn't want to acknowledge the other members of my group. They tied me to my past. I wanted to focus on the future. But when Caroline called again, the fear in her voice made me turn back. "Ren! Señora's hurt."

Hurt? That got my attention. I jogged over to the other side of the monument, where my group huddled around Señora Wallace. She was on the ground hunched over and clutching her stomach. "It's a sharp pain," she said to Lina. Hannah crouched awkwardly beside her mom, her face white. A mix of terror and compassion filled her young eyes.

My mind raced. A trickle of sweat ran down Señora's neck. The day was warm but certainly not hot. Maybe she had a fever. Maybe she had a bad cramp. Her normally rosy cheeks were pale, and her knuckles went white where she gripped her stomach. It didn't look like a cramp. Maybe she had the flu, but those things didn't usually come out of nowhere, and she said it was a sharp pain, not queasiness. This didn't make sense. Something was really wrong. Panic rose inside me again, fear for Señora, and for myself. Would she be okay and what would happen to our group if she wasn't?

"Everybody, get on the Metro." Lina pointed to a Metro sign across the street that read *Dressanes*. We hurried down the stairs to the platform, and Lina followed behind us, her arm wrapped around Señora's waist to support her.

Once the train lurched into movement, Lina left Señora's side and crouched in the aisle between me and Caroline. Andi sat with Hannah behind us. "I'm getting off with your teacher at the next stop."

"Can I come with you?" Hannah asked shakily.

"It'll be safer for everyone if you stay with the group," she said softly. "I need to focus on your mom." Hannah's expression mirrored the terror I felt, but she didn't argue. "I need you all to go back to the hotel without me. Do you remember the stop?"

"La Diagonal," I said. The others seemed surprised I produced the answer so quickly.

"And which way do you turn to get to the hotel?" Lina asked me directly this time.

"Right. Then four blocks to the hotel."

"Good." She stared into my eyes, as if assessing me, questioning my ability or my fortitude. I squared my shoulders and willed myself to face her unspoken question. I must've passed the test because she finally stood. "We might be gone awhile. Stay together and get some dinner back at the hotel."

I opened my mouth to argue, the image of the rainbow flag still flapping in my mind, but then Lina added, "Promise me you'll take care of Hannah while her mom is at the hospital."

What could I say? I may have been on a mission, but now I had an important role to play here too. "I promise."

"Thank you." She squeezed my hand briefly, her fingers soft and warm against mine. Then she wrapped her arm around Señora and helped her to the door. They hobbled up the stairs as the train pulled out again.

I stared out the window and tried not to notice the others watching me. I didn't want to see how scared they were, and I worried they'd see my fear too. I didn't want to be afraid or weak. I wanted to be the person Lina had asked me to be, the person they all trusted. I forced down the sinking feeling that I wasn't really that person, that I was an imposter, faking my confidence and knowledge.

Thankfully my bravado held up long enough to get to our stop; then in the clearest voice I could summon, I said, "Let's go."

❖

We all trudged back to the hotel in silence. I felt like I should've been more comforting to the others, but it was all I could do to keep my inner fears from consuming me. I'd gotten them all there safely, but it exhausted me physically and emotionally. We passed the hotel restaurant, but nothing looked appetizing, or maybe none of us had an appetite to begin with. I just wanted to crash.

Andi, Caroline, and I turned toward our room, but Hannah looked as lost as I felt. She seemed even smaller than she had earlier as she stood, shoulders slumped, in front of the door to her room. It took me a second to remember she was all alone. I wanted this day to be over so we could move on with our trip, but I couldn't abandon her. "I'll stay with Hannah tonight."

"Thanks." Hannah's hand shook as she opened the door. "I've never stayed in a hotel alone."

"No problem." I felt bad for her and for getting caught up in my own emotions. She had to be more upset than any of us. On top of being alone in a strange country with people she'd only known for a few hours, she had to worry if her mom was safe or seriously sick. That's a lot for anyone to handle, especially a kid.

"You want to watch TV?" I asked, hopeful for a distraction.

"It's all in Spanish," Hannah said, an unspoken "duh" punctuating her sentence.

"Oh yeah," I mumbled. "Better get ready for bed, then. I'm sure things will seem better in the morning." That logic sounded stupid even to me, but I didn't know what else to say. I wished again that I were smarter or stronger or just better all around. Instead I shuffled my feet awkwardly.

I checked in the small closet of the hotel room and found an extra pillow as Hannah came out of the bathroom. Clutching the end of the pillow in both hands, an idea flashed to mind, and I swung at Hannah's back. The pillow hit her with a light thump, and she squealed. I hit her again on her side. She laughed and ran across the room. Jumping on the bed, she grabbed her own pillow and swung wildly at me.

We chased each other around the room, pillows flying haphazardly as we went. Hannah laughed so hard tears ran down her cheeks, and I finally collapsed onto Señora's bed. Hannah landed one more blow with her pillow right in my gut, then fell exhausted onto her bed.

We both lay there on our backs, gasping for air, and let our laughter fade. I felt a bit of pride that I'd helped Hannah open up and have some fun. Who was I kidding? I needed some fun too, and she was young enough she probably wouldn't think less of me for it. I rolled over onto my side to tell her it was nice to just relax a little, but she was already asleep, her pillow still clutched loosely to her chest.

I smiled and covered her up with her blanket and then turned off all the lights, except for the bathroom one in case she woke up and forgot where she was. I didn't know how to handle a twelve-year-old. I wasn't the babysitting type, but I tried to think of what I would want someone to do for me.

With the room quiet and dark, I noticed the lights of Barcelona out the window. The city was much brighter than the nights in small-town Illinois and kind of pretty. The lights of restaurants and bars mixed with the moving taillights of cars heading downtown, maybe to Las Ramblas. Did any of those lights illuminate the rainbow flag I'd seen earlier? My heart beat faster, warring between my desire to do right by the people I cared about and the urge to race toward the future I'd come here searching for. I tramped down my insecurities for the time being, reminding myself that the flag and all it symbolized would still be there tomorrow. By then Señora would feel better, Hannah would be taken care of, and I'd get back to my mission. I'd waited my whole life for this trip. One more day wouldn't kill me.

DAY TWO

A soft knock filtered into my dreamless sleep. It took a minute to figure out where I was and what had woken me, but when I noticed Hannah asleep on the other bed, I remembered everything that'd happened the night before. I hadn't planned to fall asleep. I'd intended to stay up until Lina and Señora Wallace got back, but the pink sunlight shining through the curtains made it clear they'd been gone all night.

"Who is it?" I asked in a stage whisper.

"It's Lina." She pronounced her name *Lee-nah* with such a beautiful Spanish lilt that I would've opened the door even if I didn't know who she was.

I looked behind her for Señora Wallace. A sinking feeling settled into my stomach when she wasn't there. "Should I get the others?"

"In a minute. Let me talk to Hannah first."

I didn't know if I should stay. She didn't ask me to, but I wanted to know what was going on, so I leaned against the wall and tried to act casual.

Hannah sat up staring at us expectantly. "Where's my mom?"

"She's at the hospital, but she's going to be fine," Lina said gently.

"Then why is she still at the hospital?" The panic rose in Hannah's voice and tightened my chest.

"She needed to have her appendix removed," Lina said calmly in her soft Spanish accent, rolled the "r" on "removed."

"She had surgery?" Hannah asked.

"Yes, it couldn't be avoided. Her appendix could've burst." She put her hand on Hannah's shoulder. "She'll be okay. She did great, and the doctor said she'll have a full recovery."

"When will she get out of the hospital?" I didn't realize I'd asked the question aloud until they both glanced up like they'd forgotten I was there.

"She'll have to stay in the hospital for a while," Lina said, glancing from me to Hannah to gauge our reaction. "She'll join us in Málaga."

I quickly tried to recall our schedule. "The last day of the trip?"

"Yes," she answered. "She'll need lots of rest, but she'll be well cared for, and so will you."

Hannah started to cry, not sobbing, but quiet tears rolling down her cheeks. "I want to stay with my mom."

Lina turned to me, helplessness filling her soft brown eyes. I looked away as my own eyes brimmed with tears. I didn't know what to do or say. I didn't know how to help Hannah. I barely knew her, and I didn't know Lina at all. The only person I knew in the scenario was in a hospital room and would have to stay there for a week. My own fear mixed with sadness for Señora. She'd miss this trip she'd planned for us.

"I'll get Caroline and Andi," I mumbled and left the room. It was cowardly to run away, but what could I do? I couldn't even absorb all my own emotions, much less help Hannah sort through hers, and I didn't want her or Lina to see how overwhelmed I was.

I took several deep breaths before I opened the door to my own room. Both Caroline and Andi woke up when I came in. "What's wrong?" Caroline asked immediately. My facial expression must have given me away, and I made a mental reminder to try to appear less depressed, for the sake of my reputation and everyone else's mood.

"Señora had surgery to remove her appendix. She has to stay in the hospital for a week." The words spilled out bluntly. The terror on their faces told me I probably should've started with something more soothing like Lina did, so I added, "But she's okay."

Caroline began to cry. "What's going to happen to us?"

"Don't cry," I said, standing my ground. "Hannah's crying too."

"Of course she is," Andi said, hugging Caroline. "We're scared."

I was scared too. I honestly didn't know what would happen to us, which was why I avoided Caroline's question. I didn't know what our trip would entail now. Still, instead of letting my fear show, I got pissed. I don't do well with fear or sadness. I know it's not productive, but neither is wallowing. I work hard to stay in control or at least appear that way. I hate to feel weak, and when other people get scared or sad, I get defensive. "Well, crying about it won't make it any better."

"Geeze, Ren," Andi snapped. "Don't you care about Señora?"

"Of course I do, and I care about you guys, but we have to step up. If we fall apart, then who will help Hannah?"

"Where is Hannah?"

"She's with Lina."

Both girls ran down the hall, not even stopping to check their hair or change out of their pajamas. I followed behind them more slowly, not ready for the swells of emotion likely to follow.

Caroline and Andi both hugged Hannah, and then Lina hugged them. Hugs—I hadn't thought of that. I like hugs. I'm naturally a huggy person, but there's that control thing I mentioned earlier, and falling into an embrace with a kid or a stranger wasn't something I was ready to do, even if I wanted to. Besides, the whole lesbian thing complicated matters too. I don't ever come on to straight girls, but what if they misunderstood a friendly hug as an attempt to convert them or something? No, it was safer to keep my distance.

"Escuchad," Lina said, which means "listen." Señora Wallace says it to us all the time in class, and she must say it to Hannah at home because everyone gave her their full attention. "We'll be fine. Señora Wallace will get good care, and she'll meet us in Málaga to fly home with you all."

"We're going on the trip alone?"

"Claro que no," she answered. "Of course not. You won't be alone. I'm going with you. We'll help each other, and we're going to have the time of our lives. You can still do everything you originally planned to do in España."

That was the best news I'd heard in a long time. I was sorry for Señora, but glad the rest of our plans wouldn't be interrupted. If anything, now I'd have a real chance to gain some independence. I wasn't happy Señora was in the hospital, but I had to focus on the silver lining. If I let myself dwell on the fear and the sadness, I'd fall apart, and I refused to let that happen. If I had to fake confidence until I actually found some, then that's what I intended to do.

"Come on, you guys. Señora spent a long time getting us ready for this trip, and we can handle it," I said, perhaps a little too cheerfully, but the other girls nodded solemnly. "It'll be an adventure."

❖

Lina took Hannah to the hospital and told the rest of us to try to get a bit more sleep, but we were too keyed up to go back to bed. Caroline, Andi, and I went to get breakfast in the hotel restaurant. My friends seemed to want to stick close to me, probably because I was the only one in the group not on the verge of tears. I liked the way they followed my lead, even if I wasn't completely sure where to lead them.

"What will you have?" the waitress asked in English, but the menu was all in Spanish, and I hadn't had enough time to translate anything yet.

"Por favor, yo necesitas...necessito...huevos, con...um... toast-o."

"Toast-o?" the waitress asked in an exaggerated imitation of my American accent.

"No, um, bread, *pan* but cooked." I struggled to find the right word in Spanish before frustratingly turning to Caroline. "How do you say 'toast'?"

"Do you speak English?" the waitress asked.

"Of course I speak English," I said, causing Caroline and Andi to giggle.

"Good. It'll be easier for both of us if we stick to a language you actually know," she teased, and the girls laughed harder.

My face flushed. I hated being the butt of a joke, and I hated botching something as simple as "eggs." It's not even exotic. It didn't help that my friends, who'd looked at me as a leader earlier, now found me ridiculous. I was already on edge to begin with, and the exchange wrecked what was left of my credibility and confidence. Still the waitress waited for me to order something.

"I just want an omelet," I mumbled.

The girls continued to tease me by repeating "toast-o" and laughing like my mistake was the funniest thing they'd heard in days, which I guess given the circumstances it probably was. I tried to play it off and even said I was happy to give them a laugh, but I silently vowed to speak English or stick to Spanish I was sure about.

When our omelets finally arrived they were filled with potatoes, spices, and some other stuff I didn't even recognize.

I tried to pick it all out, but that didn't leave much. Between skipping dinner and my meager breakfast, I worried I'd starve if I didn't find a McDonald's soon. How much longer would I have to wait before something went right on this trip?

❖

We went back to the room to get ready for the day, since Lina had told us to meet her in the lobby at eleven. I needed only a few minutes to shower and change, but Caroline and Andi took forever. What takes other girls so long to make themselves presentable? I don't wear makeup, which I guess saves me time. My short, shaggy hair spills over my ears and across my forehead, so I can shake it dry or maybe scrunch in a handful of gel. The whole routine takes about two minutes. Throw on a little deodorant and a quick brush of my teeth, and I'm good to go.

I arrived in the lobby long before the meeting time, so I was surprised to see Lina already waiting. She smiled as I came out of the elevator, but she had dark shadows around her eyes. "*Hola*, Ren."

"Hi. Where's Hannah?"

"She's on the phone with her dad. I wanted to give her some privacy," she explained. "Thank you for staying with her last night."

"Sure, no problem."

"She told me you had a pillow fight."

I blushed. It sounded childish, and I didn't want her to think I was a kid. "I tried to make her feel better."

"I appreciate it, and I also appreciate you helping the other girls too. They obviously see you as a leader."

I shrugged, feigning nonchalance, but my stomach fluttered at the compliment. I did like for my friends to look up to me, but for some reason it pleased me even more for Lina to take notice.

"It's okay to be scared, though," she continued.

I stiffened slightly as my emotions rumbled toward the surface again. "There's nothing to be scared of. Señora will be fine."

"You're in a strange country, being led by someone you don't know. There's nothing wrong with being worried."

"We don't know each other, but trust me. I can take care of myself." My voice came out sounding harsher than I meant for it to.

Lina held my stare again like she had the day before on Las Ramblas, like she was searching for something more than what I wanted to say. I didn't like it even if her eyes were beautiful, so I turned away.

"Okay, Ren. I'll trust you, but I'm with you the whole trip. Maybe along the way you'll trust me too."

I didn't know what to say, so I didn't say anything. Thankfully the silence wasn't too long because Hannah arrived in the lobby followed by Caroline and Andi. As we headed out for our first full-day exploration of Barcelona, I wondered what Lina hoped I'd trust her with, and if I'd be able to live up to the trust she'd agreed to have in me.

❖

We all piled into a white minibus labeled *Costa Del Sol Tours*. It looked like an airport shuttle with a handful of bench seats upholstered in hideously bright stain-resistant cloth, a few luggage racks, and plenty of big windows to maximize our views. Lina introduced our bus driver, Jesús, who would be with us throughout the trip. He was a big man with a barrel chest, several days of stubble on his chin, and frizzy gray hair. He didn't speak much English, which is to say he didn't speak any English other than "Dixie Chicks," which was apparently his music of choice because it's what he played on the bus stereo all the way through the city. It was funny to hear country music as we wound our way through the heart of a bustling city and up into the mountains.

"We're going to the Barcelona Olympic Stadium, Estadi Olímpic de Montjuïc," Lina said, turning around in her seat and raising her voice slightly over the sound of "Cowboy Take Me Away." "You're too young to remember the 1992 Olympics, but they're still a point of pride for Spain."

When the bus pulled to a stop, we exited to a spectacular view. I could see for miles around in nearly every direction. The city below sprawled out under a sepia haze to the deep blue of the Mediterranean harbor filled with billowy white sails and massive steamships. We all pulled out our cameras to snap pictures while Lina continued her speech.

"The diving venue is still considered one of the best in the world because of the backdrop." She pointed out a few landmarks down in the city below. "There's La Sagrada Família. We'll go there tomorrow."

"Where's Las Ramblas?" I asked. It's not that I didn't appreciate the splendor of what lay in front of me, but now that we were moving on with the trip again, I was ready to move forward with my own plans too. The image of the rainbow flag was still imprinted on my memory, and when I set my mind on something, I have a hard time thinking about anything else.

She pointed down along the coast. *"Ahí está."*

I tried to see the spot she indicated, but the city was a jumble of streets and buildings with little distinction between them. I'd never seen anything so massive in all of my years of living in a small town. How would I find one rainbow flag in the midst of it all? I strained again to see the street that loomed so large the afternoon before.

"You can go back tonight if you enjoyed it," Lina said softly. "We all have our favorite spots."

I nodded. "Are we all going out together?"

"No, Hannah wants to go visit her mom, and Andi's going with us."

"What about Caroline?" I asked. Maybe I should go see Señora too, though that wasn't what I wanted.

"She can only have two visitors a night," she said. "We can set up a schedule and a room rotation so Hannah's never alone. I'll take turns with her too, of course, but she might be more comfortable if you each spent a night with her as well."

"Sure." I wasn't thrilled with the idea of babysitting every couple of nights. I couldn't cruise gay bars or pick up women with a kid tagging along, but I wanted to help out too. I'd just have to find a way to balance everything out in its own time, starting tonight.

"So I'm on my own tonight?"

"You don't have to be." Lina's tone sounded more like a question than a statement.

"No, that's fine," I clarified. Actually it was better than fine. An unsupervised night in a big city was exactly what I needed.

❖

We ate a picnic lunch under some shade trees outside the stadium and then headed back through the city to a big park. "Park Güell was created by Gaudí in 1900 and took three years to finish," Lina told us as we passed a gatehouse toward a massive set of stairs. "The mosaics are a trademark of Gaudí's, and if you look carefully you'll see them on many buildings throughout the city."

Once up the staircase I wandered aimlessly, examining the weird sculptures in little chips of tile. The place was surreal, like something out of a Tim Burton movie, but a lot more colorful. The art was pretty funky.

"Hey, Ren," Caroline called, "I bet your parents would love this place."

"No joke." Caroline and Andi had known me since we'd started kindergarten together. In a small town everyone goes to the same school, plays on the same sports teams, and takes the same dance classes. We all spent enough time at each other's houses while growing up that my parents weren't Dr. Molson or Mr. Molson but rather Mama and Papa Molson.

"Do your parents like Gaudí?" Lina asked.

"Probably. They're hippies. They like really trippy art."

"Hippies?" She smiled. "I don't know this word."

How do you explain a hippie? "They're from the '70s. They like tie-dye and leather and rock-and-roll."

"Rock music?" she asked.

"Yeah, and peace."

"Piece of what? Pie?"

"No, peace, as in no war." I held up two fingers in a peace sign.

Her face registered recognition as she exclaimed, "Woodstock!"

"Right, Woodstock was full of hippies." I smiled because she was cute with her face all brightened up and happy. She seemed young again, like she had yesterday before everything got crazy. I got that funny sensation in my stomach again, and I didn't know what it meant. It wasn't bad, but not great either, just tingly.

She stopped walking. "Your parents went to Woodstock?"

"No, they were way too young, but they go to protests and burn incense and harp on me about finding my path."

"Your path?" she asked, trailing her fingers along one of the mosaics.

"Yeah, any path will do really. I just need to pick one. Like, now."

She smiled sympathetically, then pointed to an offshoot in the brightly colored sidewalk. "How about that path?"

I shrugged as we started to walk again. "If only it were that easy."

❖

We wandered around the park for an eternity, or maybe only an hour, but my stomach growled, and all the hippie sculptures gave me a headache. I was hot, sweaty, tired, hungry, and cranky. I definitely needed a shower before I went back out, a nap wouldn't hurt either, and I had to find some real food. I wasn't sure exactly how I'd go about picking up a woman and making love all night long, but I probably shouldn't do it on an empty stomach.

Every minute we spent touring this Gaudí mess meant one less minute to spend on the search for my lesbian identity. I wasn't sure what time most gay places opened, or the best time to visit. On *The L Word* all the hooking up seemed to happen at night, but then again lesbians online and in magazines always complained about how *The L Word* is nothing like real life. Who knows, maybe lesbian dating worked like the farmers' market back home, and if I didn't get there early all the good stuff would be taken. The statues were nice, but not exactly what I'd come to Spain for. I had been patient long enough. I had to get back on track soon, or I'd lose my cool.

Finally, in an act of civil disobedience, I parked myself on the lowest step of the entrance. My parents told me about the sit-ins they went to in college, and since this was a hippie-ish place, now seemed as a good a time as any to try the concept for myself. I was done, and I intended to sit there in silent protest until the others acknowledged my demands and headed for the exit.

Caroline and Hannah joined me after a while, with Andi a few minutes behind them.

"My feet are killing me," Andi groaned.

"I miss Carl," Caroline said.

"I miss my mom," Hannah added.

I've got to find some lesbians, I thought, but that was inappropriate to say out loud.

Lina bounced down the stairs seeming as chipper as she'd been hours earlier. "Are you all falling asleep on me already?"

"Yes," we replied in unison.

"Pobrecitas," she cooed. I wasn't sure, but I thought she'd called us "poor babies." "Let's get you back to the hotel."

When we got on the bus and rode back into town, Lina sat with Hannah, giving me a chance to talk to Caroline.

"Hey, what do you want to do tonight?"

"I'll try to call Carl. If I can't get a hold of him, I'll write him a letter."

"So you don't want to go out?"

"No, sorry. I'm too tired."

"Do you mind if I go out, and maybe stay out for, like, all night?"

Her eyebrows shot up. "What are you going to do?"

"I found a gay place on Las Ramblas, and I want to go check it out." I tried to act cool, like it wasn't a big deal.

"What kind of gay place?" Andi asked.

"I'm not sure. I saw a rainbow flag."

"You're going to be gone all night because of a rainbow flag?" Caroline squeaked.

"Shh." I didn't need to broadcast my plans to Hannah and Lina. "I said *I might* be gone all night. It could be a bar or a dance club."

"Or it could be a gay men's bar or some pervert's apartment."

"Yeah, it might be, but if it is I won't be out all night," I said, frustrated. I didn't want to think about my destination as being anything other than perfect. I didn't need Andi and Caroline to babysit me, either. I needed to build confidence in my ability to find the right place and the right person. If I could do just one important thing right, surely things would start to get better, and their cutting me down only made me more determined to prove myself. "I want to go check it out. I promise I'll be careful."

"Fine." Caroline snickered. "I hope you don't end up spending the night with some big old drag queen."

I laughed. "Yeah, me too."

❖

I stepped out into the light of Las Ramblas, pleased with myself for remembering how to get there on the Metro. If the day before was busy, tonight the street felt absolutely alive. A mass of people wove in and out between jugglers and musicians as the traffic whizzed by noisily in the background. The sun hung low in the sky but wouldn't set for nearly another hour, which I found disconcerting since it was almost nine o'clock. Getting ready took longer than expected. I'd waited until Lina, Hannah, and Andi had left, but I'm not sure why. I was old enough to go out on my own, and I didn't need to explain myself to anyone, but I couldn't help feeling someone would try to stop me if they knew my real plans. This could be the night I'd waited for my whole life, and I wouldn't risk missing it.

Eager as I was to find the rainbow flag, another familiar sight caught my eye first: the golden arches of a McDonald's. Right across the street from where I stood near the entrance of Las Ramblas sat the answer to my food-based prayers. I paused only to let a pack of motor scooters zoom by, their high-pitched whines assaulting my ears. Once inside the restaurant, I had no trouble ordering in Spanish because all I said was *"número dos"* for a number two combo of a double cheeseburger and fries. I wanted to ask for no onions, but didn't know the word and didn't want to risk my good mood by repeating the ordering fiasco from breakfast. Besides, picking off onions wouldn't be such a high price to pay for American food.

I bit into my fries before even finding a table. The smell hit me first, immediately followed by the accompanying taste of fish. *What the hell?* Why did my fries taste like fish? I unwrapped the burger and hastily scraped off the unwanted onions before stuffing a big bite in my mouth. It tasted better than the fries, but still not totally what I expected. The meat tasted, I don't know, different. Maybe a little fishy, a little chewier, or just less greasy. Whatever it was, I didn't like it.

Why couldn't anything be easy on this trip? I didn't have much choice. My fishy Mickey D's was closer to American food than anything I'd found in this country. I wolfed it down, trying to ignore my disappointment so I could refocus on the elusive rainbow flag. The food served as a means to a much more important end, hopefully the end of my virginity.

Back out on Las Ramblas, the sun sank lower and would set by the time I walked to the Christopher Columbus statue. I didn't know exactly what I was searching for, but if it was a place to meet women, I should probably go there after dark. I wasn't sure how bars and dance clubs worked since I'd never been in one, but getting there too early might make me seem desperate. I forced myself to walk slowly.

Many of the flower shops and food markets had closed, but the restaurants were jumping with business. People filled patios, sipping wine and laughing over appetizers, some of which even smelled good. My stomach didn't feel great. I blamed the funky McDonald's and how quickly I'd eaten, but nervous excitement probably factored in as well. I was excited at the prospect of meeting other lesbians, but nervous because I wasn't sure what to do when I did. I hoped connecting with women like me would come easily and when the time arrived I'd know what to do.

I was born gay. It was in my blood, or my genes, or hardwired into my brain. My sexual orientation was the only thing I knew for sure. My attraction to women came as naturally as breathing, so I assumed sex with a woman would work the same way. I mean, no one taught me how to breathe, or told my heart how to beat. My body just knew. Maybe my body knew other things too. Everybody was good at something, but so far I'd yet to find anything that felt right to me except for being gay, so maybe that could be my something. I hoped to recognize a woman as the one and know exactly how I should act around her, because if those natural instincts didn't kick in soon, I'd be in trouble.

When I reached the statue, I turned in the direction I'd seen the flag, even though it wasn't visible now. The uneven cobblestone street was narrower than Las Ramblas, with high stone buildings on either side and lined with dark windows. Above them were balconies, some empty, others filled with groups of people eating, talking, and laughing. People walked along the street as well, though much fewer than on Las Ramblas. No one seemed to notice me, and no one appeared particularly gay. Not to stereotype, but there wasn't anyone sporty or androgynous or like a UPS driver. I'd heard of a sixth sense, gaydar, that helped gay people recognize each other, but I started to worry it was a myth, or even worse, that I didn't have it.

I felt like I walked miles, three blocks, then four, then five. I could no longer make out the distinctive sounds of Las Ramblas. The natural light dimmed, and even fewer people walked around than earlier. Had I gone too far? Had I missed the flag? Right, like I would absentmindedly pass the object I'd obsessed over for two days. Maybe it wasn't attached to a bar after all. What if someone had the flag on their apartment or business and took it in for the night? No, I wouldn't let myself consider failure.

I walked faster, finally hearing the low thump of bass and light laughter falling out into the night sky. That had to be my place and my people. I almost jogged around a bend in the street. When bright neon lights came into view, I skidded to a stop and stared.

Women of every age, shape, size, and race filled a patio strung with lights. They talked and laughed and drank. Some of them held hands. Others loosely draped their arms across one another's shoulders. A young woman with long, dark hair had her hands in the back pocket of another woman's jeans. Behind them an open door allowed music to drift into the street. As people came and went, they smiled and waved to each other. Above the patio, a quieter group of women occupied a balcony, some talking softly or dancing in each other's embrace. Over the whole place, one large rainbow flag floated silently on a gentle breeze.

My breath caught at the sight of the flag, like a welcome beacon telling me I'd arrived home safely. I felt an immediate connection to these women. They were like me, or more accurately, I wanted to be like them. I wanted to feel comfortable in my skin. I wanted to laugh easily and casually touch other women. I wanted to be secure and relaxed and at one with my community. I wanted to gaze into someone's eyes, feel the spark of attraction, and see it returned in her. My heart ached as I watched the women interact easily. I wanted to be that kind of lesbian.

My chest swelled with pride. I'd found this place, these women, all on my own. My instincts had carried me to exactly the right spot. I did something right, and I had the opportunity to seize all the experiences that could make me the person I dreamed of. Only, I didn't know what to do now. I couldn't walk up to some random woman and say, "Please teach me how to be a real lesbian." I may not know everything, but I knew that was pathetic.

Should I go into the bar and order a drink? The legal age in Spain was eighteen. I could drink if I wanted to, but I worried alcohol would make me more confused. Maybe I should go in and find a table to myself. If a woman noticed me alone, she might come on to me. Then again, sitting at a table alone staring at random girls might make me seem like a loser, and then no one would want to talk to me.

There might be a dance floor. Maybe I could ask a woman

to dance. *"Quieres bailar?"* I'd practiced the phrase over and over again in preparation for this moment, but which girl should I say it to? Should I ask one of the women out here, or should I find someone closer to the dance floor, and what should I do until I did? Sit down? Stand up? Walk around aimlessly, hoping to bump into someone?

Damn. I'd found exactly what I wanted, and I was still lost. I stepped back into the shadow of a balcony and watched the women at the bar. I wanted to fit in, but I didn't know how. I needed someone to teach me. How would I ever find that someone to teach me if I never found the courage to go in?

I breathed deeply and tried to calm down. *Chill out. You didn't come all this way to have a meltdown.* If I stayed outside and studied the interactions for a minute, I might learn a few things. I could wait and see how the women approached each other, maybe pick up a few pointers, or at least I could look for other single women. Aside from hiding in the shadows like a weird Peeping Tom, it wasn't a bad plan. I learned all kinds of things by watching other people. Why should this be any different? I was still in a better position than ever before.

I studied the women carefully. Some held hands or touched each other easily, clearly indicating they were taken. Others were harder to read. Some stood in groups, talking or laughing. Sometimes they hugged or brushed against each other. They might be friends, or dates, or maybe they were friends who wanted to date. Either way, they were occupied with someone else. I scanned the crowd more closely. There didn't seem to be anyone sitting alone or clearly searching for a partner. Maybe I should go inside, but I'd lose my cover. I'd be a lot more vulnerable out in the open, and I didn't want to feel vulnerable.

I decided to stay put a little longer. More people came and went the later it got. A group of women strolled up the street from the other direction. There were clearly some couples in the group and maybe a few of their friends, but behind them a woman walked alone. I couldn't make out her features clearly, but she didn't appear to be with the others. Her silhouette showed her fit physique, with a flat stomach and noticeable but not too big breasts. As she got closer, I saw she wore shorts and a dark shirt with her hair pulled back in a sporty ponytail. Then just when she came close enough for me to make out the details of her features, the group of women in front blocked my view.

I couldn't see the woman's face, only one tanned arm and one toned leg, from the cuff of her shorts down her smooth calf muscle to her painted peach toenails peeking out beneath the straps of her sandals. My heart beat faster. This was the girl for me, I could feel it just like I hoped I would. She felt familiar somehow. Even before I saw her face, I recognized her as the one I'd waited for. My instincts worked after all. My excitement overpowered my nervousness.

I moved forward out of the shadow to get a better view through the crowd, but as I did someone breezed past my shoulder, headed quickly toward the bar. I barely registered her presence until the woman called out, "Lina."

I froze, and the group of women parted to reveal my tour guide. Her eyes widened in recognition, and a big smile spread across her face as she focused on the woman coming toward her. The two of them met in the street, and Lina hugged her before kissing her on each cheek. She wrapped her arm around the other woman's waist, and they went inside the club. I stepped back into the shadows and rested my back against the wall.

So, Lina is gay. My brain went into overload trying to absorb that. So much for knowing a lesbian when I found one. Why hadn't she said something? How hypocritical to have lesbian clients and not come out to them. Of course…I hadn't told her I was gay. But I didn't hide it either. Surely she knew. I had been out to all my friends for years. Then again, maybe she was out to her friends too. She was my tour guide, not my friend. Still, she was supposed to watch us while Señora was in the hospital, not sneak out to meet women.

Now who's the hypocrite?

"Shit," I muttered and slapped my hands against the wall. What should I do now? I couldn't go in the club with Lina there. What would I say to her? Would she send me back to the hotel? She couldn't do that, though. She might not have been my friend, but she wasn't my mother, either. Maybe she'd tell Señora. That would be awkward, but I had just as much right to be there as she did. Then again, even if she didn't rat me out, how could I pick up women with a chaperone around? No one would want to take me home if they had to clear it with my babysitter first.

No.

My night was over.

❖

I trudged back toward Las Ramblas, my heart as heavy as my feet. I was so absorbed in my own depression I didn't even see Jesús until I ran into him. I bounced off his shoulder and would have fallen over if he hadn't caught my arm with one of his big calloused hands.

"Sorry," I muttered. "What are you doing here?"

He smiled and nodded.

"Oh did you drop Lina off?"

"Lina," he repeated with another nod, then pointed toward our bus parked at the end of an alleyway.

"Okay, well, good for you."

He cocked his fuzzy head to the side and then gestured toward the bus with his thumb.

A ride? I sighed. "Why not?"

We boarded the little bus and I flopped into the seat behind him as we started through the streets of Barcelona.

This sucked. Why did I have to go back to the hotel, alone,

while Lina and her friend, or girlfriend, or lover, or whoever stayed at the bar to do everything I wanted to do? My dreams, so close minutes earlier, now seemed completely out of reach.

"Shit," I said aloud, causing Jesús to glance at me in the review mirror. "Sorry. I've had a bad night, or a bad couple of nights really."

He nodded.

"It wasn't supposed to happen like this, you know. Nothing's going the way I thought it would, and I'm not just talking about tonight. Hell, it shouldn't have gotten to this point in the first place, you know? If I could've pulled myself together sooner, I wouldn't need this trip, I would've moved on two years ago like normal people do."

Jesús smiled and continued to nod sympathetically as he turned a corner, but gave no indication he understood anything I'd said. But, what the hell, I needed to vent, and he didn't know enough to judge me.

"It's okay, you don't have to understand. No one does. No one knows how it feels to be stuck in purgatory for two years while your friends go off on great adventures. Or what it's like to spend two years at a community college and still not know what you want to do with your life." I slouched lower in the bench seat, dejection weighing heavy on my shoulders. "I have one month to make a decision about a major, and two college professors for parents to lay on the pressure, but I still have no idea what I want to study."

Jesús continued to nod.

"Some parents want their kids to become doctors, or lawyers, but my parents aren't like that. They just want me to do something, *anything*. Hell, I'd rather they'd just tell me what to do. At least then I'd have something to go on, but no, I have to find my own passion."

I leaned back and rested my head on the window. "My passion. What does that even mean? The only thing that ever made me stand out is my gayness. I know, that's not exactly going to get me a career or a major, even, but seriously, that's all I've got."

Jesús turned a corner that looked suspiciously like one we'd passed earlier. Was he going in circles? Surely not. He knew the area better than I did.

"So I'm a lesbian, which makes me unique, at least where I'm from. It's supposed to give me an identity and a community, but it doesn't, because liking women and knowing what to do with them are two totally different things. Back home I can't even find gay women. Now I've traveled across half the globe to find this club, a place where I could finally become myself without worrying about looking like an ass, and I can't even go inside." I raked my hands through my hair and blew out an exasperated breath. "This is supposed to be the easy part. At least I know I'm gay, but if I can't handle something I'm sure I want, how will I ever succeed at school or finding a career when I'm genuinely unsure of myself?"

I looked out the window again as we passed a store I knew I'd seen a few minutes ago. Why were we going in circles? Was I imagining things, or was this ride home mirroring my life? Or did Jesús realize I needed more time to vent?

"How did I get so lost tonight, Jesús? I found a lesbian bar by myself. I stood mere steps from the world I wanted to be part of, with all the opportunity I've craved, but the only woman I felt attracted to all evening ruined my night."

The words shocked me, spilling out before I'd had a chance to process them. Was I really attracted to Lina? I didn't know she was Lina at the time, but I totally checked her out, and liked what I saw. I even felt excited about approaching her until I realized who she was. How weird that the first hot lesbian I met was a big, hot downer.

No, she wasn't the downer. I was, and that was the real problem. With my friends, I could still pretend to have it all together. I might know I was a fraud, but at least they didn't, and as long as I did my learning on my own, down side streets and in bars, I could get the experience I needed without anyone ever being the wiser. But if Lina got too close she'd see through me. She could expose all my failures and shortcomings just by comparison.

Leave it to my body to react to the only lesbian in all of Spain who could blow my cover. I shook my head, trying to somehow dislodge my mind from this vicious loop. Now not only was I stuck traveling through a foreign country without Señora and dragging a twelve-year-old kid behind me, I also had to hide from my cute lesbian tour guide in every city.

"Damn, Jesús, there's no justice in the world."

He only nodded.

DAY THREE

The next morning I stayed in bed after the alarm went off. Andi spent the night in Hannah's room, but Caroline got up and took a shower. I lay on my back and stared at the ceiling while I listened to the water run. I was too tired to move, but that didn't stop my mind from wandering. How would it be to see Lina today after seeing her at the bar last night? Would she seem different? I already felt different about her because yesterday I didn't feel much of anything. Now I felt a lot of everything. I was angry she'd ruined my evening, suspicious she hadn't come out to me, curious about what she could teach me about being a lesbian, and nervous because I found her attractive. Mostly I worried she'd see through my attempts to act confident. When I mixed everything together, the overwhelming result was confusion.

"Hey, Jackass, the shower's all yours," Caroline said as she came out wrapped in a towel. That caused me to hop up and head for the bathroom. Nothing gets me moving in the morning like a straight girl in a towel. I mentioned it before, but it's worth repeating. I try to avoid anything that might seem like I'm coming on to a straight girl, and watching them dress definitely qualifies. Caroline had a great sense of humor, but why push my luck, right?

I showered quickly and dressed, then went back into the room to get my camera and my wallet for our sightseeing trip. "What time did you get home last night?" Caroline asked.

"About eleven o'clock. You were already asleep."

"Yeah, I fell asleep writing a letter to Carl."

They'd dated steadily since high school. Caroline wanted to study journalism, and she could've gotten into a good university, but she'd chosen to stay in town at the community college with him. I thought she was crazy, but I envied her certainty about their future. "Did you tell him you love him and miss him and want to have his babies?"

"No, but I told him you did."

I laughed. "I bet he'll love that."

"You weren't out late. What happened? You didn't like the big, hairy drag queen you went to see?"

I didn't know what to say. I couldn't tell her I found a lesbian bar and chickened out. I couldn't tell her about Lina, either. One of the few things I knew for sure about lesbians was you weren't supposed to out them. "Naw, it was a bust."

"Sorry," Caroline said seriously. "I don't know how you do it. I couldn't pick up a stranger in a bar. Carl and I were friends a long time before we started going out, and even then I was still nervous."

"Yeah, well." My voice caught a little bit as I tried to keep my tone light. "I don't need to fall in love. I've got a lot of women left to meet."

Caroline laughed. "You're such a player."

I slipped on my sunglasses and did my best impression of confidence. "Players are people too."

It bolstered my confidence to know some people still believed I was in control. I just wished I could be one of them.

❖

I avoided Lina's eyes when we boarded our little bus, and Jesús fired up the Dixie Chicks for the drive. I sat with Andi and stared out the window as the city passed by.

"Where're we going today?" Andi asked.

"Some church," I grumbled. The idea didn't appeal to me. I wasn't particularly religious, and people who were made me uncomfortable. Of course, my hippie parents taught me to respect people who practiced their religion out of love, and honestly I'm kind of envious of people who are secure in their beliefs. Lord knows I'm not sure about anything in this life, much less the next one. Still, I always worry about people who use God as an excuse to commit hate crimes or start wars.

"We're going to La Sagrada Família," Lina said, turning around in her seat. Her deep brown eyes met mine for a moment, and I turned away quickly in an attempt to squash my attraction for her. The last thing I needed was to develop a crush on her. She was the same person she'd been the day before, only more confusing, and I hated being confused.

"That means 'Holy Family'?" Andi asked.

"Yes, it's a church designed by the same architect who built the park we were at yesterday, Antoni Gaudí. He started work on it in 1882, and it's still not finished."

"What a waste of time," I mumbled.

Lina looked at me questioningly, but Caroline drew her attention away. "Are we going to Mass?"

"No, we'll tour the completed part of the church. The architecture is like nothing else in the world. We'll focus on that, but we'll enter the main temple. We can pray there if you want."

I snorted. "Yeah, right."

Jesús stopped the bus and we all got off. Lina watched me carefully as I passed her but said nothing. I stepped into the bright sun and saw the mammoth structure in front of us. Actually what I saw turned out to be only a small portion of the church. I lifted my gaze slowly over the massive doors to the intricate carvings climbing story after detailed story into arches and cavernous spires before they continued skyward to peaks adorned with heavily sculpted crosses. I craned my neck so far I actually stumbled backward a few steps. Just as I thought I'd fall over, I felt an arm wrap tightly around my waist. "Still think it's a waste of time?" Lina whispered as she steadied me.

"I, um…" I couldn't think of a witty comeback with my body going crazy. Goose bumps ran down my arm from the warmth of her breath on my neck, and my stomach did that weird clenching thing. I pulled away quickly. "It's okay."

The other girls hadn't seemed to notice the exchange as they excitedly ran toward the entrance of the church. I followed at a slower pace, trying to figure out what had just happened. I was thrown off by the lingering press of Lina's body, by her arms wrapped protectively around me. It felt good, but why? I didn't need protecting, and I certainly wasn't supposed to like it. I wasn't vulnerable. When I came to Spain looking for a woman, I expected it to be different. Meeting a young, sexy, vibrant lesbian should've made me feel in charge, strong, confident. She was everything I thought I wanted, but she didn't make me feel any of those things. Being near her made me feel frustrated and disoriented.

I hung back as we passed through the ticket office. The tour operators provided us with tickets, so I didn't have to embarrass myself further by trying to order anything in Spanish.

I know it's juvenile because I was having the opportunity of a lifetime to see so many amazing places, but I was too cranky to enjoy them. It's hard to relax when you feel off-kilter.

My friends followed Lina around the church, wandering from room to room as she pointed out the stone faces of saints and martyrs, but I couldn't focus on the artwork. It was all so old, so cold, so hard, tributes to a God I didn't know, and who, I'd been taught, didn't care to know me.

"The Central Nave won't be open for worship for another

year, but after 126 years of construction, that doesn't seem too long to wait," Lina joked lightly, but I didn't laugh with the others. I had waited for this trip for twenty years and I didn't want to wait another minute to get what I wanted. I couldn't imagine waiting over a century.

"Right now they're holding Mass in one of the side naves, and between services you can pray there." She led us through heavy doors to a cavernous room flanked by massive stone pillars that rose several stories before joining in huge archways and intricate domes. At the end of the room a gingerbread style sculpture in the wall interspersed with flashes of brightly colored stained glass casting an array of blue and green light across the floor. There were several pews and altars throughout the room as well as a section of little candles in rows of tiny dancing flames that gave off barely enough light to illuminate their tiny corner of the nave.

"I want to light a candle for my mom," Hannah said.

"That's a great idea," Lina replied and followed her. Caroline and Andi walked to the other end of the room and snapped pictures of the stained glass. I chose to stay near the door and lean up against one of the pillars. Hannah lit her candle, stared at it for a moment, and then moved on, but Lina lingered before kneeling and crossing herself. She closed her eyes and folded her hands. Serenity washed over her features. I felt voyeuristic watching something so personal, so intimate, but I couldn't turn away. I imagined that's what she'd look like asleep, her lips slightly parted and her hair shining in the dim light as it cascaded around the features of her peaceful face.

How did she find peace in this place? Why didn't she feel the nerves and the restlessness that consumed me? Was it an act? Or denial? Could someone ever be that comfortable in her own skin? It didn't seem fair. How could this woman, not much older than me, do all the things I couldn't? She was able to breeze into the places I wanted to go, talk to the women I wanted to know, and feel all the things I lacked. I started to hate her a little bit. I would've hated her more if she weren't beautiful. Still, even her beauty made me mad. What right did she have to take my breath away when I was angry at her?

I forced myself to turn away from the source of my emotional overload. She shouldn't be there. She shouldn't pray to a God I feared, and I didn't want to admire her while she did. I focused on the various statues within my line of view, but none of them held the appeal of the woman I'd been drawn to moments earlier. I studied the image of a man carved in the sand-colored stone. His lifeless eyes and square-cut chin tilted down at me mournfully. Was it Jesus, a saint, or a worshiper? Either way, I doubted he'd think highly of me right now, and I didn't care. I didn't think much of him, either.

"Te gusta?" an old man asked, startling me out of my stare-down with the statue.

"No," I answered flatly. I didn't like it.

"Por qué?"

Why? I didn't know how to explain I was using the statue as a scapegoat for all my shortcomings, for all of Lina's complexities, and for the very idea of a condemning God. I certainly didn't want to try to say it in Spanish. "I don't speak Spanish," I replied brusquely.

Sadness, or maybe pity, filled the old man's eyes. *"Lo siento."* He apologized, then shuffled off quietly.

"That was rude," Lina said from nearby, her arms folded across her chest and her cheeks colored pink with anger or perhaps embarrassment. "Señora Wallace said when you apply yourself, you're one of her best students. I know you can speak Spanish."

"I don't want to speak Spanish," I grumbled.

"What's the matter, Ren?" she asked softly.

I faltered a little at her concern, but then my anger rebounded.

I didn't need the pity of someone who should've felt the same way as I did here. "This place is irrelevant to me."

"Irrelevant? I thought you came to Spain for the 'culture and stuff.'"

"Culture, not religion."

"In Spain, our religion is part of our culture. It's shaped our history for a thousand years."

"The Catholic Church is still living in the dark ages. They don't allow women priests, they don't believe in safe sex, and they condemn gays and lesbians." I watched closely to see if my statement registered any shock, but her eyes stayed steady on me, her expression unchanging. I hated seeing her so calm while turmoil ripped my insides. Why did she get to stand there self-assured while I floundered? She was a lesbian too, or did she conveniently forget her sexual orientation when she wore her tour guide persona? I couldn't stand it, and the words spilled out before I thought them through. "What kind of self-hating lesbian admires Catholic churches?"

She didn't flinch. She didn't wince. She didn't even blink. She smiled. "Are you angry because you're a lesbian, or because I am?"

"What? No." That didn't make sense. Of course I wasn't mad I was a lesbian, and it'd be silly if I got mad at her for being one too. I was mad at her though. "I'm mad about this hypocrisy."

"What do you mean?"

"I mean, I mean—" *Damnit, what did I mean?* "All this church business. You doing the Spanish Catholic routine and not telling me you're gay."

"Oh," she said, clearly trying to fight a smile. I admit that wasn't the most articulate statement I'd ever made, but she frustrated me. "You didn't tell me you were gay either, and yet we're having a conversation about being gay, so neither of us did any hiding, did we?"

"Yeah, well." She had a point. "But the church tour, and you kneeling and crossing yourself?"

"The church is a national landmark and an architectural treasure. I'd be a bad tour guide if I didn't bring you here, but aside from that I'm also a very real Catholic."

"You can't be a gay Catholic."

"Says who?"

"I'm pretty sure the pope."

She threw back her head and laughed so loud people turned to stare. Did they see the beauty in the gentle curve of her neck and the little lines at the corners of her mouth when she smiled? "Well, I don't agree with everything the pope says."

"Then why are you a Catholic?"

"I don't agree with everything my mother says either, but I still love her. Besides, when I kneel at the altar, I don't thank the Pope. I pray to the Creator of all of this." She opened her arms with her palms up and glanced around the cavernous room to millions of etchings and details carved in stone. "I thank the One who gave us the power to dream and build and love. Being gay is part of my identity. My Catholic faith is another part, and so is my job as a tour guide. I can't let one part of me overshadow all the others, or I wouldn't be me."

I didn't know what to say. I didn't have all those things in my life. I didn't have any hobbies or special abilities, but being a lesbian made me unique among my friends. Wasn't that enough? Did there have to be more? If so, what? Should I try to find multiple important parts of me? I struggled to find even one. I didn't have a job. I didn't know what I wanted to study after two years at college. I wasn't a person of faith. I didn't sing or play an instrument or excel at sports. Honestly, I wasn't even a good lesbian.

"Ren, do you want to talk about something?" she asked, resting her hand gently on my shoulder.

"What? No." I shook off her comment and her touch. As

much as her words had shaken me, I wasn't ready to cave. I had too much invested in the do-it-yourself mentality to fall apart the first time a pretty girl offered a sympathetic ear. This trip was my last chance. I wouldn't admit defeat after two days. I had to stay strong and independent. I had to become the person I'd always wanted to be. I shook my head and prayed my voice wouldn't crack. "I'm sorry I snapped at you, but I really can take care of myself."

❖

That evening Caroline asked if I'd watch Hannah so she and Andi could do some shopping before we left Barcelona. I wasn't thrilled with the idea, but I had gone out the night before while the others had stayed in. I didn't have a good excuse for asking them to give up another night. I considered going back to the same bar off Las Ramblas, but running into Lina wasn't a pleasant prospect. I didn't want her judging me or my abilities to pick up women, especially after my little meltdown at the church. I also considered trying to find another lesbian bar, but I didn't know where to start. As much as it pained me to lose valuable time, I agreed to waste a night babysitting.

I packed my stuff and knocked on Hannah's door around six o'clock. She let me in, and we both stood there awkwardly. "Hi," I said, not sure how to handle this. "I'm staying with you tonight."

"Sorry," Hannah said. "You don't have to."

I felt guilty for making her feel bad. None of this was her fault. "No, I didn't mean it like that. We'll have fun."

"Yeah?" She seemed skeptical. "What do you want to do?"

I shrugged. I couldn't tell her what I really wanted to do tonight. "We can do whatever you want."

"I've only been on the tours and in the hospital."

"Oh," I said, floundering. How was I supposed to learn how

to be cool and confident with women when I couldn't even hold a conversation with a twelve-year-old? "We could get something to eat."

"The food here sucks."

I laughed. At least we'd found some common ground. "Pretty much, but I found a McDonald's last night."

Hannah's eyes lit up. "For real?"

"Yeah, it's not totally like American food, but it's the closest thing I've found."

"You have to take me there." Hannah took my backpack and threw it in the room before grabbing my hand and dragging me toward the elevator.

When we arrived at our subway stop, I hopped up and led her into the night. "Wow," she said at the bustle of activity around us, "this place is pretty cool."

I grinned, glad she felt the same way I did. I enjoyed sharing a connection with someone, even a kid. We made a break for the double arches and both managed to order our combo numbers in Spanish. I wasn't sure if I should pay for her or not, but she pulled out a wad of euros and counted the right amount. She acted more comfortable with the transaction than I did.

"You did good," I said as we found a table.

"My mom's a Spanish teacher. I've been able to count in Spanish since I was, like, two."

Her reasoning made sense, but it didn't make me feel any better.

Hannah bit into a fry and wrinkled her nose. "This tastes like fish."

"Yeah, and the burger will taste funny too. I told you it wasn't perfect."

She frowned and her shoulders sagged as she sat back in her chair. "I wanted something to go right on this trip, you know?"

"Yeah." I could sympathize, but I wanted to make her feel better, not worse. "But we're going to Madrid tomorrow."

"My mom's not."

So much for cheering her up. The kid was obviously scared about going to a new city with a bunch of strangers while her mom lay in a hospital. The realization made my problems seem smaller. "It's going to be okay."

"Everyone keeps telling me that."

"I guess it sounds pretty stupid."

"Yeah, I mean, just because my mom is going to get better doesn't make it okay. We planned this for a long time, and now it's all messed up."

Hannah had just said everything I felt but was too insecure to put into words. "I know what you mean. It's not what I expected either."

"Is that why you were such a jerk to Lina today?" she asked, taking another bite of her burger.

I frowned "I disagreed with her, but I wasn't a jerk."

"You were."

"It's complicated." Who did this kid think she was? Never mind the fact that I thought she was spot on a minute ago.

"Why is it complicated for you?"

It didn't seem age-appropriate to tell her I didn't know how to pick up women and I was tired of feeling like a loser. Even if I could tell her, my problems seemed petty compared to hers. "It just is."

"Are you upset about my mom too?"

"Yeah," I lied. Honestly it upset me more to realize how self-absorbed I'd been. Señora would miss the whole trip, Hannah was scared and lonely, and I hadn't even thought about them all day. I'd been too wrapped up in my own issues to care about anyone else, and even worse, apparently I was a jerk to Lina. By pouting and not making the most of this trip, I'd been a jerk to everyone.

"I miss my mom," Hannah said with tears in her eyes.

"I do too, but you know what? Your mom wouldn't want us

to mope around. She'd want us to"—I did my best impression of Señora Wallace's teaching voice—"experience España."

Hannah burst out laughing. "You sound exactly like her."

Seeing Hannah enjoy herself for a minute made me feel better than I had all day. Maybe Lina was right about needing more to my identity than being gay. I didn't have to give up my quest for lesbians, but there wasn't anything wrong with enjoying a night off. Hannah needed someone to take care of her, and I needed to loosen up.

"Come on," I said. "We've got a whole night on our own in one of the most beautiful cities in the world. Let's have some fun."

DAY FOUR

I woke up more rested than I had been since arriving in Spain. I had fun with Hannah the night before as we'd wandered Las Ramblas buying souvenirs and soaking up the celebratory atmosphere like kids at the county fair. We'd laughed and joked the whole way back to the hotel, then I fell exhausted into bed, with only the hint of disappointment at missing an opportunity to become super lesbian.

I slept well without the turmoil I'd suffered the night before and was ready for a new day, almost as if I was getting a do-over on my arrival in Spain. And it did feel like a do-over as I showered and pulled on a fresh pair of jeans. We were headed to a new city where I'd get a fresh start, now three days older and a little wiser. I slipped into a tight blue polo and tucked my shaggy hair under a St. Louis Cardinals hat. The ensemble gave me a boi-ish charm. Maybe the ladies of Madrid would eat that up.

As usual, I was the first one in the lobby. I snagged a few candy bars and a Coke from a vending machine and flopped into an oversized hotel chair where I could wait for the others. I was halfway through a Snickers bar when Lina joined me.

"I see you're a fan of healthy breakfasts."

I shrugged. "The Coke is warm, but the rest of it tastes familiar."

"I guess we all need the comforts of home occasionally."

I didn't know how to take her comment. Was she suggesting I was homesick or not up for this adventure? Why did she always make me second-guess myself? Maybe because her deep brown eyes bored into mine like she could see more than I wanted to show her.

Thankfully the others entered the lobby dragging their luggage behind them. Lina collected our room keys and got us checked out while we greeted Jesús and loaded our stuff into the bus.

"Get comfortable, *chicas*," Lina said. "We've got a six-hour bus ride."

We all groaned. When Jesús grinned and said "Dixie Chicks," we groaned louder, but he didn't seem to notice as he cranked up "Wide Open Spaces" and shifted the bus into gear.

I don't mind traveling. I get antsy and claustrophobic if I'm not on the go, so the constant vibration of the bus soothed me. Outside my window, the city blended into suburbs and slowly faded into open countryside. It was pretty, a lot more pastoral than I'd expected, and very hilly. Not too different from the Midwest. Vast swatches of greens and browns spread endlessly beneath a pale blue sky, but at home the fields were covered in corn this time of year. Here things were more open.

"May I join you?" Lina asked.

She had plenty of open seats to choose from—for instance the one she'd been sitting in close to Hannah—but I scooted over anyway. When she sat down, the bare skin of her arm brushed lightly against mine, and I got goose bumps. I hoped she wouldn't notice her closeness made my body react in all kinds of crazy ways.

"Do you like my country, Ren?"

The sincerity of the question caught me off guard, but I'd started to expect that from her. "Yes, I do."

"Good." She smiled brightly. It felt good to make her happy after the tension I'd caused yesterday. It made me happy too.

"Do you see that?" She reached her arm across me to point out the window. I smelled her lotion or perfume, sweet but subtle, not like the girls I know who smell like they bathe in plumeria. This carried a hint of something citrus, and I took another deep breath before realizing I was smelling her arm like some nutcase. I glanced out the window quickly and hoped she hadn't silently judged me as some lunatic arm sniffer.

I scanned the rolling countryside to see where she pointed. High on one of the grassy hills stood a huge, black, bull-shaped statue, or maybe it was flat like a billboard. I couldn't tell. "What is it?"

"A long time ago, the bulls used to be advertisements for a cognac company. They put them all over the country, and no one ever took them down. They've been adopted as a national symbol of Spain. The people are proud of *los toros*."

I thought of American billboards, brandishing brightly lit, garishly colored homages to fast food and strip malls. None of them managed to capture the spirit of the nation and would certainly be replaced with something newer and tackier the moment their companies missed a payment. That simple black bull served as a pleasant reminder I was in a truly foreign country, a place with its own standards, ideals, and values. This was a country secure in its identity. If I could've been a place, I might've chosen this one.

"Tell me more," I said, turning back to face her.

"About the bulls?"

"About the bulls, about Spain." *About you*, I added silently.

"We'll take turns. I'll tell you about Spain, you tell me about yourself."

I found the prospect thrilling and terrifying. I was excited she wanted to know about me, but nervous about what she'd find out. What if she learned what a failure I was as a lesbian? Or as a person in general? What if she found nothing interesting or outstanding about me? What if I actually did open up to her and she wasn't interested anymore?

"What's wrong?" she asked, brushing her hand across my shoulder and breaking me out of my downward spiral of what ifs.

"That's not a very fair deal," I said brushing off her touch. "You're a tour guide. It's your job to teach me about Spain. I don't see why I have to answer questions in return."

The corners of her mouth turned down slightly, and a flicker of hurt registered in her eyes. I was being a total jackass. The urge to apologize was swift and overwhelming, but before I could say anything, she forced herself back into cheerfulness. "Okay, I'm tour guide extraordinaire until you tell me otherwise, but the peace offering will remain on the table until you're ready to accept."

What did that mean?

She launched into a discussion of Spanish history, but I didn't hear much of it. What had she offered, and why didn't I accept? Could I accept now? How? And why? Did I need to make peace with her, or did she need to make peace with me? What did we need to make peace for? The argument in the church? Or was she alluding to something else?

You know how sometimes when you wake up and you know you had a dream but you can't quite remember it? You don't even know what you're reaching for, but you want to know, like maybe it was something good or important. Right then, I suspected she knew what I was searching for, and she was waiting for me to find it.

❖

We stopped at the side of a busy street, and Lina ushered us off the bus. We followed her as she did the tour guide backward walk, facing us rather than the objects she pointed out. I was sure she'd run into someone or crash over a curb, but she never faltered. I barely managed to walk forward without tripping over myself.

"We're in Zaragoza, Spain's fifth largest city. It's a beautiful example of my country," she said, beaming with pride. "It is a modern capital of industry and home to a large automotive industry Its people are educated and affluent with all the modern sensibilities of the new millennium." She indicated a suspension bridge and large office buildings to prove her point. Traffic passed loudly around us as we followed her around a corner, and everything stopped. The noises, the activity, the modern cacophony faded behind us, and she smiled broadly. "We're headed toward a bright future, but we never forget where we came from."

We appeared to be in an old town square. Large stone buildings surrounded us, and on one side large cathedral spires towered over the entire scene. "That's the Basílica del Pilar." She pointed to the church. "And we're in La Plaza del Pilar. On El Día del Pilar the people from this region dress up in traditional dresses and head scarves, and they cover this entire plaza with thousands of flowers. The colors are overwhelming."

The exuberance in her voice transported the sights she described right into my imagination. I had to admit, I loved seeing this country through her eyes. They were much more attentive than my own.

"I wish we had time for a full tour, but we're only stopping for lunch. Grab some food for yourself and the pigeons, and soak up the atmosphere."

We all had our cameras out as we bought sandwiches and snacks from a little café and sat on the ground facing the square.

I bought a bag of potato chips and fished one of the candy bars from the hotel out of my pack back.

"I see you keep up your healthy eating all day long, Ren," Lina teased as she sat down next to us. She stretched out her tan legs, letting the sunlight caress them, and I got the urge to caress them too. They were perfect. Long and graceful, toned and deeply tanned, and *oh my God, I can't stop staring at her legs*. This wasn't some random chick in a bar. Lina didn't seem like the type of woman who appreciated being ogled. I forced my eyes away from her legs in time to see her give me a playful smile.

"What?" I asked sheepishly.

"Have you read *The Spanish Pearl*?"

"No." I hadn't, but the way she smiled when she said it made me want to.

"What's it about?" Caroline asked.

"It's about a modern woman who goes back in time to find the woman of her dreams living in Aljafería Palace right here in Zaragoza."

"It's a lesbian time-travel romance?" Andi asked. "How cool is that?"

"Very cool." Lina chuckled. "Cool enough for even Ren."

Andi and Caroline laughed along with her. "She's onto you, Ren. She can tell you're a babe magnet already."

"What about you?" Hannah asked. "Do you have a girlfriend?"

Wait, how did Hannah know Lina was gay?

"No, I am single now for over a year, but I'm still searching these castles," she said lightly, but the words echoed through my body. The woman at the bar wasn't a lover.

"How old are you?" Andi asked.

"Twenty-four."

I did the math in my head quickly. She was only four years older than me. How was that possible? She looked young, but she acted much older. Would I be as steady in four years? Did age guarantee growth, or did I need more experience? What kind of experience did she have that made her comfortable with herself?

"I graduated from the university early so I could lead Americans around the country I love."

"Only Americans?" Andi asked, and I marveled at her openness. These were the questions I'd wanted to ask on the bus. I'd wanted her to open up to me, and I'd had my chance, but I'd been too afraid to take it. I'd let my fear of being discovered as a fraud prevent me from getting to know her. Now the others were having the conversation I should've had.

"Americans and Brits mostly, since I'm fluent in English."

"How'd you learn to speak English?" Caroline asked.

"My father was born in America. It was important to both of us that I communicate with him in his native tongue. We used to visit his parents in Chicago. I spent many summers there while growing up."

This discussion appeared easy, safe, and devoid of conversational land mines, so I finally got the nerve to join in. "Does your dad still take you there, now that you're grown up?"

She met my eyes. A brief flicker of sadness crossed hers, but her smile stayed in place as she spoke. "He passed away several years ago. I haven't been back since he died."

Shit, this is exactly what I feared. One simple question dredged up more emotion than I was prepared to deal with. I imagined her as a teenager, tears rolling down her young face as she learned she'd never see her father again. My chest ached for her, and my eyes watered, but I slammed the emotions shut inside me and mumbled, "I'm sorry."

"Don't be sorry," she whispered and rubbed her hand against my arm. "It makes me happy to remember him, and it would make him happy to have you compliment my English. As a little girl I would read his books and memorize his phrases. I'm always excited to learn new words, like 'hippie.'"

I cracked a smile, and my aloofness cracked along with it, but the distant chime of church bells interrupted our tenuous connection. Lina jumped up. "Jesús!" We all stared at her, startled by the religious exclamation.

She laughed and motioned for us to follow. "We're late to meet Jesús. Come on."

We jogged through the narrow streets of old Zaragoza and into the newer, busier ones, where Jesús incurred the wrath of fellow drivers by stopping in the middle of traffic. Lina jumped on first and then gave us each a hand, pulling us into our little bus. I was the last one aboard, and she clutched my hand, her eyes meeting mine, as our laughter blended together, then faded. We stood staring at each other as the bus began to move. I felt like she was waiting for something, waiting for me. I should've asked her to sit with me. I should've taken her up on the peace offering she'd mentioned earlier. It wasn't that I didn't want to. I wanted, maybe even needed to be close to her, but I couldn't let myself need anyone right now. I had to learn how to make women want *me*, not the other way around. I sat by myself and tried not to think about how empty the seat felt without her beside me.

❖

We arrived in Madrid a little after five o'clock and checked into the Hostal Madrid, which wasn't actually a hostel. The building was pretty modern, though not fancy. Our room had three small beds with bright green plaid bedspreads, a tiny dresser, and a lamp in the corner but no other furniture or decorations. Our tiny bathroom didn't have a bathtub, only a shower.

I didn't bring my laptop with me, and data racked up insane fees on my cell phone, but I spotted a computer in the lobby while I waited for the others to get ready for dinner. I glanced around nervously before approaching the keyboard. What I intended to type might not be suitable for public viewing, but I was the only person around. I entered "Madrid Lesbian Bar" into Google's search engine. I got 473,000 results and almost fainted. I quickly clicked on a random result. I scanned the page, which was mostly in Spanish, so I only understood parts of it, but I learned Madrid had a gayborhood called Chueca. I'd never heard the word before, but most of the gay and lesbian nightlife was in that part of town.

I heard someone enter the lobby from outside and quickly closed the browser.

"*Hola*, Ren," Lina greeted me. "Sending some e-mail?"

"Yeah, you know, telling my parents all is well." I immediately regretted lying. Lina hadn't done anything to suggest she'd boss me around or get parental about gay bars. If anything, she'd been more open about her sexual orientation than I had. But I still wasn't comfortable telling her my plans for the evening.

"Good," she said with a smile. "Hannah went to get Caroline and Andi. They'll be right down."

"Are you staying with Hannah tonight?" I asked.

"Yes, it is my turn. We called her mom earlier, and she said to eat some paella for her."

"That sounds like Señora."

She laughed. "You do know Señora is not a name, right? It's a title, like you would say *Miss* in English."

"Yeah, we all know that, but we've only ever called her Señora. We wouldn't do it to anyone but her. It's kind of like her nickname."

"A nickname?"

"Yes." I'd never thought about the term "nickname." I didn't know why people called it that. Maybe because *Nick* is a nickname for *Nicholas*? "It's like a shortened name, or a funny name, something you call someone that's not their real name. Like my full name is Rennick, but that's just awful, so everyone calls me Ren."

"Rennick?" She tried the word out loud, and for the first time in my life it didn't sound absurd. In fact I actually liked the way she rolled the *R*.

"It's my hippie mom's maiden name, so she wanted to pass it on, but everyone calls me Ren."

"Then I have a nickname too." I could tell she liked saying "nickname" because she grinned every time she did. "I'm Evangelina, like *mi abuela*, but we can't be called the same thing, so I'm Lina."

"Evangelina." It was my turn to repeat a new name. I didn't like it as much the way I said it, but it was still nice. I repeated it, though this time it was more of a whisper, "Evangelina." The name gave me a little chill, and I wondered if she felt it too because I noticed her breath catch.

"Woo-hoo. Earth to the ladies," Caroline called.

We both jumped back. How long had they been there? I don't know why we acted guilty. Nothing happened, but it seemed like something could have. What was it about Lina? She was pretty, sometimes even beautiful, but there was more. When I was alone with her I got a feeling I couldn't quite explain. It felt like potential, or maybe anticipation, like something truly great or totally awful could happen. I'd arrived in Spain thinking I could handle anything, but when she looked at me with those searching eyes, I wasn't so sure.

She led us a few blocks to the Puerta del Sol, which is like the center of the center of the city, or more accurately the center of the whole country.

"We're at Kilómetro Cero." Lina pointed to a small plaque embedded in the gray stone pavement. "All the distances in Spain are measured from this point in our capital city.

"There's the symbol of Madrid." She pointed to a black statue of a bear climbing a tree. Hannah snapped a few pictures, but I checked my watch. It was almost eight o'clock, and I wondered how much longer this tour would take. Spaniards ate dinner late, and the bar in Barcelona didn't get busy until after ten o'clock, but I got jittery knowing I was close to a gayborhood. I didn't want to wait any longer than I had to.

"And that's Charles the Third," she added, pointing to a statue of a man on a horse. "He established the capital and many of the roads we still use today."

She beamed as she shared these facts. She clearly loved everything about Spain and was eager to share it with us, almost like a little kid who wants to show everyone her artwork. I felt guilty for not caring about Charles the Third or what he'd done. I felt worse about plotting my escape when she was having so much fun being our guide, but unfortunately, she couldn't lead me where I needed to go tonight.

I was really starting to like Lina, but she confused me. She made me feel lost and unsure of myself, and that's exactly what I came to Spain to escape. Maybe after I got some of the experience I craved, she and I would be on more equal footing. I wanted to be able to relax around her, but that couldn't happen yet. I needed to find my community and my place in it, and I couldn't do that here in Puerta Del Sol. I needed to get to Chueca.

Thankfully, she wrapped up her formal tour by stopping at a subway station and pointing to a map. "You can catch three different Metro lines here."

"Didn't some trains get bombed in Madrid?" Andi asked.

Lina nodded solemnly. "Yes, 11 March is much like your September 11. Terrorists bombed four local trains and killed almost two hundred people, a huge number for a country as small as Spain. They weren't exactly subway attacks, but many of the trains connected to the Metro."

We stared at the steps disappearing into the dim light of the station. None of us ever worried about terrorism in our little Midwestern cocoon. It was sobering to think hundreds of people had walked down steps like these and hadn't come out alive. Suddenly, I wasn't in such a hurry to catch the next train to Chueca.

"Niñas," she said softly, "there's danger everywhere, on trains, on busses, crossing the street. Even where you come from, accidents and illnesses end lives. Here in Spain the terrorists took the lives of many, but we refuse to let them steal our way of life. We live every day in defiance of them. Each time we gather in the streets or board a train, we tell them we won't be ruled by fear."

"Cool," I said. "It's like your country is standing up to a bully."

"I'm not surprised you think that way, Ren. You seem like the kind of person who lives defiantly."

"You have no idea." Caroline laughed. "Ren wouldn't be afraid to ride the train all day long."

"I bet she'd do it buck naked," Andi added, "and laughing."

I straightened my shoulders and lifted my chin, bolstered by my friends' misplaced confidence in me. I wanted to be as confident and strong as they thought I was. "That's me, defiant, naked, gay subway rider. Show me to the train."

Everyone laughed, but Lina shook her head. "Hannah and I are going to La Plaza Mayor. Do you want a tour?"

"We want to shop till we drop," Caroline said.

"Well, if you want to drown in shopping, you should go to El Corte Inglés. It's the biggest store in Spain. It takes up several buildings and has everything, with many specialty stores inside."

"Sounds perfect," Andi said, her eyes getting a little wide with excitement as she no doubt envisioned shopping heaven.

I couldn't be less interested in shopping for hours, but I saw my chance to escape. "How do we get there?"

"Get on the yellow line Metro and go up one stop to Callao. Then when you get off, it's right there," Lina said, adding, "If you want us to ride up with you we can show you the way before we go to dinner."

"No thanks," I answered a little too quickly. "We can do it."

"Okay, then I'll see you back at the hotel."

I led Andi and Caroline down the stairs to the Metro platform and immediately scanned a large map of all the Metro lines.

"We need the yellow line," Andi said.

"I'm looking for something more my style."

"What do you mean?"

"There's a gay neighborhood I want to check out while you're shopping. Go ahead and get your tickets, I'll catch up before the train arrives."

They both acted nervous, but neither objected. Once alone, I traced my fingers along various lines on the subway map, first the yellow, then the blue. Finally I saw it, the word "Chueca" in bold print on the green line. My heart beat faster as I stared at my finger pointing to the word.

"Ren?"

I spun quickly to see Lina standing behind me. Did she notice what I'd been pointing to?

"I came down to give you my phone number in case you get lost."

"Okay," I said and accepted the small slip of paper from her. "I'm sure we'll be fine."

"Do you need directions to somewhere else?"

"Um, no." I didn't even sound convincing to myself.

"If there's something you want to see, I'd gladly show you. You don't have to go alone."

For some reason the phrase struck me. My chest and my throat tightened. I wanted to tell her how badly I wanted to be cool and strong and sexy. I wanted to say I didn't know what to do, and I wanted to become much more than I was, but she couldn't do any of that for me. She was wrong. I did have to go alone. "No, we're fine. Thanks."

She nodded sadly, and before turning to go she said, "Be safe, Ren."

I watched her walk up the stairs and out of sight before I went to meet Andi and Caroline. I was headed off to a whole neighborhood of gays and lesbians. I'd dreamed of a place like Chueca for so long. I tried to envision the hundreds of lesbians there who would teach me everything I needed to know, but the only woman I could think of was the one I'd sent away.

❖

I left Caroline and Andi at the Callao stop and got on a green line train, proud of myself for finding my way on the Metro without any guidance. It was a good first step to independence. Not many people from Darlington, Illinois, could hop a train in Madrid without fear, but I had. Well, maybe I was a little nervous, but certainly not afraid. It was more like anticipation of my first date. In a way it kind of was my first date. I'd tried to date a few boys as a teenager, but that was awkward for everyone involved instead of a magical, love-struck experience. This would be different, though. It had to be.

I ran up the stairs of the Metro station and found myself in a square pretty much like all the others I'd seen throughout the city. I don't know what I expected, but not plain red and sand brick buildings lined with wrought-iron balcony rails. I'd hoped for something gayer. Where were all the rainbow streamers and drag queens with feather boas? A few boutique stores with darkened windows lined the square, but none of them sold anything overtly gay or lesbian. Maybe I needed to look harder.

At well after nine o'clock, the sun was setting, but the patios of a few restaurants were packed with people waiting to eat dinner. The smell of food made my stomach rumble. Maybe I should've gotten something to eat with Lina and Hannah before going out. I fished my last candy bar from the cargo pocket of my shorts and ate it while wandering around the square. The Twix had melted from the heat and didn't fill me up, but it took the edge off my hunger. I knew I should probably try some of the local food at some point, but after my first disaster I didn't want to waste any time when I could be cruising the gayborhood.

Chueca. The word gave me chills, and I didn't even know what it meant, which is to say I didn't know its English translation. To me it meant freedom, culture, and opportunity. It meant I could roam the streets with my head held high and purpose in my step. I could make eye contact with a girl and give her a smile, or maybe a nod of recognition, and while we wouldn't actually know each other, we'd know about each other. It meant I could finally feel at ease with myself.

I began to notice signs of queer culture popping up around me. Pretty boys in trendy clothes ate in clusters while several women were paired off together on one of the patios I passed. As it grew darker, the street traffic picked up too. Several people held hands, casually chatting with other members of the same sex. Boyfriends with boyfriends and girlfriends with girlfriends mingled as part of larger groups. I got chills watching them. They looked comfortable, relaxed, and sure of themselves. I wanted to be like them. I wanted to hold someone's hand while we laughed and talked about a movie or dinner plans.

Another group of young men and women not much older than me approached. One of the boys in skinny black jeans and a bright yellow polo slung his arm loosely around the waist of another guy. Behind them a few women jostled and joked with each other in Spanish. They all came right by me. I stood frozen in my spot. While I was dying to jump into their group, I couldn't follow random gay strangers around the city. I wasn't desperate enough to stalk anyone yet, but after they'd passed, one of the girls turned back around and smiled at me. The little grin of acknowledgment made me want more. Maybe I *was* desperate, because I quickly abandoned my no-stalking policy and followed from a distance, trying to act nonchalant.

They stopped in front of a plain building. Even in the darker part of the square, I could tell they were getting money or IDs out to show someone at the door. I kept my distance but grabbed my wallet. My nervousness welled up again. The last time I actually tried to enter a gay bar was two years ago in St. Louis. I snuck down to the city with a fake ID and presented it proudly to a bouncer who took one glance at me before laughing. She shouted at a few friends to check out this horrible fake and sent me away humiliated. Needless to say I hadn't tried since. Being alone quietly was better than being mocked as a massive loser.

But tonight, I wasn't a fake. In Spain I was old enough to get into the places I wanted to go. I reminded myself I belonged here and approached the bouncer with a bit more confidence.

"Cuatro euros," the woman on the stool said with a smile. She wore black jeans with a white T-shirt and red suspenders. She looked more like a mechanic than a doorkeeper. I pulled out a few bills, unsure if I needed an ID as well. She hadn't asked for one, but I still hesitated, unsure of what to do next.

"Americana?" she asked with a thick accent.

"Yes," I answer shyly. I wasn't sure whether she'd seen my passport or if she'd read my uncertainty, but I might as well have had a big red "tourist" stamp on my forehead. I hadn't even gotten inside yet, and I was already sticking out like I didn't belong.

"Bienvenida a Truco," she said and nodded for me to go ahead.

"Thanks," I mumbled. I'd been welcomed to a place called Truco, which sounded vaguely like a vocabulary word from some Spanish quiz, but I didn't remember what it meant. I made a mental note to ask Lina if the opportunity arose.

The entryway opened into a large room with a bar along one wall and tables and booths around the other three. The music was loud, but not obnoxiously so. The constant thump of bass would've had potential to become annoying fast anywhere else, but nothing could ruin this place for me. I was finally in a lesbian bar. A few men mingled throughout the crowd, but the girls outnumbered them. Skinny girls in tight pants and low-cut shirts. Stocky girls with muscles and tight T-shirts. Athletic girls, lean and taut, wearing ball caps and sneakers. There were girls everywhere, and I leaned against the wall to steady myself.

In this crowd of femmes, butches, and everything in between, there had to be someone who'd love to give a first-timer a fair chance. I was young, decent-looking, and eager to please. Plus, deep inside me lived a suave lesbian lover dying to be released. If I found the right person to give me a chance, I could become everything I wanted, everything I pretended to be. I felt the immense potential of the situation. This was the place for me to get some experience, build my confidence, learn all the skills I needed to be successful with women. I wouldn't start college as a confused, pathetic, virgin loser of a lesbian. I was going to become a chic, sexy, world-traveling lover.

So, what should I do now?

I slipped into a seat at a table for two. Should I get a drink? Should I look for a woman I was interested in? Should I wait for someone to approach me? My hopes dimmed. Why weren't there any written rules for these things? For straight girls, in general, the guy asked you to dance or buy you a drink. I think some lesbians have a more masculine type and a more feminine type, and they let that shape some of the interactions, but what about when both women were femme or butch? What if I wasn't either? Would I offend someone if I asked a butch to dance? Would a feminine girl wait for me to make the move? What about women like me who fell in the middle? Would we sit there all night waiting for the other to do something?

There wasn't much of a dance floor, but a few women got up to dance in an open space where a few tables had been pushed aside. The music was a mix of Spanish and American songs, and I tapped my toe. The vibe in the room was great, and I enjoyed myself because I'd never seen women dance together. At school dances I went with friends, and occasionally we'd all dance in a big group, or a guy friend would dance with me occasionally for fun, but I never got to hold anyone in my arms or rest my head on anyone's shoulder. I'd never put my hands on the curve of a hip or the small of a back. I'd never pressed my body against someone else's without worrying about giving them the wrong idea. It thrilled me to see women interact with each other in all the ways I longed to, but it was also disappointing that no one had asked me to dance yet. To top it all, my stomach started to rumble. I should've eaten something other than candy and potato chips all day, but it was too late now. I didn't want to leave for fear of missing my chance.

I would get a chance, wouldn't I?

I'd been in Chueca for an hour, and had only made eye contact with one girl—a sporty brunette. I quickly scanned the crowd and saw the brunette with her arm around another women's waist, her mouth bent low near her dance partner's ear, whispering something that made the other woman throw her head back and laugh. I suffered a pang of jealousy. I wasn't naïve enough to think a woman owed me anything simply because she'd smiled at me. But I was jealous of any woman who could smile at me so easily and not think anything of it, or who could ask a woman to dance without obsessing, or who could hold someone close without worrying about doing it right.

I assumed the women dancing with each other did so easily. Then again, maybe they felt as self-conscious as I did and just hid it better. Maybe I needed to drum up some artificial courage, to pick a girl and take charge. I could do that, couldn't I? I could approach someone and say, *"Quieres bailar?"* I could wrap my arms around a stranger and luxuriate in the press of her body against mine without giving a second thought to anything other than the physicality of the moment. Right?

Was it okay to want a woman for her body? I didn't want to be a jerk or a womanizer, but I didn't have time to go slow. Hopefully romance would come later, when I had more to go on. Couldn't I be the confident, quiet, sexy type just for one night? That couldn't just be a straight thing. I could have a practice girl here in Spain and then start at the university much more experienced. I needed to fake it till I made it, and then I wouldn't have to fake it anymore. I'd have experience. Once I lost my virginity, it would be gone forever. No more embarrassment, no more bumbling or wondering how to do things right.

I worked myself up with a nice little pep talk, and my heart beat faster. I closed my eyes and exhaled slowly, then opened my eyes and scanned the room. Who would be the lucky lady? I locked eyes with a woman standing a few tables over.

I smiled.

She smiled.

I gave her a slight nod of acknowledgment. She returned the gesture. I felt like we'd started some ancient lesbian dating ritual. My stomach churned with excitement, accentuated with a little bit of queasiness from eating junk food all day. I held my ground and didn't look away as she walked over.

She approached at a casual pace and stopped at my table, resting her hand on the empty chair and asked, *"Necesitas esta silla?"*

I thought she asked me if I needed the empty chair. Maybe I mistranslated and she is actually asking if anyone is joining me.

"No." Okay, not the most brilliant conversationalist, but hopefully I wouldn't have to do much talking once we got started.

"Puedo cogerla?" she asked with a grin. She wasn't what I'd call pretty. Her smile was plain and didn't light up her face.

She wasn't a dud or anything but certainly not vibrant like Lina. Damn, why was I thinking about her?

The woman had asked me a question. *Puedo* meant "can I" or "may I." I knew from asking for things in Spanish class, but what did *cogerla* mean? Oh hell, what did it matter? She'd asked for something, and at this point in the evening, I'd say yes to anything any woman asked of me. I gave her my best smile and my most enthusiastic *"sí."*

"Gracias," the woman said and then quickly walked off with my empty chair.

What the hell? What did I miss? She'd asked if anyone was sitting there, and then she asked if she could… Damn, she'd asked if she could take the chair. I'd said yes, and she'd taken it right back over to her girlfriend so they could cuddle together at their own table.

I was gutted. What an idiot. I'd smiled like a crazy woman while getting blown off. The woman I'd been willing to give my virginity to had been more interested in an empty chair than me.

Great. I must've projected my loser status, so clearly she realized no one would be joining me tonight. Everyone else could probably sense it too. I was a virgin fool who didn't fool anyone. My face flamed, and I was glad for the dim light. I'd already shown myself to be a failure with the ladies. They didn't need to see my embarrassment about it too.

My stomach clenched in frustration, and the queasiness multiplied. Afraid I might permanently seal my status as the unsexiest woman in the room, I decided to leave before I actually threw up.

❖

"Ren?" Lina said as soon as I entered the hotel lobby. She sat on a little couch with a magazine on her lap.

Had she waited up for me? Something about the way her eyes swept over me suggested this meeting wasn't coincidental.

"Hey." I tried to force a smile but didn't succeed. I imagined it turned out more like a grimace or maybe some weird face spasm.

"Are you okay?"

"Yeah, just a little queasy."

"Come sit down." She patted the seat next to her.

"I'm not in the mood for company. I want to go to bed." *And curl up and die of embarrassment.* I'd trudged to the subway and ridden back without drowning in my own dejection, but I didn't know how much longer I could go on.

"Please, talk to me for a minute," she pleaded.

There was no use trying to resist when she looked at me with her big brown eyes. I may be a crappy lesbian, but I was still a lesbian, with a soft spot for pretty girls. I flopped down on the couch next to her.

"I worried when the other girls came home without you."

"Oh yeah? Well, I'm home safe."

"I'm glad, but your safety was only part of my concern."

I wasn't sure what she meant, but I wanted her to let me go to bed, so instead of asking questions I said, "I'm sorry."

"What are you sorry for?"

Why is she asking so many questions? I closed my eyes and tried to swallow the bile rising in my throat before speaking. "I'm sorry you worried."

"Have you been drinking?"

"No." But now that she mentioned it, I wished I had been. Maybe if I drank I wouldn't be afraid, or timid, or embarrassed. Alcohol might numb the anger at my own stupid inability to act, or better yet, maybe it would kill my inability to act in the first place.

"You don't have to lie." She placed her hand over mine.

"You're old enough to drink, though I wish you wouldn't make yourself sick."

"I'm not lying," I said as clearly as possible, but I had a hard time mustering any indignation when she touched me. Her skin was soft and warm against my hand, like a soothing blanket. How would it feel to be wrapped up in her completely?

"What did you eat for dinner?" she asked suspiciously.

"A candy bar."

"*Dios mío!* No wonder you're sick. I haven't seen you eat a real meal in two days. You're smarter than that. You can't survive on junk, and even if you could, it's not healthy." She continued rambling as she crossed the room. "We're going to get you some real food."

"I don't like Spanish food."

She stopped a few feet from the reception desk and turned around. "We'll deal with that comment tomorrow."

I waited while she talked to an older woman behind the desk, who then disappeared around the corner before returning with a banana.

She handed the fruit to me. "Eat this. Slowly."

I wasn't sure I wanted to eat anything. I was in the weird stage of queasiness where I either really needed to eat or really shouldn't eat, but if I guessed the wrong option I'd pay dearly. Still, she looked awfully serious, so I took my chances with the banana.

I nibbled and swallowed cautiously, then made another attempt to smile. This one must've gone better than the earlier face spasm because she relaxed a little.

"That should settle your stomach," she said, "but what about the rest of you?"

"Huh?"

"You left your friends. You're out until midnight in a strange city. One minute you're vibrant, the next you're reclusive, and I always feel like you're looking for a chance to escape. The people around you really love you, but you hold them at a distance."

I took another bite of the banana because it tasted good and it bought me time. Part of me wanted to tell her everything. She was sweet and caring and obviously paid at lot of attention to me if she noticed things my friends and parents never did. Maybe she'd understand. Maybe she could even give me some pointers, but I still wouldn't have figured anything out on my own. Turning to her would confirm to both of us I wasn't good enough or strong enough or sexy enough to attract a woman on my own.

Even worse than losing out on a woman, though, would be losing Lina. She clearly knew something was wrong, and she might think I was a bit of a mess, or stubborn and reckless, but I preferred that to her thinking of me as a loser. I couldn't stand it if she pitied me. I'd rather spend my life as a lonely virgin than as someone's charity case.

"I'm sorry I worried you." I chose my words carefully, trying not to sound rude, but also attempting to come across as strong. "But nothing's wrong. I'm just a bit of a loner."

She shook her head slightly, her lips pursed together in a little frown. "Okay, Ren, I'll let you be alone, then. For now."

"Thanks. I'm going to go get some rest." I ignored the last part of her statement. Hopefully by the time she brought this up again I would have regrouped and would feel more secure in myself.

DAY FIVE

I stared at the ceiling, wishing for something different. Not a different ceiling, but a different feeling or outlook on life, a different me. I expected to be much further along by now. I thought I'd feel better about myself and my future. My friends had all decided what they wanted to do with their lives. So many of them had relationships, and even if they didn't, they at least had enough experience to know what to search for. This was supposed to be the best time of my life, and I was missing it. Now I was blowing my chance on this trip too.

Today marked the halfway point of our travels, and time was running out both on this trip and on my time before starting college. My constant stream of waiting and failing exhausted me. Last night I'd blown my best opportunity yet. Shots like that didn't come along often, and who knew when I'd get to a gay neighborhood again. And if I couldn't make myself act in a bar full of lesbians when I had nothing to lose, how would I ever find the courage this fall at school when I really had everything to gain?

I rolled out of bed and hopped in the shower. Caroline had spent the night in Hannah's room, so I was alone with Andi as we got dressed.

"Lina said we're going to a palace today, no blue jeans

allowed," Andi said as she held up two skirts. "Wanna borrow one of these?"

"Uh, no." I grimaced. "I haven't worn a skirt since my grandma's funeral five years ago, and even then it made me look like a drag queen."

Andi laughed. "You always were a tomboy."

I selected a pair of khakis and a cream-colored polo while I wondered why people called you a tomboy at ten and a dyke when you were twenty.

"Are you okay?" Andi asked. "You've got your brooding face on." She noticed things like that, and she'd known me long enough to recognize my moods. She'd actually been the first person I came out to. She'd noticed my withdrawal over a period of time and finally cornered me about it. I was so nervous about telling her but she barely managed to act surprised. She said she liked me before I told her, and she didn't see why anything should change because of something that didn't affect her in any way. Her reaction helped me feel comfortable telling other people. Who knows, if my first coming-out experience had gone differently, maybe I would've stayed in the closet. I wondered what she'd think if I told her my problems now. I doubted she'd be able to help this time around. Telling someone you're gay and telling someone you're a complete loser are two different things.

"Sorry," I mumbled. "Did you guys have a good time shopping?"

"Yeah, I got souvenirs for my whole family, and I got this new shirt for me. What do you think?"

The red and cream swirled shirt fit tightly to Andi's body, hugging all those straight girl parts I wasn't supposed to stare at. It was a shame, because she really was pretty. The shirt showed off the tan she'd gotten in this sunny climate, and the way the shirt clung to her showcased her figure, but I couldn't say any of that to a straight girl. I nodded and casually said, "Yeah, it's nice."

"Does it make you want me?" she teased.

"I don't do straight girls," I said as confidently as I could and headed for the door before the joke could go any further.

As I left the room, I remembered Lina's comment the night before about holding my friends at a distance. She and Caroline always asked me about women and teased me about being a Casanova. I was always the one who played it serious. I didn't want to make anyone uncomfortable, but then again it had started to seem like the only person uncomfortable in those situations was me.

❖

We all boarded the bus to Palacio Real with Jesús singing away to "Not Ready to Make Nice." I couldn't decide who grated on my nerves more, the Dixie Chicks or the driver.

I flopped into my seat, and Lina took the one in front of me. As soon as we got rolling, she turned around, her arm resting on the back of the seat and her chin on her arm. The pose made her look younger but no less beautiful. "Feeling better?"

"My stomach's okay," I answered honestly, but left out the fact that my overall state was pretty run down. A banana couldn't fill the hole in my ego.

"You'll eat better today," she said, and then rummaged through her bag for an apple.

"Thanks." I bit into the apple. "That's good."

"Spain produces some of the best fruit in the world. Valencia's known for its apples and oranges."

"Señora told us that, but I guess I forgot. I've only had a green omelet the first morning, and then Hannah and I had some bad McDonald's."

"Bad McDonald's?" She laughed. "That's…how do you say, 'means the same thing'?"

"Redundant."

"Yes, redundant. You're not talking about Spanish food, you're talking about Spanish people cooking American food." She pointed to the apple. "The *manzana* is Spanish food."

The apple was good, maybe the best apple I'd ever eaten, but apples are pretty hard to screw up. That didn't mean I'd like a full Spanish meal. She must have realized I needed more convincing because she said, "Give me time, Ren. I'll win you over."

My mouth went dry when I tried to swallow. Surely she was talking about the food, but I felt like it meant more, and that scared me. She could win me over, and not just in my opinions, but I couldn't let that happen. She wouldn't like the real me right now; I still had a lot of learning to do. I couldn't let myself get distracted by someone like Lina.

❖

We unloaded at Palacio Real, and once again pulled out our cameras. I'd already gone through one SD card and started on another, but I wondered if I'd be able to remember what everything was when I got home. I'd seen some pretty amazing sights since arriving in Spain, but somehow it didn't feel like I'd really been there. Part of my disconnect came from the fact that it was almost too big to absorb. How do you really process a whole new continent with art and architecture ten times older than your entire country? Still, I could've done a better job of paying attention. My preoccupation with meeting women affected my ability to concentrate on my surroundings. Today was no exception.

Lina led us through the gray stone courtyard past black iron gates with ornate gold tips. The palace walls rose all around us, cascading up to high-arched balconies. We headed toward a section topped by spires and a gleaming silver dome. We entered through heavy doors, the kind you see in medieval movies. "El

Palacio Real," she said in her tour guide voice, "is the biggest palace in Europe."

She led us to the base of a richly decorated staircase. "It's the official residence of the King of Spain, but King Juan Carlos doesn't actually live here. He and his family live in El Palacio del la Zarzuela and use this one for formal functions."

I tried to focus on her words. Really, I did. I didn't want to be some sex-crazed, self-absorbed manic, and even if that's all I was, I wouldn't get laid at ten o'clock in the morning. I might as well enjoy my day before going back to Chueca.

Chueca. I thought of the disaster there the night before and my face flushed with embarrassment. What a loser. How would I get any experience if I was too nerdy to get a girl to notice me, and how could I get cooler around women if I didn't get any experience with them? It was a vicious cycle.

Lina talked excitedly about famous kings and emirs who lived in the palace at one time or another. I remembered a bit of the history from Spanish class, but mostly we'd studied vocabulary words, grammar, and pronunciation, so I was pretty sketchy on the Spaniards-fighting-the-Moors information. Lina certainly knew a lot about it, and her emotion and excitement made me want to learn more. She seemed to care about everything, and she made me wonder if there was more to life than I'd previously thought. I was still pondering her comments about her sexual orientation being one part of her whole identity. It made me feel a little guilty. I should probably try to learn more about this amazing country she loved, but how could I ever grasp something so foreign when I couldn't even get a handle on my own identity?

"Here's a painting by Velázquez." She pointed to the image of a white horse with its front feet kicked up. "He's one of Spain's most treasured artists, but you'll learn more about him this afternoon." I stopped to glance up at the painting. Maybe because horses were a familiar sight to me, or maybe a painting was easier to take in than thousands of years' worth of history, but I liked this Velázquez guy. He was uncomplicated at a time when I needed something concrete to latch on to. Apparently Lina liked him too, because she lingered beside me while the others went ahead to the next room. Finally I looked away from the painting and toward her. She still gazed up at the horse as if studying it for the first time, her eyes dark and focused, her lips parted and her head titled back. She turned to me and smiled one of her slow, knowing smiles that stuck in my chest the way it had in the church a few days ago. I got that sinking feeling again, like she knew something I didn't, but before I could ask what she was thinking, she quietly walked away.

So much for uncomplicated.

❖

We passed through one gaudy room after another. Crystal, gold, silver, and granite all blended together before Lina ran out of information. By the time we left the palace around noon, Hannah's feet were dragging, and even Caroline's and Andi's eyes glazed over, but Lina continued excitedly relating funny stories of monarchs and Moorish leaders. We got back on the bus with Jesús, who had progressed to "The Long Way Around," and hummed along with his big grin and even bigger curly hair bouncing to the beat as he zipped through Madrid.

"Where're we going now?" Hannah asked, sitting down in the seat in front of me and resting her head against the window.

"I don't know, but I hope it involves lunch," I said.

"I thought you hated Spanish food," Lina said mischievously.

"Touché. But bad food is better than no food at all."

"Good, because we're going for a picnic in El Parque del Retiro."

"We went by there last night. It's huge," Caroline said, sounding simultaneously impressed and worried "We're not going to see the whole thing, are we?"

Lina laughed. "No worries, friends. I won't make you walk the whole three hundred acres."

"Thank you," Hannah sighed.

"It's got some amazing views, but we're going to experience it for its original purpose."

"What's that?" Andi asked.

"A retreat from the palace." Lina smiled her kid-like smile, and I sensed a tour guide story coming on. "'El Retiro' means a retreat. King Phillip set aside the park as a retreat for the royal family to relax in, and even though he needed to relax from a different palace than we're leaving, it's still a nice tribute."

It was a nice idea, and the way Lina took joy in drawing connections between the past and the present made me feel connected to it too. Perhaps a little bit of her educational information was sinking in after all.

We spread out a big blanket under some large trees, making use of the shade and what little breeze we had. The temperature had crept up near ninety and was expected to get even higher as day went on. After all the walking we'd done, none of us wanted to explore anything other than the boxed lunches Lina unpacked for us.

"Ham and cheese?" Hannah asked, unwrapping a sandwich.

"Ren mentioned perhaps some of you needed something more familiar."

Hannah threw her arms around my shoulders. "Thank you."

I stiffened at first, not sure what to do, but when I caught Lina's eyes she gave me a little nod. What did that mean? Did I do something right, or did I need to do something right? Unsure, but not wanting to let her down, I loosely put my arm around Hannah's back and patted a few times. "You're welcome."

"It's not completely American," Lina said. "The ham is cured in the Spanish tradition. It's saltier than you're used to."

I took a bite. It did taste different, definitely saltier and also chewier than I was used to, but the flavors of the cheese and the sesame seed bread balanced out the taste.

"The cheese is Manchego. It's a Spanish sheep cheese."

"Maybe there are some things you shouldn't tell us," Andi said, laughing at the expression on Hannah's face.

"Yeah, I could've done without the sheep part," Hannah said, wrinkling her nose.

"What does it matter where it comes from if you like it?" Lina asked. "You enjoyed it a minute ago. Why should the name change that?"

"I don't know," Hannah admitted. I was glad she was having this conversation so I didn't have to, but also a little worried I thought more like the child in the group than the worldly, graceful lesbian. "Why can't things be normal?"

"What's normal?" Lina asked gently. "And who says normal is the best option? Sometimes things we expect still disappoint us, while the surprises are the most fulfilling."

She wasn't watching Hannah anymore. She'd turned to me, her deep brown eyes soft and questioning. Did she want me to understand her? Did she want me to agree with her? Or did she want something more?

"I like it," Caroline said, breaking the spell. I didn't know whether to thank her or curse her. She made Lina smile and took the pressure off me, but I couldn't shake the feeling it should have been me to take a stand instead of drowning in my uncertainty. I'd missed the chance to do something important. Then again, maybe something important had happened, only I couldn't figure out what it was.

❖

"There's no way to see this whole place in one day." Lina said as we entered the cavernous corridor of a white stone building.

We'd walked to El Prado from the park. Along the way she'd told us about the art museum and how it housed one of the world's best collections of European art with over ten thousand pieces. The more she talked, the more animated she became, her hands gesturing rapidly and the inflections in her voice peaking with excitement, but the bigger she made this museum sound, the more dejected my friends looked. European art wasn't something we knew much about, and I doubted any of us considered that a big loss. Where we came from, the nearest museums were hours away, and when we did visit a city, it was for shopping or restaurants, not paintings. Even my college professor parents stopped dragging me to museums when I was old enough to say I didn't want to go.

"We're going to focus on Spain's big three of painting. The first is Francisco de Goya," she explained, leading us to a smaller offshoot of the museum and standing between two paintings until we all clustered around. The portrait to her right featured a woman reclining stark naked. The one on the left showed the same woman in the same position and fully clothed.

"That, *amigas mías*," Lina said, "is the first fully nude woman in European art. She's called *La Maja Desnuda*, or *The Nude Woman*."

None of us said anything. What can you say about the first naked lady on canvas that doesn't sound prudish or immature?

Lina chuckled. "People of the time were not as silent about the painting. They were outraged and demanded Goya paint clothes on her, but he refused to cover this painting. He compromised by painting the one next to it, called *The Clothed Woman*, but he didn't destroy the original and faced the Spanish Inquisition for it. He lost his official titles and was removed as the royal court painter."

I studied the painting closely, not because it was a naked

woman, but because I wanted to see what Goya saw in her that made him willing to give up everything for her. Sure, censorship sucks, but why not cover her up? Was it about the art or the woman? I couldn't stop comparing the two paintings and wondering if I would've stood my ground in his position. Would I ever feel so strongly about a girl, or anything else for that matter? Did I even want to? Could I face the Inquisition over some naked woman? I couldn't even stand up for myself at a gay bar.

"What do you think, Ren?"

I blushed at the question and the way all my friends turned their focus on to me.

"The painting is beautiful."

"But?" she prodded.

"She doesn't do straight girls," said Andi and Caroline in unison before dissolving into giggles.

"Come on, that's not funny." I was frustrated, confused, and depressed about my lack of progress with meeting women and learning about myself. Now on top of my own insecurities, my friends made fun of me in front of Lina.

"It's a little funny, stud," Caroline teased.

"Stud?" Lina asked with raised eyebrows.

"Ren's a stud. She just hasn't gotten the chance to prove it yet," Andi told her.

"Shut up," I growled. They had no way of knowing they'd hit a nerve, but I was still pissed. Who were they to talk? The whole world was set up for them and their relationships. TV shows, books, billboards, even the institution of marriage itself catered to them. They knew what role they were supposed to fill, and they didn't have to play guess-and-check in some bar to find out if they were doing things right. They could have sex for fun, they could find love, or they could save themselves for marriage, and any way they chose, they had role models. How dare they make fun of me for being lost?

"Okay," Lina cut off the conversation. "Let's move on to Diego Velázquez."

We followed her through a maze of hallways to a huge painting of a man painting the picture of a little girl while a bunch of servants waited on her. "This is *Las Meninas*. It's a portrait of the artist painting a portrait," Lina said with the little quirk of a smile that showed how clever she found the concept.

Still fuming, I couldn't appreciate the concept or its execution. Lina gave the history of the painting as I stood in front of her with my jaw set and my fists jammed into the pockets of my khakis. I had to do something soon, or I'd explode. I couldn't handle any more rejection. I needed to make my own chances tonight.

We followed Lina around the gallery as she pointed out several works of art, but I noticed I wasn't the only one having a hard time focusing. Hannah sat down on a bench in the middle of the room and rubbed her feet while Caroline and Andi looked like they wanted to do the same. Lina must've noticed her audience fading because she quickly moved us to the next room.

"The last artist I want you to see is El Greco. You'll hear more about him tomorrow, but you'll appreciate it more if you see his work here."

I shuffled along at the back of the group, sulking too deeply to pay much attention to the paintings until she stopped us in front of a large canvas. It must've been ten feet tall, with its subjects robed in the richest colors I'd ever seen in a painting. The reds and blues shone, lush against the thick charcoal background. I stifled the urge to touch them. I involuntarily stepped backward to take in the entire work of art. It was a group of men and women with flames over each of their heads, and hovering over them all was a dove that showered them all in golden light.

"It's *The Pentecost*," Lina said. "The reception of the Holy Spirit."

I wasn't certain what that meant, but I stood transfixed. The bodies were elongated as if their very substance actually stretched beneath the vibrant colors of their billowing clothes.

"El Greco uses color like no one else of his time, and not even many modern artists have mixed bright and dark with such captivating results." Lina stared in admiration much the same way I did.

"Great," Hannah said. "So that's the last one?"

Lina and I both looked at her, the spell broken. What an adolescent thing to say. I reminded myself she was a kid and didn't know better. I'd just about excused her indifference when Caroline asked, "When will Jesús pick us up?"

I couldn't believe it. Sure, I'd wanted to leave a few minutes earlier too, but how could anyone skip out on a masterpiece like this? I noticed El Greco's touch on the other paintings around me, and I wanted to study them but now feared Lina would rush us along.

"We're not scheduled to leave until five o'clock."

The others groaned. "That's over half an hour."

"We won't get back here. Don't you want to explore some more?"

"I want to explore the bench I saw in the other room," Hannah grumbled.

"You can do whatever you'd like as long as you meet us out front by five."

The others agreed and left the gallery, but I inspected another painting. This one was titled *Baptism of Christ* and pictured a naked man, probably Christ, being sprinkled with water while the dove from the other painting hovered below an old man, obviously God. I missed the religious significance, but I couldn't stop staring. Angels in hazy blue surrounded a God figure, and his robe shone with a pristine white almost too bright to stare at.

The next painting, *Annunciation*, showed a band of angels playing over a larger angel and woman. The larger angel wore a green so deep I thought it might swallow me.

"She's Mary, the Virgin Mother," Lina said lightly in my ear, causing me to jump, but she steadied me with a hand on my biceps.

I might not go to church, but I'd certainly heard of Mary. "She's a pretty big deal, huh?"

She chuckled. The low, rolling sound made me hot and cold at the same time. "Yes, she is. There she is again, being crowned the Queen of Heaven." She nodded toward another painting of the same girl, but this time Mary sat among the clouds between Jesus and God while they placed a crown on her head.

"Wow, I didn't know heaven had a queen."

Lina gave me a conspiratorial grin. "I can't imagine heaven without a whole bunch of queens."

It was the first joke she'd made in allusion to our shared sexual orientation, and I couldn't help but smile with her.

I turned back to the painting. Mary and Jesus wore matching attire, which was kind of funny when you thought about it, but their red robes with blue sashes were too vibrant to be trite. "I can't get over those colors," I whispered reverently.

"They're almost five hundred years old," she said. "Can you imagine what they looked like freshly painted?"

I couldn't imagine how anything could be more vibrant than what I saw now, but before I could say so, the others interrupted. "It's almost five o'clock," Hannah whined. "What are you guys doing?"

"We're admiring the art," Lina said, seemingly unperturbed. Didn't anything shake her?

"I don't get it," Caroline said with a shake of her head.

"What's not to get?" I asked, looking up at the Queen of Heaven again. How could someone miss the beauty in that? "It's flawless, and the colors are transfixing."

Andi and Caroline stared at me like I'd lost my mind. "Who are you and what've you done with Ren?"

I rolled my eyes and tried to shake off their disbelief.

"Seriously," Andi continued, "did you decide to go for the artsy lesbian appeal with extra granola, please?"

"Maybe she identifies with the virgin." Caroline snickered. "Ren, our Lesbian of the Perpetual Virginity."

"Yeah, that's a plan for you, Ren. If you lock yourself in here with all these painted women, you won't have to worry about the real thing anymore."

The words hit me like a kick to the stomach. Was my interest in the paintings another sign of my loserdom? What did it say about me that I'd completely forgotten about Chueca when I saw my first El Greco painting? Caroline and Andi liked to tease me, but they were both pretty clear they found the museum boring. Maybe I wasn't the suave, charismatic lesbian but instead was some weird, nerdy, lesbian abnormality. *Oh God, I'm never going to get laid.*

I had to pull it together. I'd let myself fall so far from the image I tried to project that my friends didn't even recognize me anymore. I didn't want to be artsy lesbian or nerdy lesbian. I wanted to be cool, confident, sexy lesbian. Sure, I liked the paintings, but that wasn't enough. I wanted to like myself too.

"Earth to Ren," Andi said. "You still with us?"

"Yeah." I pulled myself out of my own thoughts and tried to focus on acting cool. "Learning about the local art might help me tonight. You know, a little conversation starter."

The others laughed, all except for Lina. "That's the Ren we know and love," Caroline said and nudged me toward the door.

The Ren they know and love? I didn't even know who I was anymore, and I certainly didn't love myself. I guess it didn't matter, though, if I was convincing to other people…right?

❖

It was Andi's turn to watch Hannah, and Caroline was going to go out to dinner with them. I hadn't heard what Lina had planned, but I was avoiding her. I hoped to slip out unnoticed. I felt awkward with her on the way home from the museum and back at the hotel. A subtle sadness hung over us since I shifted back into being who everyone expected me to be and left behind the connection we'd shared earlier. I don't know why it felt like I'd rejected her. I just had bigger issues and couldn't waste time worrying about her opinion of me.

I told the girls where I was going, and I still had Lina's phone number in my wallet in case I got into trouble, but I couldn't imagine using it. Tonight was about proving myself. I had to learn to be confident and independent, and to do that I needed to take charge of my own destiny. No more passiveness, no more timidness, no more waiting for other people to bail me out.

I slipped into the tightest pair of jeans I owned and pulled on a form-fitting black T-shirt. I glanced in the mirror and wished I was a little taller than my five-foot, four-inch height, but my stomach was flat, my arms toned. My blue eyes were my best feature, and I liked the way they peeked out from underneath wisps of brown hair that fell over my forehead in a windblown style I hoped made me appear casual but defiant. I wasn't devastatingly handsome or model beautiful, but at least good-looking. Maybe someone would notice tonight.

It was dark when I left the hotel, but I clearly recognized the silhouetted figure leaning against the wall outside of the front door. Lina's beauty showed even in the dim streetlight. She had a perfectly sculpted physique, lean and lightly toned, the kind of body you'd hate if you weren't attracted to it. I stopped in the doorway, frozen by both her beauty and my fear of having to explain myself to her. I considered backing up and trying to sneak out a back door, but it was too late.

"You look nice tonight," she said.

"Thanks," I mumbled. "You do too."

"Do you have plans?"

"Um, not really," I lied. I knew exactly where I had to go

and what I had to do when I got there. I intended to go directly to Truco to approach the first woman who caught my eye, and ask her to dance. I'd put my hands on her waist and on the small of her back. I'd kiss her slow and easy and build up from there. After that, the details got hazy, but surely either instinct or the other woman would take the lead. Anyway, the details didn't matter as much as the end result. I would wake up tomorrow a new woman, but she didn't need to know that. "I thought I'd do some exploring."

"I'm going to meet a friend. Would you like to join us?" she asked.

"No, thanks. You have fun, though." I started to walk away.

"Ren," she said, catching my arm. "If there's something you want to know about Madrid, any part of Madrid, you can ask me. You don't have to explore alone."

I stared at her hand where it touched the bare skin of my arm, strong but gentle. The heat of her touch spread up my arm and into my core. My mouth went dry and I nodded. "Thanks, but I'm good."

"Are you sure?" She practically pleaded. "Some things don't translate the way we expect. It's nice to have someone who's been there before to guide you."

At this point I knew we weren't talking about the city anymore, and for some stupid reason tears stung my eyes. I blinked them away. She was offering help I couldn't accept. I didn't understand why she kept doing this. Why did she have to make it hard for me to remember what I wanted? A few seconds earlier I'd been sure of myself, but now with her soft skin and her pleading eyes on me, I wasn't sure of anything.

"What does Truco mean?" I asked hoarsely.

She exhaled slowly, as though trying to remain calm. Her mouth formed a flat line, and a subtle flash of recognition lit her eyes. "It means 'trick.'"

"Like trick-or-treat?" I asked, in a bad attempt at levity.

"No, not at all," she said solemnly. "'Trick' is a derogatory word for someone you pick up for a one-night stand. It's not a respectful term."

My heart hammered inside my chest so loudly I could barely hear myself say, "Okay, just wondering."

"I hope so, Ren." She finally let go of my arm. Then she added more softly, "I really hope so."

❖

I arrived at Truco and gave my euros to the same door-woman as the night before, and she grinned. *"Necesitas más, Americana?"*

"Sí," I answered. I did need more. Much more.

The bar was busier than it'd been before, and the crowd had a stronger sense of purpose to it. I didn't get the sense most of these women were relaxing. There was a more sexual tone to the music, dancing, and talking, or maybe I projected my own agenda onto the people around me.

This time instead of sitting at a table, I went right to the bar. I didn't want to be relegated to a corner like some lonely sap. I wanted to be a woman on the prowl. I almost faltered when the bartender walked over and smiled.

"Hi," I said.

"Hola." She kept on smiling, but it appeared more forced the longer she waited for me to order something.

I understood drinking and sex made a bad combination, but I didn't want to be a prude and drink water at the bar. Maybe a little alcohol would help me loosen up. I didn't have to get drunk. I could just chill out, but on what? I hated beer, and none of the farm parties I'd attended ever served much of anything else. There had to be something classier, something sexier. I scanned the special board above the bar, not recognizing any of the words until I reached the middle of the list, then I saw it.

"Sangría, por favor," I said confidently. It sounded uniquely Spanish. No one where I came from drank sangría, and saying it made me feel sexy.

The sangría looked sexy too when it arrived in a tall, thick glass. The deep red liquid glinted in the dim light of the bar and beckoned to me. I sipped tentatively, unsure what to expect. It was sweet, fruity but not in a fake way. It tasted like real apples and cherries with a hint of warmth that didn't burn my throat, but rather spread slowly through my chest and arms. I liked it, a lot, and finished more quickly than I intended to, but I didn't taste much alcohol. The next time the bartender came by, I ordered another.

This time I sipped more slowly with my back resting against the bar. Already more relaxed as I scanned the crowd of women, I didn't get overwhelmed with worry. These were my people, my community, and tonight I would prove I belonged here. I would start college cool, confident, experienced, and worthy of any woman who came along in the future. That made me think of Lina, but I pushed her image quickly from my mind. I was too close to getting what I wanted to get distracted. I just needed to find the right woman to make it all come together.

My eyes settled on a group of women by the dance area. Several of them looked pretty young, maybe twenty. All of them had good figures, and none of them appeared paired up, but I couldn't tell for sure since a few of them had their backs to me. I took another sip of the sangría. I didn't want my courage to fail me now. When one of the women shifted, my eyes met with the woman she'd been blocking, and I froze.

Her dark hair was cut close to her head, and she wore dark jeans and a black leather vest over a white T-shirt. She wasn't as young as the others, maybe in her mid-twenties, and her dark eyes made her seem even older. She blatantly scanned me up and down, then smiled. It wasn't a sweet smile, nothing like Lina's.

No, this smile was slower, more deliberate, less friendly, but it still made my stomach clench.

She wove her way slowly through the people around the bar until she stood next to me, so close I felt the slight rise and fall of her shoulders with each breath she took but she didn't say anything. She flagged down the bartender and ordered two sangrías. My heart sank. It was a repeat of the chair misunderstanding. The woman next to me was obviously buying drinks for one of her girlfriends, and I just happened to be standing in the space she wanted to occupy. I downed the rest of my sangría in an attempt to burn away my embarrassment before it caused me to flee. I forced myself to stand firm and try again, but before I could turn my attention elsewhere, the woman faced me and placed one of the glasses in my hand and then clinked it lightly with hers.

My heart beat faster and my palms started to sweat. She'd come onto me when I'd given up hope. Totally unprepared and worried my nervousness would blow my only chance, I sipped the drink to buy some time to think. I hoped she couldn't see my hand tremble as I lifted the glass to my lips.

"*Gracias,*" I said. "*Me llamo Ren.*"

Her smile broadened in a way that somehow didn't seem genuinely happy so much as predatory, but I wasn't about to complain.

"*Americana, Ren?*"

"*Sí,*" I answered, wondering if my nationality would be seen as a good thing or a bad one.

"*Qué bien,*" she said and finished her drink in a few swallows.

Okay, I guess that was a good thing.

"*Baila conmigo.*"

I recognized the words "dance with me" as a command more than a request, but I didn't care. It would've been nice if we could've talked more, but I didn't speak much Spanish. It was probably best we moved on.

I downed the rest of my third drink and let myself be led onto the floor. The woman didn't waste any time wrapping her arm around my waist and pulling me close. The strong bass beat made the floor vibrate and if the alcohol made me unsteady, I wouldn't have known because the rocking of my hips was being guided by the firm hands of the woman in front of me.

It wasn't what I'd expected. She wasn't as gentle as I thought a woman would be. There weren't any tender caresses, and I didn't get much chance to hold her, but maybe that's the way it goes when someone else leads. I'd always thought of myself as the leader, but in this case perhaps the best way to get around my inexperience was to let someone else set the pace. What did Lina say about using a guide? *Damnit, why did I have to think of her?* I finally had a woman in my arms, or I was in hers as we headed quickly in the direction I wanted to go. I shouldn't think about anything else.

The song changed to another pulsing techno beat, this one slightly slower, and I tried to throw myself back into the moment by putting my arms around the other woman's neck and pulling us closer together. I couldn't feel her body as well as I'd hoped because of the leather vest with its zippers and buckles, but I still detected softness somewhere beneath all those barriers, and it soothed me a little. I had a real live woman pressed against me. She ran her hands up my back, and for the first time in my life, I felt desirable. Someone wanted me. Someone chose me. She found me attractive, and she was sexy too. She was solid and confident, and she took what she wanted. She wasn't everything I wanted, but she was certainly everything I wanted to be. I'd waited for this exact experience, why didn't it feel right?

We danced without stopping for several songs, and every time the beat changed, my dance partner got bolder. First she leaned her head against mine. Her breath rushed warm against my skin as she began to place quick kisses along my neck and earlobe. Next, she slipped her fingers under the hem of my shirt and kneaded the bare skin above my jeans. Despite being uncomfortable with how fast we were moving, my body reacted. My skin tingled, and my senses heightened the way I'd only read about before. The new feelings scared and excited me, but they were mostly a relief. They served as confirmation there wasn't anything profoundly wrong with me. I was capable of a normal lesbian interaction. Every brush of her fingers or lips made me breathe a little faster and my head get a little lighter. Maybe the sangría had some effect on me because I couldn't focus on anything other than her body touching mine.

Finally, she lifted my chin and took my mouth with hers. The kiss didn't start slowly or tenderly. There was nothing to savor. Her tongue quickly pushed past my lips and into my mouth, startling me with its forcefulness. I felt a mix of emotions starting with confusion. I didn't know a kiss could start so fast and hard, but then again I didn't know much about kissing at all. I tried to tell myself moving quickly worked in my favor, and I should be grateful someone else took the lead because left to my own impulses I'd never get laid. At least this way I'd get the experience I wanted.

Once I'd adjusted to the pressure, and kissed her back, I wrapped my tongue around hers, sucking and nibbling her bottom lip. She apparently liked that and clutched me tighter. A wash of pleasure surged through me. I turned someone else on. I felt proud and strong and aroused. Emboldened by my first success, I moved my hands up to her hair and sank my fingers in around the base of her neck. Short and filled with product that made it kind of spiky, there wasn't much hair to hold on to, but the woman moaned in my mouth, so she must've liked it more than I did.

We'd all but stopped dancing, and the woman backed me off the dance floor. She broke our kiss and, without a word, grabbed my hand and pulled me behind her as she worked her way through the crowd. I agreed we needed to get out of there since things were obviously headed in a direction not fit for a dance floor, but I was concerned she didn't ask me if I wanted to go back to her place. Then again, I assumed that was where we were going since she hadn't exactly told me. Maybe we'd get a chance to talk on the way. Despite the language barrier, we could at least cover the basics, like her name.

Shit. I was about to leave a bar in a foreign country with a woman whose name I didn't know. I panicked and slowed down. When I did, my head spun a little and I leaned up against the wall to steady myself. Before I could catch my breath, the woman pounced on me again. She growled something in my ear in Spanish, but I was too off balance to try to translate. Then she was kissing me again, rougher this time, biting my lip and pressing hard until my back flattened against the wall.

This corner of the room was almost completely dark, the sounds of the bar muffled. Even though I couldn't see them or hear them clearly, there were other people nearby. The woman's hands roamed over my body. She pressed her palm against my breast through my shirt and squeezed a little too roughly. I squirmed, trying to lessen the discomfort, but I couldn't say anything with her mouth firmly over mine. She must've mistaken my discomfort for arousal because she slipped her other hand up under my shirt. My brain fought to send me a message through the haze of lust and alcohol, but somehow my body didn't hear the metaphorical warning bells. When I tried to push her away, my hand connected with her breast and only managed to press halfheartedly.

The woman broke away from my mouth long enough to groan, and then she dove into the crook of my neck, sucking and biting along the sensitive flesh. It was good at first, and I could catch my breath. I focused on getting control of my body and remembering my goals, but the longer the woman sucked on my skin, the more it stung. Someone brushed past not far to my right, and I remembered that whether I was enjoying myself or not, we weren't alone. I didn't know much about sex or how these types of hook-ups generally happened, but I thought what we were doing should be done in private, not in some dark corner.

"Stop," I panted, but it only came out as a hoarse whisper, and if the woman against me heard it, she gave no indication. I tried again more loudly, this time catching a handful of her shirt. "Slow down."

That got her attention but didn't appear to register any sort of understanding because she looked at me with the same predatory grin and thrust her hips into me quickly before closing in on my mouth again. I tried to settle back into the kiss, attempting to assert a little control over the tempo, and at first she responded. Instead of frantically attacking my mouth, she eased back, allowing a little space between our bodies. I relaxed. Maybe she was taking the hint. No longer scared, I attempted to enjoy the kiss. It wasn't unpleasant when she stopped suffocating me.

I actually started to feel a little sexy again when her hands slipped down the waistband of my jeans and popped open the top button, but my eyes shot open as she moved farther, pressing hard as she went. This wasn't what I wanted. I mean, it was, but it wasn't. I wanted to lose my virginity. I didn't have any unrealistic fantasies of flowers and candlelight, but I expected a bed and a little privacy. I didn't have any illusions of love, but I wanted to know her name. I didn't expect reverence, but this hurt. Her calloused hands pushed roughly against my most sensitive body parts, and I winced. Trying to pull away, I inadvertently threw myself back into the wall and hit my head, causing a flash of pain followed by a wave of dizziness, but the woman didn't let up. She pushed harder, thrusting and scraping against me, trying to get a better angle until suddenly she was gone.

A rush of cold air hit the bare flesh of my stomach, and

I sucked in a deep breath through my swollen lips. I squinted through the darkness and my own haziness to see Lina, her eyes wide with terror and looking as shaken as I felt.

"Are you okay?"

I nodded, my throat clogged with too much emotion to speak. The fear plainly crossing her features only magnified my realization of how much danger I'd been in. I trembled from the mix of adrenaline and icy mortification running through my veins.

Lina then turned on the other woman and yelled at her in Spanish. The woman had the good sense to look ashamed and made only a minimal attempt to justify herself. Lina clearly didn't want to hear it. She gestured to me and made a comment I didn't understand, but I heard the phrase "too young" and winced.

"I'm not too young," I said. My voice sounded weak and scratchy.

"What?" Lina snapped.

"I'm not too young. She didn't force me. I asked for it."

Her shoulders sagged. "You asked to be treated like that?"

The dejection on her face was too much to bear, so I stared at my shoes. The situation was more complicated than her question, but I couldn't explain myself, not here, not now. I just said, "Yes."

Her anger flashed again. She caught me by the scruff of my shirt and dragged me out the side door where she quickly hailed a cab. "Get in."

I mustered only a sliver of defiance and said, "What if I don't want to?"

"If you want to finish your tour of Spain you don't have a choice. You acted like an idiot tonight, and you made me feel like a fool for letting you. You won't get another chance to do either of those things. Get in the cab."

❖

We flew through the streets of Madrid, causing everything to spin around me. The streetlights blurred together as I slouched against the window. The panic I'd felt moments earlier still buzzed through my body, but as it began to subside, new emotions swept in. I was overwhelmed by dejection, desolation, depression, and the realization I'd failed in the most ultimate way. I was out of excuses. I'd had the opportunity to seize everything I'd ever wanted, and I'd blown it. I'd freaked out, and instead of enjoying and learning and getting past my first time, I'd fallen apart. I couldn't even get laid when someone tried to force me. I wasn't supposed to be scared or helpless. Sex should be the one thing that came naturally, the thing to prove I wouldn't be a loser or a fake for the rest of my life. Now what? I still didn't have the slightest clue how to act around women. I still didn't have any confidence in myself. Hell, if I wasn't a good lesbian, I didn't even know who I was supposed to be.

"Damnit!" I shouted, making both Lina and the driver jump. "What am I going to do now?"

"Cristo," Lina snapped, "are you drunk?"

"Yes." I didn't see any point in lying. The sangría was clearly affecting me, but that was the least of my problems.

She rubbed her hand vigorously over her face as if trying to scrub away the situation. "I can't believe you did this to me."

"To you?" I snorted. "You're the one who barged in on me and…and—"

"You don't even know her name."

"She doesn't matter. It's not about her. Why doesn't anyone understand that? It's about me."

The cabbie pulled up to our hotel and shooed us out of his car. I'm not even sure if he made Lina pay him, he was so happy to be done with us. The spinning wasn't as bad if I stood still, but I didn't get the chance to enjoy that for long. Lina dragged me upstairs while I stumbled and tripped my way along, trying to keep up.

She never let go of me as she unlocked and pushed open the door to her room. I finally managed to squeak out, "You're going to make me fall."

"You're going to fall because you're drunk." She shoved me into the shower, clothes and all, then turned on the cold water.

"Shit!" I shouted and tried to squirm away from the frigid spray, but I slipped and slid back into the tub, soaking myself further. I kicked and thrashed for a few seconds to right myself, but the water hit me directly in the face. I tried again to push myself up, but my arms wouldn't support my weight. Between the alcohol and exhaustion from my earlier terror, I was too weak to fight anymore. I'd lost, yet again, and I sank down, wishing the water were deep enough to drown in. As soon as I stopped struggling, my head began to clear. The room wasn't as blurry, and my body stopped swaying against my will. I shook now from the cold, not from the lack of stability.

I looked up through the water cascading over me and saw Lina, her arms folded across her chest and her lips pursed in a thin, hard line. "Ask me for help," she said quietly.

"What?"

"Do you want out?" she asked, her voice flat.

"Yes," I mumbled.

"Then ask me to help you."

"I want out."

"That's not good enough," she said.

I rolled my eyes and tried again. "Help me out."

She shook her head. "That was an order, not a request."

Why was she doing this? Was she some kind of sadist? I shivered and tried to give her a hard stare, but I kept having to blink the water out of my eyes.

"*Dios mío*, Ren, you can't do it, can you?" She threw her hands in the air. "You have to be perfect? You have to be better than everyone else? You have to do everything on your own?"

"You don't understand."

"You keep telling me that," she shouted. "*I don't understand.* What don't I understand? That you're superwoman? You're a stud? You're too good—"

"I'm not good enough!" I screamed.

"What?" She stared at me, eyes wide, mouth open.

"I'm not too good! I'm not good at all. I'm not smart or strong or confident. I'm not cool or crazy or funny. I'm not a stud. I'm not suave. I'm not attractive."

"Okay." She knelt beside the tub.

"No, it's not okay." Once I started I couldn't stop. Everything I'd tried to hide from everyone poured out of me. "I'm a loser. I have no idea what I'm doing. I don't have any skills, or even any interests. I have no idea what I'm doing with my life. I'm confused constantly. Every time I get close to doing something right, I screw it up. I don't belong anywhere, and I'm tired of not knowing what to do. I'm never going to get better if I don't change, and I don't know how to change if I can't figure out how to be better. Tonight was my chance to learn, and I blew it."

"Blew what?" she asked softly.

"My chance to learn how to act around women. My chance to lose my inexperience, lose all my insecurities, lose my virginity."

"Your what?" She gasped. "*Madre de Dios*, you were about to spend your first time being complicit in your own rape?"

When she put it that way, it didn't sound at all like I'd planned. I didn't want to say yes, but I couldn't deny what I'd gone to the bar looking for. "I'll do anything to not be like this anymore."

"You were so eager to throw away something you'll never get back because you thought it would make you feel better about yourself?"

Why did it seem like such a good idea in my head but sound

so stupid when she said it? I was tired of answering questions that made me feel dumb.

"Was it working, Ren? Did you feel better when you were drunk up against a wall with a stranger? Did you find the answers you were searching for?"

"No." As much as I wanted to deny it, I hadn't liked any of it. "I already told you, I'm a loser. I didn't know what to do. I'm a terrible lover. I'm a bad lesbian, and I'm going to end up alone."

"What you did in there had nothing to do with loving, and you don't become a lesbian in the back room of a bar." She pushed herself back into a standing position. "But you're right about one thing, if you don't learn to admit you're human and ask for help, you *will* end up alone." Then, without giving me another look, she left the room.

I lay there, no longer feeling the cold water that had long since soaked through my clothes. The deep chill settling over me now came from the echo of Lina's words. She was right. Nothing I'd done over the last five days had helped. I was the same pathetic person I'd always been. I was still a wreck of insecurities and pretending I wasn't. Trying to force myself to fake control had only put me in a dangerous situation. Maybe it was time to give up.

My tears started to fall. I hadn't cried in years, but now the frustration at having to give up, the sadness of my failure, and the relief of letting go welled up and spilled out of me. I used my last steady breath to call, "Lina, will you please help me?"

She was beside me in an instant, pulling me out of the tub. She wrapped me first in a towel and then in her arms, pulling me tightly against her as the sobs continued to rack my body. She whispered soft shushing sounds in my ear and stroked my wet hair. "It'll be okay now, *nena*."

I don't know how long I let her hold me, but I somehow managed to pull myself together enough to put on some dry clothes and get into the bed Lina turned down for me. The exhaustion was almost unbearable, and I drifted off before I even lay down. But as I did she said, "You're going to feel better tomorrow."

"I don't want to *feel* better. I want to *be* better," I mumbled and turned over.

I couldn't be sure but it sounded like she whispered, "You're already so much more than you know."

Day Six

My head throbbed before I even opened my eyes. I lay still, trying not to remember why I felt awful, but the memories rushed back anyway. My muscles were bruised from the tension of being literally up against a wall. My eyes burned, my nose clogged from sobbing. Worst of all, my chest ached, a deep, suffocating constriction caving in on the spot where my heart and ego once resided. I didn't know how to face the day ahead with no purpose, no sense of self, and no hope of improvement. I didn't even have my façade of bravado to hide behind after my breakdown the night before. I felt raw, exposed, like my skin was thin and translucent. A shell of myself, I feared if I moved I'd crack and crumble to pieces.

"Ren," I heard a soft voice whisper. "It's time to get up."

Someone sat on the bed beside me, then placed a hand on my shoulder, not shaking me, but rubbing gently. I opened my eyes slowly to see Lina smiling down at me. My breath caught in my throat. She was the most beautiful thing I'd ever seen. Her dark hair spilled over her shoulders and her brown eyes filled with concern. *"Buenos días."*

"Morning," I replied, my voice hoarse and my throat scratchy. I wasn't sure about the "good" part yet, but waking up to her eased some of my pain.

"Cómo estás?" she asked.

"Así así," I responded automatically.

The answer sparked a huge grin out of her. "You spoke Spanish."

"Did I?" I tried to sit up, but the pounding in my head made me groan and lean back against the headboard.

"Sit still." She grabbed a glass of water off the bedside table. "Drink all of this."

I lifted the glass to my mouth, hoping the trembling in my hands wasn't too noticeable, but then again, a little shaking was likely the least of my worries. I probably looked as bad as I felt, if not worse. I couldn't believe the first time I woke up to the sight of a beautiful woman I looked and felt like crap. Wouldn't I ever catch a break?

"Better?" she asked when I finished the whole glass.

"A little."

"Bien," she said, then stood. "Get up slowly, then go get ready. We leave for Toledo in an hour."

The prospect of another bus ride or walk in the heat was enough to make me flop back into bed. "Maybe I should stay in today."

"Lo siento, that's not an option for you anymore. You stay with me until I can trust you again."

My face flamed with embarrassment, and I started to say I was twenty and didn't need a chaperone. Then I remembered the look of terror on her face when she'd pulled the woman off me the night before. I threw off the covers, gathered my things quickly, then bolted for my own room.

"What happened to you?" Andi asked as soon as I walked in.

"I don't want to talk about it," I grumbled and turned on the shower.

"Are you okay?" Caroline called out from the other side of the bathroom door.

"I'm fine," I lied as I caught a glimpse of myself in the mirror.

No wonder they'd freaked out. My hair was matted. My normally blue eyes were pale and rimmed red. Lina's clothes hung loosely across my chest, and the pants were too short. Worst of all, a series of violent red marks ran down the side of my neck. I pulled off the shirt and examined myself more closely. The bite marks extended across my shoulders, and a series of raised scratches ran down one side of my abs.

I felt the woman's hands on me again, her nails digging in painfully as she pinned me helplessly to the wall. I hung my head in my hands and took several deep breaths, attempting to keep the panic at bay. Once steady, I quickly showered and scrubbed myself raw with soap and scalding hot water as if I could somehow wipe away the reality of what I'd almost done. Lina was right: I couldn't be trusted. I didn't even recognize myself in the mirror. Not only was I uncool and unattractive, now I was unsafe to be left alone.

❖

The ride to Toledo lasted an hour, and I sat alone in the back of the bus. Occasionally one of my friends glanced back at me, but they could obviously tell I wanted to be left alone. I didn't know what to tell them. I didn't know how to relate to them without pretending to be the carefree, independent, reckless baby dyke they admired. I never believed I was the person everyone else did, but I hoped I could be. Now I'd lost that hope. I'd done everything in my power to turn into a strong, sexy, independent lesbian and failed. After last night's disaster, I understood I wasn't lacking in motive or opportunity, but rather some key component to my character was insufficient or missing altogether.

Jesús stopped the bus in the middle of nowhere and opened the door. Lina motioned for us to follow her outside, I didn't know why, but I was done second-guessing her.

The five of us stood on the roadside under gray clouds. A

warm breeze stirred our hair and sent waves shimmering through the tall grass on the surrounding hillsides. Below, a river moved swiftly among rocks and over little drop-offs. On the other side, its bank rose steeply to meet a city wall, tan and gray like the buildings behind it. Something sparked my memory, a foggy image in comparison with the view before me. The picture in my mind didn't have the roads or cars, but seemed too similar to be coincidental.

I glanced at Lina and found her watching me carefully, the hint of a smile quirked at the corner of her mouth, giving me the familiar suspicion she was waiting for something.

"It's the *View of Toledo*," I said.

Her smile broadened exponentially, and for a moment I thought she would throw her arms around me. Instead she cleared her throat and said, "You're right. We're standing in roughly the same spot where El Greco painted one of the most famous landscapes in history, four hundred years ago."

"Señora has the painting in our classroom," Caroline said.

"The Met in New York has the original, but many people who love España choose this as their image of our country. Now that you've seen this place, you'll notice the painting in a great many places, and each time you do, you'll remember this moment. Take some photos, and take some time to imprint this moment on your memories."

She stepped back while the others talked in hushed tones as they snapped pictures. I'd have to get copies later because I had too much on my mind to play amateur photographer. Instead I chose to sit on a stone and soak up the scene.

I closed my eyes and breathed deeply. The smell of impending rain soothed me like the warm towel Lina had wrapped around me the night before. I'd been so broken I opened myself up in every way. I'd needed a moment's relief and hadn't intended to fall apart completely, but once I let my guard drop, everything poured out. My fears and failures, the insecurities I'd hidden roared to the surface the way the river rushed over the stones trying to impede it. The tension of carrying that weight for so long wouldn't give me temporary rest. When I tried to loosen my burden, it crushed me completely. I couldn't pick it up again or put the pieces back together, but I didn't know how to move forward without them.

Without my bravado to sustain me, or the barriers I'd erected to protect myself, I didn't know how to function. Without my image of myself, I didn't know how to relate to others. Without my search for community, I didn't know where I belonged, and without the lessons I hoped to learn, I didn't know where I was headed. I was ready to let go of my former sense of self and all the dreams that came with it, but could anything fill those voids or would I always carry this overwhelming emptiness?

I felt Lina sit down before I even opened my eyes to the scene before me once again. "I'm sorry."

"I accept your apology, Ren." I marveled at how she said it without hesitation. I doubted I'd ever accept anything about myself with such ease.

"Did you know El Greco wasn't Spanish? His name means 'The Greek.'"

The change in topic was abrupt, but welcome. "You said he's one of Spain's biggest artists."

"He is. He adopted Spain as his home, and the country in turn adopted him. He learned the formal art of painting in Italy, but never lived up to his potential under their restrictive schools. It wasn't until he found the nurturing heart of this country that he created true masterpieces."

She was throwing me a lifeline. She'd been trying to do so all along, and I'd refused her every time. She offered me a chance to see this country through the eyes of someone who loved it, and the prospect made me the slightest bit less empty than before.

"Thank you," I said. "For everything."

She wrapped her arm around my shoulder. This time I didn't

pull away. I had nothing left to prove or to hide. I relaxed into my surroundings and into her.

❖

We drove through the ancient heart of Toledo with the modern din of cars and busses, winding our way through century-old stone buildings and narrow one-way streets. Lina pointed out churches and monuments along the way, reciting history of Roman occupiers, Moorish caliphs, and Spanish lords.

"Those people fought each other all the time?" Andi asked. "Until Spain finally won?"

Lina shook her head. "It's much more complicated. There wasn't a Spain back then. The Romans built much of Toledo and turned it into a major center of commerce for the area, but when their empire fell, the Visigoths brought the Nicene faith. In the eighth century, the Moors conquered Spain and led a golden age where Christians, Jews, and Muslims lived in peace. Toledo became rich in economy and culture. Its wealth along with its location made the city a central site for battles between Moors and Christians during the Reconquista."

We stared at her, overwhelmed by the whirlwind history lesson. She grinned, and it seemed like she was looking at me more than the others. "Don't worry about the dates or even the names. Just remember this city has been a center of major cultures for over a thousand years, and every group left an impression on it. Those influences blended together to make a distinct culture all its own."

I thought about her words in light of what I'd experienced over the last few days. Was it possible I didn't have my own culture, but rather a mix of identities? It was a nice idea, but kind of far-fetched. How could I master more than one community when I couldn't navigate any one of them successfully?

We exited the bus at a stone building with a tan brick

bell tower. The line of windows in the bell tower were cut and engraved like the decorations I'd seen on TV reports of Muslim countries. I began to understand what Lina meant about the mixing of cultures.

"This is La Iglesia de Santo Tomé," she said, leading us inside. The church wasn't anything like the one we'd seen in Barcelona, but small and sparsely designed. I started to wonder what we were doing there at all when she led us into a side room. A massive painting covered an entire wall. I immediately recognized the style as belonging to El Greco and silently congratulated myself when Lina confirmed my knowledge, saying, "This is *The Burial of the Count of Orgaz* painted by El Greco."

The painting was almost too big to take in. The upper part showed a heaven scene with angels and God and Mary and a bunch of other people, while the bottom half depicted a funeral scene. On closer look, though, some of the people at the funeral appeared heavenly too.

"What's it mean?" I asked reverently, a little awestruck by the enormity of both the painting and its subject.

"It's a depiction of a legend from this part of the country. Supposedly Count Orgaz was such a righteous man, St. Augustine and St. Steven descended from heaven and buried him with their own hands, much to the astonishment of the funeral attendees," she said in her tour guide voice.

"Cool," Hannah said. "Where're we going next?"

Lina's shoulders slumped a little, but her voice never wavered from its professional tone. "We're scheduled here a little longer, then we'll head to a steel factory."

"Can we wait outside?" Andi asked.

"Of course," she said and turned back to the artwork. She'd probably seen the painting a thousand times and would see it again with the next group she brought through, and yet she would still spend every minute of her allotted time gazing at the masterpiece, while my friends, who'd never seen it and would probably never see it again, moved on in a matter of minutes. What did she see, and more importantly, could I see it too?

"Ren?" Caroline held the door open for me.

I shook my head. This time they made no jokes about me being an art dyke or wisecracks about the Virgin Mary. Maybe they could sense a change in me, maybe they were still afraid of what I'd seen in the mirror this morning, but Caroline shrugged and walked away.

"You can go with your friends," Lina said as I stepped up beside her, both of us looking at the picture.

"That's okay. I like the painting."

"What do you like about it?"

She waited quietly while I tried to find the words for concepts I'd never considered before. "I like the colors," I said, feeling stupid for not coming up with something more brilliant, but she gave no indication of judgment. I pointed to a figure in the lower half of painting. "Like the priest, his robe is black, but his shawl is this see-through white. You can still see the black underneath, but it's not gray. Both the white and the black show through perfectly at the same time. That shouldn't be possible, right?"

"What else?" she asked, still staring at the painting, but the corners of her mouth quirked upward like she was trying to hide a smile.

I scanned the looming masterpiece. "The difference between heaven and Earth is clear because of the differences in location and color, but at the same time, they aren't really separate." I chewed on my lip, thinking of a way to be clearer. "There's no ground, there's no sky, the heavens and the people on earth melt into each other, and even before I knew what was happening, I understood some of the people below belonged to heaven because of their size and brightness."

This time she turned and gave me her full attention. "What will you study at your university?"

My stomach lurched. "I don't know," I admitted, dejected once again for knowing so little about myself.

"Maybe you should consider art."

"I'm not artistic."

"You may not be an artist, but you have the eye of one. The things you described are the things great art critics and historians point out when they're in this room."

"Yeah?" I didn't know there was such a thing as an art historian.

"They use different terms, but the concepts are the same, and most of them have spent years in school. You have a natural ability to see those things."

"I don't know about that." I flushed at the compliment.

"I do. You proved it with what you saw," she said, then added, "and you saw those things yesterday too, didn't you?"

I nodded, embarrassed to admit it.

"Why didn't you say so?"

"I don't want people to think I'm a nerd."

"People?" She raised her eyebrows.

"Yeah, the girls, or women in general." I hung my head. "It's not sexy, you know?"

"No, I don't know. A woman who's passionate about something, a woman with natural talent and eye for beauty is very sexy."

My breath caught, stifling any response. All I could do was blush profusely and stare at my shoes.

"You have a lot of things you're still discovering about yourself. Embrace every step of your journey." She hooked a finger under my chin and lifted it until our eyes met. "Because I'd hate for you to hide any part of the amazing woman I see emerging in you."

❖

My stomach was improving but still a little uneasy from the remnants of the sangría in my system, a reminder of my stupidity the night before. Despite Lina bolstering my confidence, I still felt dangerously exposed. It took all my fortitude to consume a small box lunch while we drove through more modern parts of the city where the old brick and stone structures gave way to large concrete warehouses and the occasional factory. I tried to focus on my surroundings rather than my internal turmoil.

As Jesús drove, Lina explained Toledo had a long tradition of producing high-quality iron and steel goods and still produced some of the world's best swords and knives.

"While the production of iron changed over the centuries, a few factories use the traditional Toledan forging process to make swords. That's what we'll see today."

"Swords are cool." Hannah stated the obvious. As much as I enjoyed the art museums, swords did sound sexier than paintings, though judging by my recent luck, I'd probably chop off a finger.

Once we were inside a small factory, a local guide took over, leading us into a small room filled with iron sheets and bars. The metal was blunt, dirty, and awkward for the guide to wield. He spoke about the properties of the material, but my mind wandered when I caught the smell of Lina's perfume, light and citrus, as she stood near me. She hadn't hovered, but she stayed close all day. Her attention probably stemmed from one part concern and the other part distrust. My previous behavior justified both. I'd scared her the night before. I'd been scared too, so it hadn't really struck me at the time. Then there was anger, like a fire burning her deep brown eyes and hardening her normally soft features. Anger I understood. I was angry too, angry for failing to see the danger in the situation, angry for not being stronger, and angry at the injustice of having no model for how to relate to my own people.

The next emotion should've been disappointment, or maybe

pity. Either would've followed logically, and I expected both today. I thought she'd be disappointed I behaved badly and because I wasn't who I pretended to be. I thought she'd feel sorry for me after my meltdown. I wouldn't have blamed her if she'd gone parental or treated me like a kid needing to be led through basic interactions. I'd certainly shown myself unworthy of respect, freely admitting how pathetic I was. I expected her to treat me that way; instead she was sensitive and attentive, without a hint of pity. She'd shown caring but no condescension. She'd stayed close to me, but it felt more like friendship than obligation.

We moved to the next room where a man forged long strips of iron over blazing-hot coals in what looked like a huge stone oven. The heat became overwhelming, and we stayed only long enough to see the blade take shape. The room was loud with the whirring of blades being polished, the black burn patterns melding into a dull gray as the metal started to resemble a sword. When the blade was fully formed and sharpened, the artisans dipped them in nickel for protection and shine.

"What do you think?" Lina asked as we watched the handle being attached to a sword.

"It's beautiful," I said.

"The process always amazes me. It's the same material from the first room, no?"

"I suppose so."

"It's been through fire, ground down, and picked up a few things along the way, but its core makeup is the same. The metal possessed every necessary property at the beginning, but the transformation refined it to something we recognize as an object of strength and beauty."

I grinned at her thinly veiled analogy of my own trials.

"What?" she asked.

"Are these lessons getting less subtle, or am I simply more open to them?"

She playfully bumped her hip into mine. "Maybe both."

The contact was fun and lighthearted, and I smiled in spite of the reminder I'd gone through fire the night before. I couldn't be dreary when she looked happy.

As our tour ended, we entered a large room lined with swords, axes, and battle armor. "Imagine that. We exit through the gift shop," Caroline said.

"Reminds me of the good ole USA," I quipped.

"The need to sell and buy products we'll never use is not a solely American virtue," Lina said.

"Who says I won't use a sword?" Andi jumped onto a large green mat in the display area and drew one of the display swords.

"You never know when you're going to need to run someone through," I said, grabbing a sword of my own and leveling it at Andi. "This world is full of weirdos."

"Weirdos? What about scary predatory lesbians?"

"You offend my honor," I said in my best knightly impression. "We shall duel."

"En garde." Andi lunged at me. We swung our swords carefully and with great theatrics, tapping them together then spinning away dramatically, making our own clinking and crashing sound effects. We acted like big kids chasing each other around the backyard. The realness of the swords only made the entire exchange more extravagant.

The others stood at the edge of the mat cheering while we whirled and clashed. "My money's on Andi," Caroline laughed.

"I don't know. Ren is more butch." Hannah giggled in a way that made me think she'd never used the term "butch" before.

"Ren's all mouth and no trousers," Caroline said.

"Ah, you wound me with your tongue sharper than a blade." I stumbled and clutched my chest. Andi seized her opportunity to finish me and drove her sword along my side where I trapped it with my arm to make it appear I'd been run through. I fell to the mat with a thump, then glanced up to see Lina standing over me, her eyes bright with laughter.

"M'lady…" I coughed and sputtered in the exaggerated throes of a stage death.

"My dashing knight." She giggled as she knelt beside me.

I groaned, trying to stifle a laugh. I hadn't been so happy in I don't know how long, like this little moment of letting go allowed another small part of my emptiness to fade away. Still, I was supposed to be dying, so I tried to muster up some seriousness for the role. "I was slain."

She shook her head, her beautiful features lit up with joy. "Yes, but you looked good doing it."

"Who knew all I had to do to win your attention was get run through with a sword."

She pulled me to my feet, then tousled my hair. "You fought a valiant but unnecessary battle," she said, stepping closer under the guise of brushing some dust off my back, then whispered, "you've had my attention all along."

My stomach tightened, expelling all the air from my lungs as I watched her go. My whole body buzzed, and I couldn't form a single complete thought through the mix of emotions and physical sensations overwhelming me. How did she manage to make such a mess of me, then walk away completely unaffected?

I picked up the sword Andi had dropped after my fall in battle. It was beautiful and strong, both rugged and refined. I glanced across the room at the beautiful woman with the dark laughing eyes, and knew that while the piece of steel in my hands didn't remind me of myself at all, it belonged with me nonetheless.

I carried it to the counter, relishing the sight and weight of its handle in my hand for a second longer before handing it to the cashier. *"Esta espada, por favor,"* I told him. *It's the one for me.*

"Why this one?" he asked, ringing up the purchase.

I shrugged and glanced at Lina one more time before answering, "She slayed me."

❖

After we got back to Madrid we all went to our rooms to unwind before dinner. I was thankful for the chance to rest up after the physical and emotional disaster of the night before. Andi wrote in her journal, and Caroline wrote to Carl. Neither of them asked again what happened, and I didn't offer. How could I tell them everything they knew about me was a façade of confidence that only covered dangerous insecurities, and the shell of protective bravado had failed me in a monumental way? I chose to be thankful for the space and silence they gave me.

I drifted in the space between zoning out and sleeping when Lina knocked on the door. Andi let her in.

I sat up and scooted over, giving her space to sit down on the bed. Andi and Caroline gave each other a look I didn't understand. I made a note to pay more attention to them. "Do you have plans tonight?" Lina asked.

"Not really," Andi said.

"It's my turn to watch Hannah," I answered. "I guess you'll want to keep an eye on us."

"Yes, I thought we could all stay together tonight, but instead of seeing it as babysitting, we could just enjoy each other's company."

While her phrasing sounded nicer, it didn't change the facts of the situation. "Sure, what'd you have in mind?"

"Tapas."

"Um, well." Andi seemed embarrassed. "We tried tapas the other day, and it didn't go well."

"What do you mean?"

"We went to a restaurant and asked the waiter for tapas," Caroline said. "He stared at us like we were crazy and kept asking what we wanted. We kept saying tapas and then he asked what we wanted again and we said tapas."

Lina bit her lip trying to hold in her laughter.

"He finally brought us beer nuts and two hard-boiled eggs," Andi said.

"What did you expect?" Lina asked, a little giggle escaping at the end of the question.

"I don't know. Señora told us Spanish people ate tapas, and they were like snacks."

This time Lina laughed outright. "She should've been more specific, but it's easier to show than to tell. If you'd like I'll take you to La Taberna del Alabardero."

"Tapas, take two," Andi said enthusiastically.

I didn't share her optimism about Spanish food, but I found the prospect of going out with friends strangely comforting after my pressure-filled misadventures of previous nights.

"*Bien*. We'll wait for Hannah to get off the phone with her mamá, and then we'll go."

"How's Señora?" Caroline asked.

"She's recovering well, and she's excited for Málaga, but she misses Hannah."

I felt a little pang of guilt. Despite the fun I'd had with Hannah in Barcelona, I'd completely ignored her here in Madrid. "I bet Hannah misses her too. I'm glad I'm staying with her tonight."

"Actually, we're all going out together, but she'll sleep in here, since you and I are going to be roomies."

"We are?"

"I think that'll work out best for everyone," Lina said cheerfully, but with certainty that didn't leave room for discussion. "Why don't you take a few minutes to get your stuff settled in my room, and then we can all meet down at the bus."

Another questioning expression passed between Caroline and Andi. It irked me that Lina didn't trust me even though I hadn't given her any reason to. Frustration welled up in me, and my temper flared as I tossed some clothes and my toothbrush into my backpack. I could feel my friends' eyes on my back and sensed their questions. My pride made a stubborn attempt to rebound, but lashing out at Lina wouldn't change what she'd seen, so rather than say something I'd regret, I grabbed my things and left.

Hannah was leaving the room as I entered. I took a few minutes to collect myself before heading downstairs.

I was the first one on the bus with Jesús, and he greeted me with his big grin. *"Hola."*

"Hola. Everyone else should be down in a minute."

He nodded, causing his big mop of frizzy hair to bob up and down.

"Lina's taking us all out to dinner," I said, fully aware that he wouldn't understand. Still, it didn't feel comfortable just sitting silently with him.

"Then she's going to babysit me all night whether I want to or not," I added in a bit of pout.

His smile faded but he continued to nod, probably sensing another venting session coming on.

"The thing is, I don't really mind hanging out with her. We had a great time today, and Lord knows I am not going back to Chueca tonight." I checked to see if the name of the gayborhood registered anything with him, but his expression remained attentively blank.

"Anyway, why should it matter that she's going to keep an eye on me? I get it, I really do. I can't take care of myself, I'm not who I pretended to be, and I'm not trying to fake it anymore. I brought this on myself, but it still feels terrible, you know?"

Lines of either worry or confusion creased his deeply tanned forehead, but he didn't speak, leaving me to fill the silence.

I sighed. "I just liked it so much today when we were hanging out together and joking around. I would love more of that, but I don't know if she really wants to be around me or if she feels like she has to. I mean, she hasn't made me feel like a bother, but what if I'm just a professional obligation to her?

"I guess I don't have any choice really." I shrugged. "But damn, she makes me feel so good one minute, then like a complete idiot the next. I mean I was afraid she'd hate it if she knew what a loser I was, but now it's so much more complicated than that. I don't feel like she hates me at all. It seems like she may actually like me more today. There's this weird vibe between us now that feels so good sometimes, and then I remember why we had our little breakthrough, I mean what I did, and what she saw, and hell, I don't know. I just feel like crap again."

I was going around in circles just like I always did, but now I felt close to something, like if I could just jump the track I was on I might have a shot at something real, but I didn't know how to do it. Instead of making any sort of meaningful change, I was left venting, once again to someone who couldn't understand me. Then again, at least he couldn't judge me either. There was a certain safety in that.

I looked up to see the others exit the hotel. I was out of time and out of the energy to fight anymore. "I guess some things are just out of my hands, Jesús."

He gave me a skeptical look, then shook his head. I felt bad for unloading on him and leaving him confused, but confusion was all I could muster right now.

❖

We all sat around a table on the patio of La Taberna del Alabardero and watched the people pass in the orange light of dusk. The waiter brought a basket of heavily crusted bread. Hannah knocked her roll against the table, and it didn't bend or indent. She then made an exaggerated attempt to bite it, which looked more like a mouse trying to gnaw through a rock.

"I'm pretty sure four out of five dentists wouldn't recommend this," Hannah said.

We all laughed. Despite a few childish moments, she'd handled the whole trip really well and still kept her sense of humor.

"Try this." Lina held a roll in her strong hands and broke it in two with a crisp crack. She then uncovered a small dish of olive oil in the middle of the table. The oil smelled strong and rich. I could almost taste the fragrance. She dipped the bread and then brought it to her mouth, closing her eyes as the bread touched her tongue and clearly savoring the feel of it. I glanced at my friends to see if the simple demonstration affected them the same way it did me, but none of their hands trembled, none of their muscles appeared tense, and if the sound of their own pulses rushed through their ears, it didn't show. Instead they all reached for the bread and oil as though the food inspired them, while the woman had no effect.

Okay, it was only me, then. I guess that wasn't unreasonable since I was the only lesbian in the group, but I'd seen plenty of women eat, and none of them looked so sexy. Why did I fixate on her hands, her mouth, and the way she closed her eyes?

Thankfully the waiter interrupted by bringing us our drinks. He was young, probably close to our age with thick, dark hair, an easy smile, and a name tag that said "Esteban." The girls practically swooned every time he came by, and he seemed bolstered by the attention. He pressed a little too close when he poured their water, and his eyes wandered a little too far when he answered questions about the specials. He spoke English in a thick accent to Andi, Caroline, and Hannah, and they all melted. I envied him. He was kind of cheesy, but that was his right. As a handsome young man, he knew what he could get away with. His flirtations appeared effortless, stemming either from some natural instinct or plenty of opportunity to practice. I watched with amusement as he played his part with my friends.

When he turned his finesse toward Lina, my reaction changed. His playful qualities were no longer comical, or boyish. When he leaned in to indicate an item on the menu, his shoulder grazed hers casually but intentionally. His voice dropped and his broken English turned to deep, rolling Spanish as they discussed various options. His eyes never wavered from her while he took her order, and made no move to write down her request, as if to show he committed her every word to memory. My envy turned to jealousy, and what appeared sweet with the others tasted bitter when directed at Lina. I set my jaw and ground my teeth, frustrated he could easily move from simple flirtation to signaling of genuine attraction, while I floundered in the former category. My own encounters with women ranged from bumbling to predatory with nothing in between, and here in a matter of seconds, this boy flawlessly demonstrated everything I couldn't. His success mirrored my failures, and I hated him for reminding me of what I'd probably never be.

"He was flirting with you." Hannah giggled when Esteban left.

"He wasn't good at it," Lina said flippantly, giving more attention to her water than to the conversation.

"He seemed to do a pretty good job from where I'm sitting," I said flatly.

She raised her eyebrows over the rim of her glass. "How so?"

"His posture, his tone, his eye contact, he used them perfectly. He gave all the right cues he was interested."

"Exactly," Lina said. "He gave all the cues and didn't pay any attention to the ones I sent him."

"What cues were those?" I asked.

"You didn't pay attention to me either? I guess that'll teach you who to watch next time."

The other girls burst out laughing. "She got you there, Ren."

I blushed because I had been watching him and not her, and because she'd called me out in front of my friends. Still, even in the flush of embarrassment I couldn't muster any real resentment when she talked to me so playfully. Her lightheartedness undercut my brooding in a way that was both frustrating and endearing.

"What did you order us?" Andi asked.

"I ordered a sampling of some of the local favorites."

"I thought we were having tapas." Hannah pouted.

Lina laughed. "We are. Tapas aren't a specific food. They're a method for serving food. Tapas means you get small portions of several things. You get less of each item than you would in a meal, but you get to taste a wide variety of foods."

"Like appetizers?"

"In a way, but tapas aren't only starter foods. They can be casual or fancy and made up of meats, fruits, or cheeses, more like tiny meals than snacks."

The waiter arrived again with a large tray of food, which he set on a folding stand. He said the name of each item as he set it on our table, but I didn't pay much attention to him this time and instead watched Lina interact with him. More accurately I watched how she didn't interact with him. When Esteban reached over her arm to put a plate in front of her, she shifted slightly out of his line of contact. When he asked her a question in an attentive voice, she answered him with a short and polite *"Bien,"* not leaving room for further conversation. Finally, when he lingered, his smile wide, waiting for her to return his eye contact, she smiled, not at him, but at *me*.

"Te gusta?" she asked, the playful lilt in her voice leaving me to wonder if her question referred to her food selections, or the subtle way she'd dismissed our waiter's attention.

Either way, my answer was the same, *"Sí, me gusta mucho."*

❖

Stuffed from our tapas, we waddled more than walked toward La Plaza Mayor. The others had spent more time in the square over the past few days, so they wandered around some stores that lined the perimeter, talking, joking, and picking up a few final souvenirs, but I wanted to see the sights I'd missed during our first visit. I'd been too preoccupied to take in the beautiful stone arches and red brick walls. The sun had set, but the space was well lit by the soft golden haze of streetlights and the glow emanating from wrought-iron balconies. One bright light focused on a Spanish flag flying in the center of a wall under a large Spanish crest engraved in the stone.

"That's the crest of Juan Carlos Primero," Lina said, following my gaze. "It represents the regions of Spain with the emblems of the various provinces he ruled."

"Which one's yours?" I asked.

"Mine?" She stood close to me, in the muted light, and I enjoyed the illusion of solitude the surrounding dimness provided us.

"Which emblem represents your home region?"

"It's represented in the center of the crest. It would've fallen under the region of Granada then, but it's considered Andalucía now. My home's outside the city of Málaga." Her voice sounded wistful.

"Will you take me there?"

"To Málaga? *Sí*, it's on the tour. Most groups enjoy it because they get to spend the day at the beach." She nudged me gently, and we walked slowly across the square to join the others.

"How will you spend the day?" I didn't know what had come over me. I would've avoided this type of conversation a few days earlier. Maybe I'd grown more comfortable with her, or perhaps my desire to enjoy our closeness outweighed my insecurities.

"I'll visit *mi madre*, have a siesta in a hammock, maybe visit one of my favorite cafés in the evening, and watch the sun set behind the mountains." I could only see her face in silhouette, but I heard a smile in her voice.

"Will you take me with you?" I asked again.

She stopped and faced me. "Tell me honestly, Ren, where would you rather be tonight, here or Chueca?"

The mention of Chueca shocked my system and caused a shiver to course through me. I hadn't thought of trying to get there, I didn't miss the place or my quest for the things I associated with it. How was it possible to be more comfortable in a presence of straight friends than I'd been with lesbians the two nights before? The one lesbian with me tonight held more allure than the entire crowd of women in Truco. I'd learned more from her too. I wasn't sure what that said about me, or my future, but I did know my answer to this particular question.

"Here."

I didn't know how to say it more clearly, and if she'd pushed me, I couldn't explain my reasoning, but she didn't ask. Instead she wrapped her arm around my waist, and we started walking again.

I loved the feel of her beside me, the citrus scent of her perfume, and brush of cotton-clad skin yielding against my own. My every sense went into overdrive, but not the paralyzing kind that had clouded my judgment at the bar. These sensations consumed me in the way one could disappear into the warm steam of a shower or sink into the plush covers of a king-sized bed. While the feeling was foreign, it also held something familiar, something fitting, something that couldn't be verbalized, and didn't need to be.

When we joined the others, she moved her arm and started an innocuous conversation with Hannah about the earrings she'd bought for Señora. Caroline and Andi reviewed pictures on their digital camera. Somewhere in the dark distance, a street musician's traditional Spanish guitar mingled with faint sounds of city traffic. I breathed deeply, letting go of my impulse to overanalyze our brief connection or the ease of our silence. I didn't know what the moment meant to her, or what the shift signaled in me, but for the moment I didn't have to. Even if I didn't know where I was headed, for now I was where I wanted to be.

DAY SEVEN

I awoke to the sound of the shower running and muted tones of Lina singing. I propped myself on my elbow and listened. I didn't know the tune, but I was pretty sure she was off-key, which made me inexplicably happy, like somehow the little imperfection made her more perfect.

For a second it occurred to me the direction my thoughts had just taken might be a dangerous one. Lina was sweet and wonderful and understanding and beautiful, but she was also twenty-four, and Spanish, and not at all the type of woman who'd fall for a twenty-year-old American tourist. Then there was the realization I wouldn't know what to do with a woman even if one did fall for me. I didn't want to repeat all of my failures just when I started to make peace with them. All those things should've concerned me, and they probably would have if I'd let myself dwell on them, but instead I flopped on my back and continued listening to her.

The words of her song turned to humming when the shower turned off, and I wondered what she was doing now. Drying her long dark hair? Choosing something to wear? Putting in her contacts? Did she wear contacts? I knew so little about her and she knew less about me. Then again, there were a lot of things I didn't know about me either. Shouldn't I focus on those things, and not on whether or not she wore contacts?

The bathroom door opened, and she stepped out wearing a sky-blue scoop-neck T-shirt, light khaki shorts, and sandals, with her hair in a ponytail. A single silver chain with a delicate cross rested light against the deeply tanned skin of her neck. She spotted me staring at her and flashed one of her bright smiles.

"Buenos días."

"Hola," I croaked, my throat dry from a mix of my lingering sleepiness and a large dose of attraction.

"Early start today," she said, tossing a few things in her suitcase.

I tried to remember our trip itinerary. "Seville?"

"Sí, Sevilla awaits." She said the name of the city as *say-vee-ya*.

"Don't want to be late for that." I swung my legs out of bed and headed for the shower, passing close to her in the narrow space between the bathroom and the closet. I tried to slip by as she stepped back to grab something off a hanger. Our bodies bumped lightly together, and she stumbled. I instinctively reached out to steady her, my hands firmly closing on her hips to balance her. It was a completely innocent gesture, but when my fingers tightened around the curves of her waist, something changed. Something sharp and strong shot through me—an impulse, a connection, a deep understanding of where we were headed. She gasped at my touch and turned slowly to face me.

Our eyes met, bodies grazing against each other as we stood face-to-face for seconds that stretched for hours. I noticed the heavy rise and fall of her chest, the expanding pupils of her dark eyes, the way she lightly bit her lower lip. Her fingers twitched at my side, and I knew on some gut level it took a lot of restraint for her not to touch me. She was fighting something, but what?

This? Us?

The soft click of a key in the door lock thundered through

the tense silence. We both jumped, startled and guilty, not for actually having done anything wrong, but for the potential we shared for…what had we been about to do? The feeling of the inevitable slipped away like a dream fades from memory as you open your eyes.

"Hey, what time are we—" Hannah stood in the doorway, Caroline and Andi in the hall behind her. They looked at us, a unified turning of heads from me to Lina, and then to each other.

Andi finally spoke. "We wanted to know if we had time for breakfast."

"If you do it quickly," Lina said. "Jesús will arrive at seven thirty."

"We'll be back before then," Caroline said, tugging on Hannah's arm.

"Why don't I go with you?" Lina quickly zipped her suitcase and returned to her professional tour guide tone.

"Are you sure?" Andi asked. "We're fine. There's a bakery down the block."

"I'd like to get some fresh air before the long bus ride." Lina turned to me for the first time since we'd been interrupted. "You'll meet us in the lobby?"

I nodded. "I need a quick shower."

She left, and Hannah and Andi followed quickly behind her. Caroline hesitated briefly. "You okay?"

"Yeah." What else could I say? Nothing was wrong, except something finally felt completely right, which complicated things more than I could comprehend.

She seemed skeptical but didn't push. "Okay, Jackass. Just be careful."

I showered and dressed with a constant loop of images replaying through my mind. I was almost certain we'd been about to kiss, and I'd wanted that. The same energy radiated from her, but she held back, and somehow her indecision froze me as well. I'd learned to trust her instincts more than I trusted my own.

Still, if we hadn't been interrupted, would her resistance have weakened or strengthened?

There was no way to know now, and rehashing the event wouldn't change anything, but I'd probably spend the rest of the morning doing just that.

❖

Jesús was his normal, cheery self even before eight o'clock in the morning. He pulled up with the Dixie Chicks blasting "Sin Wagon" and hopped out with a wide, toothy grin to help us load our bags onto the bus.

"Hace calor," he said to Lina.

"Sí, siempre hace calor en Sevilla."

The exchange happened quickly and completely in Spanish, but I didn't miss a word. Jesús remarked on the heat. She agreed, saying it's always hot in Seville. It wasn't a major conversation, but I understood it without effort. Maybe I'd picked up some Spanish, or I'd at least gotten used to hearing it around me.

We settled in for a nearly five-hour bus ride. Caroline and Hannah both fell asleep, and Andi put on her headphones, no doubt attempting to drown out the Dixie Chicks so she could write in her journal. Lina sat a few seats ahead of me and I watched her reflection in the glass while she stared out the window. The city faded behind us, turning from suburbs to open, rolling plains, but her expression never shifted from its steady pensiveness. Was she thinking about me? Did she regret what we'd almost done, whatever that was? Did she wish the others hadn't interrupted? Did she wonder what might've happened, or did she know?

I wished I could read her mind. I wished I could sort out my own thoughts, but since neither of those things would happen in the near future I had to consider more realistic options. Could I go to her? Could we talk about what had or hadn't happened? Could we talk about anything else? Did she want to be left alone?

I didn't. I wanted to go to her, but what if she dismissed me the way she had the waiter the night before?

Courage hadn't been my strong point during this trip, and even when I'd managed to find some, it'd been laced with sangría and stupidity. But this was Lina, not a stranger, or some dark, predatory figure. On some level deeper than my own fear of failure, I could trust her even if I couldn't trust myself. My instincts about her were clear and correct every time. Maybe I needed to have faith in myself, if only about her.

I swallowed my insecurities and took the three steps necessary to meet her. She bestowed a slow but genuine smile and nodded toward the open space beside her. She didn't say a word, made no grand gesture, but there was an unflinching, easy welcome in her reaction.

It was comfortable to sit by her. Even if we weren't solving any problems, I wasn't dwelling on them, either. Being near her calmed me, and when we did finally speak, there was none of the tension I'd feared, just the easy, natural conversation I'd come to expect between us.

"I wish we could open these windows," she said. "This is the part of the road where you begin to smell the olive groves."

"What do they smell like?"

"On a hot, breezy day, the scent is thick and rich like you're tasting warm olive oil drizzled over freshly baked bread." She closed her eyes and inhaled deeply as if she could smell from memory alone. I closed my eyes, wanting to be enveloped in her memory too. Instead I remembered her at the table last night, eyes closed, lips slightly parted, and her chin tilted slightly upward. Was this what she'd been thinking about? Was I building those kinds of memories here too?

"You'll smell them soon," she said. "When we get farther south, the groves will surround us, and the smell will seep through the vents."

"We don't have anything like that where I grew up. We grow

corn and beans, which don't have much of a scent in the fields," I admitted, a little sheepish about my pedestrian upbringing.

"I grew up smelling the sea. The thick salt air drifts into the hills on summer nights and surrounds me like a blanket. I always love sleeping with my windows open even after *mi madre* says it's too cold."

"I know what you mean," I said, feeling our connection deepen. "I love the smell of a thunderstorm brewing in the moments before the rain falls. Where I live, you can smell it coming for miles across open prairie fresh and clean, mixing with the smell of earth and water. I loved to sit on our front porch and breathe it in."

She covered my hand with hers and squeezed gently. "I used to drive this road on the way to university when I went to school in Madrid. The city would smell stuffy and sharp, and I'd leave my windows closed until I got here. When I'd reach the point where I could smell the olives I finally felt like I was headed home. Then when I smelled the sea, I knew I'd arrived."

"You didn't like Madrid?" I asked, surprised. I'd yet to hear her hint at anything less than wonderful about Spain.

"I enjoyed parts of Madrid at the time, but I love it more now that I'm able to see it the way I want to and share it with others. At the university, I worked too hard."

"Is that how you graduated early?"

"Yes." She frowned slightly. "I knew what I wanted to be and rushed to become that person. I didn't stop to enjoy the journey."

My stomach tightened with a sickening familiarity. "What do you mean?"

"When my friends went dancing, I studied. They dated, and I kept to myself. I didn't get distracted. I worked for a tourism company to gain experience instead of joining clubs. I took myself too seriously and missed out on a lot of experiences and a lot of friendships."

"Was it worth it?"

"Sometimes." She shrugged. "This life can be lonely, but I do love the work, and I've met many wonderful people. I've learned to soak up every minute and every detail."

"Are you the woman you want to be now?"

She laughed. "No, I still have goals, but I'm not in a hurry anymore."

"Must be nice," I muttered.

"It is." She bumped her shoulder into my mine playfully. "You should try it."

I smiled in spite of the fact that her advice was easier said than done. It couldn't hurt to try. I stared out the window, trying to slow down my mind and take in the scene around me. Row after row of olive trees stood short and dark against the gently sloping fields. I took a deep, full, centering breath. The scent of olives, fresh, rich, and warm, flooded my nose and mouth. I couldn't believe I hadn't smelled them sooner. Lina's eyes met mine, and our smiles mirrored one another, broad and exuberant with our shared understanding.

❖

We arrived in Sevilla at one o'clock, and the oppressive heat hit us as soon as Jesús opened the bus doors. By the time we'd unloaded our bags, we were wilting. The hotel consisted of a sprawling set of low buildings and we had to walk outside again to get to our rooms. When we passed the pool, I wasn't the only one who cast a longing glance at the clear blue water or the thatch-roofed cabanas circling it. We stopped outside our rooms while Lina ran over the itinerary for the day.

"We'll go to the Plaza de España, then for a stroll though a scenic part of town."

"Um," Caroline interrupted nervously. "Are those things outside?"

"Yes," Lina admitted, like even she found the prospect daunting.

"I want to stay here," Hannah whined.

"We don't want to miss out," Andi said more diplomatically, "but it's got to be a hundred degrees. Is walking around in the sun for hours a good idea?"

"You think lying by the pool would be a better way to experience Sevilla's culture than to see her famous landmarks?" Lina asked in her best teacher voice, but the corners of her mouth twitched upward.

"Yes," the girls said in unison.

She laughed. "Well, I'm a tour guide, and I'll tour the sights, but if you do not wish to be tourists, I won't stop you from playing sunbathers today."

"Thank you," Hannah and Caroline said, and Andi added a *"gracias,"* which got a nod of approval from Lina before she headed into her room.

I followed her and tossed my bag on the bed next to hers before I fished out my camera and a ball cap. I looked up to see her watching me.

"You aren't going swimming?" she asked.

I shrugged. "I'll go with you."

"Ren, you've been on good behavior. I trust you."

Lightness spread through me at her vote of confidence. "Thank you. That means a lot, but I'd still rather see Sevilla with you than see the pool with my friends."

Now it was her turn to stand a little straighter. "Okay, then I'll give you an especially personal tour."

My breath caught, and I struggled to banish the double entendre from my mind. I'm sure she hadn't intended to sound intimate. Maybe it was one of those language things that didn't translate exactly, but I liked the sound of it anyway.

We rode the subway from near the hotel to La Plaza España,

and she gave me background information along the way. The plaza was one of many landmarks built for the Spanish American Expo in 1929 and showcased the Moorish roots of the city. The plaza was designed to be an impressive display of Spain's glory, and standing at the entryway I had to say the architects succeeded.

The plaza formed a huge semicircle around a cobblestone courtyard. Beyond a large fountain, a moat flowed beneath a series of bridges parallel to the arc of a long, palatial building that rose in terraced layers of sand-colored bricks and brightly hued tile mosaics. The scene reminded me of an ancient desert castle, with arches, spires, and ornate works of art embedded in the walls.

Lina stood quietly while I tried to absorb the view and document its immenseness through the lens of my camera. No picture could capture the magnitude of what I saw, but I tried anyway.

"It's stunning," I finally said.

"Wait until you see the details." She beamed and headed for one of the bridges near the end of the plaza. I followed, happily trailing along in the shadow of majesty and the wake of beauty.

Across the bridge I saw the mosaics under each archway formed a series of U-shaped benches. Every alcove and bench was decorated with ceramic tiles forming unique pictures. As I explored the perimeter inspecting the artwork, I noticed each one had a heading with a name spelled in tiles. Barcelona, Cádiz, Córdoba—all places in Spain. Lina followed close behind as I walked along, seeing the depictions of places we'd passed and places I'd only heard of, Ciudad Real, Granada. The pictures offered a complete tour of Spain in alphabetical order. As I neared the middle I found Madrid, and next to it Málaga.

"This is your home?" I asked.

She nodded, her smile turning shy. "You remembered."

"Por supuesto," I said. "Of course I remembered something that important."

"Why's it important to you?"

"Because it's important to you."

Her blush was immediate and mine followed quickly when I realized how much I'd given away in the unguarded honesty of my answer. What could I say now? Should I try to minimize the comment? Even if it left me exposed, the statement was true. I cared about the things she cared about, and I cared for her. I wanted to know more about her, to be close to her, to savor every minute together even if these minutes were all we'd ever have.

I leveled my camera at her. I snapped the shot before she had time to react and caught her looking natural, pleasantly surprised, the faint color of blush still visible in her cheeks. Behind her the details of a mosaic rose into the majesty of the Plaza de España, a backdrop befitting her beauty.

"What was that for?" she asked.

"For me," I answered, the honesty coming a little easier this time.

She reached out her hand and took the camera, then motioned for us to change places. She snapped a picture quickly before I could strike a pose. "That can't be good." I laughed. "I wasn't ready."

"It's *perfecto*," she said, smiling at the digital display, then held it for me to see. She'd caught me looking at her, amusement and lightness in my eyes, my smile clearly directed at the person holding the camera. "Will you send this to me when you get home?"

"Sure," I said still studying my expression in the picture. There was something there I'd never seen in me before, something easy and free, but also meaningful.

"Ren." She touched my hand. "Promise me."

I met her eyes, deep brown and swirling with an emotion I

couldn't read, or maybe I just wasn't ready to put it into words. I tried to convey my understanding as seriously and clearly as I could. "I promise."

"Thank you." Her expression softened, and she threw her arm around my waist, in that comfortable, easy way that always amazed me. This time though, instead of freezing up or holding my breath, I draped my arm around her shoulder. We walked together through the rest of the plaza, the magnificence of the setting completing the mood of the moment.

❖

We strolled side by side through the park surrounding La Plaza España with Lina pointing out important sights along the way. No longer on the planned tour, we wandered through narrow streets, ancient squares, and centuries-old gardens, like oases in the desert heat. In the Santa Cruz neighborhood, she showed me a church that had originally been a synagogue.

"This used to be the Jewish quarter before the Reconquista. The neighborhood was founded five hundred years before Christ."

"I can't believe how old everything is," I said. "My house is a hundred years old, and my parents are proud they didn't get something new."

"Your country suits you. It's still finding its identity in the world. My country settled into its place hundreds of years ago."

"But your country shaped my country's identity. Christopher Columbus, your Cristóbal Colón, sailed from Spain."

"Sí," she acknowledged. "Spain had a hand in the formation of your nation, but it wasn't a defining factor. Cristóbal simply let people see potential for growth. Others realized that potential. My involvement was merely a starting point for future development."

Her slip of using "my" instead of "Spain's" confirmed we'd

shifted from world history to the subject of creating personal histories. "Who decides what factors define us? Don't I get a say?"

"Ren..." Her voice trailed off while she wavered between personal and professional.

I waited as I had earlier that morning to see which would win out. Would she say what she wanted to say, or would her restraint reassert itself? Wasn't there something I could do to tip her internal scale in my favor instead of holding my breath in anticipation?

"There." Her professional façade fell back into place as she took her arm off my waist to point at a statue ahead. "That's Don Juan Tenorio."

I sighed heavily. I'd missed my chance, our connection severed, and Lina's intimate tone and easy touch were lost to her tour guide's professional friendliness, and I didn't know how to cover the distance between us now.

I wasn't interested in going back to the role of tourist but didn't see another option. "Don Juan?" I asked grudgingly.

"A legendary seducer of women."

"Lovely." I stared up at his black marble face. What a perfect reminder. They erected statues to memorialize men like him, men of action and charisma. But what hope was there for me, a person who struggled to even talk about what she wanted, much less seize it?

"He's not what you think," she said softly.

"How do you know what I think?"

"I see how you look at him. The same way you looked at the subway map to Chueca, like a path to heaven."

"It's a monument to a great lover. How am I supposed to view that and not see my own shortcomings?"

"I didn't say he was a great lover," she corrected. "He slept with many women, but he only gave his heart to one, and for that he paid a heavy price."

"What happened?"

She smiled sadly. "It depends on who you ask. Some say he was dragged into the pits of hell to pay for his sins. Others say the one woman, the true love, bargained her own soul to save them both."

"Still, he had to be pretty impressive for someone to bargain her soul against his."

"But he slept with hundreds of women, and none of the others were willing to give themselves up for him. He was a trickster to them. He didn't become a lover until he fell in love."

She regarded me with her searching eyes, but this time I sensed an urgency I hadn't before. She silently begged me to understand something. My pulse pounded through my ears, and my insecurities threatened to suffocate me. I was going to fail her. How could I not? I'd yet to do anything right when it came to women I didn't even care about, and I had less at stake in those situations. My doubts began to overwhelm me. It would've been easy to give in, but this time she willed me to be strong. I breathed deeply, exhaled slowly. I silenced the what-ifs and focused on the woman in front of me.

"I'd like to take you out to dinner." The words spilled out painfully simple but heartfelt. The sentence held no answers, no grand speeches, or flowery sentiments, only a genuine statement of my own desires.

"I'd like that very much." Her joy returned along with her radiant smile, and a new set of emotions surged through me: relief, pride, and most overwhelmingly, happiness.

❖

We walked farther into the Santa Cruz neighborhood. Whitewashed houses with brightly painted trim angled so close together they left little more than alleyways between them. People sat on balconies and on wrought-iron bordered patios; many of them nodded to us as we passed. I was proud to have such an amazing woman on my arm for my first date. I'd managed to ask a girl out, and she'd miraculously said yes. Unsure whether to be ecstatic or terrified, I decided to simply savor the moment.

We wound our way down narrow, cobbled streets until we happened past a small, scenic square lined with orange trees. Across from us a small restaurant opened onto a sun-streaked patio.

"What do you think?" I asked, nodding at an empty table.

"The food smells amazing," she said, "but I've never eaten here before."

"Good, we'll make a new memory in an old city." I pulled out a chair for her.

Lina, pleased with either the comment or the gesture, gave me a sweet smile. A waiter came by, polite but not overly interested in us. He kept glancing back to the soccer game on TV in the bar. He brought us water and a small pitcher of sangría, though we hadn't asked for it.

"I should stay away from that stuff," I said. "My first experience with it will probably be my last."

"No," Lina said gently, "Sangría isn't the same here. It's served for refreshment, not intoxication. This is for sipping."

She poured us each half a glass, then watched as I raised it to my lips. This recipe wasn't as thick or as strong as I'd previously tasted in Madrid. My glass contained more big chunks of real fruit and ice than wine, but I still took tentative sips, not wanting anything to lessen my senses right now. She was beautiful sitting across from me with golden patches of sunlight filtering through the orange trees behind her. I wanted to burn the image in my memory so I could hold on to it forever.

The waiter approached and asked for our order, but I'd been too busy staring at Lina to look at the menu. "We need a few more minutes."

The waiter stared at me blankly. It was a little bit of a shock. Everyone I really tried to communicate with spoke enough English to get by. It was amazing I'd gone seven days in Spain before having to speak Spanish, but I wished this point hadn't come when things were going so well. My fear of embarrassment crept back as I mumbled, *"Un momento, por favor."*

When he left, I quickly picked up the menu, hoping to hide my discomfort, but Lina was too attentive. She reached across the table, covering my hand with her own. "Why don't you like to speak Spanish?"

"I'm just not good at it."

"When you're relaxed, your Spanish spills out beautifully. You stumble only when you're self-conscious," she said emphatically. "You shouldn't be so hard on yourself. Do you think I spoke English perfectly from the beginning? Even now I'm still learning new words like 'hippie' and 'nickname.'"

"I don't want to mess up."

"You can't let not knowing stop you from trying to learn." She gave my hand a little squeeze. "Do you know how to say 'waiter'?"

"Camanero?" I said, more as a question than a statement.

"Close, it's *camarero*."

"Camarero." It sounded different than what she'd said coming from me, flat, almost choppy, compared to the smooth way it slid off her tongue.

"Cah-mah-ray-ro. Let the *R*s roll off your tongue."

"I can't," I admitted, feeling very Midwestern in the face of her beautifully rich accent.

"Yes, you can. It's an important sound. Without it we couldn't say such beautiful words like 'Ren.'" She grinned, and I wondered if she could see my blush. "Try. Say '*Me llamo Ren.*'"

"Me llamo Ren," I repeated, trying to roll my *R*.

"Better. Try again. Say it like 'Ren.'" She drew out the sound, more like a purr than a letter. It was the sexiest thing I'd ever heard.

I took a drink to soothe the dryness in my throat then mustered all the control I had left and tried one more time. *"Me llamo Ren."*

It didn't sound like her pronunciation, but it must've been passable because she beamed at me with a mix of pride and something slightly more intimate. *"Qué bonito nombre."*

"Gracias." I never thought of my name as beautiful, but then again I'd never heard it said like that before.

"You're welcome. Now call the waiter."

"What should I order?"

"Do you trust me?"

"I do." I trusted her more than I wanted to. I could've tried to play cool, but that never worked in the past. She saw past all my defenses—surely she knew I'd deny her nothing.

"Bien." Her smile turned playful. "You call the waiter. I'll order."

I gave only a brief second thought to my early disasters with Spanish food before I met her impish grin and called out, *"Camarero."*

The food arrived in waves. First came a plate of Spanish breads and cheeses. Nothing looked or smelled scary, and my relief must've been palpable because she smiled and asked, "You expected something more foreign?"

"I expected something more Spanish."

"This is very Spanish." She handed me a piece of bread topped with a thick spread of creamy cheese. *"Este queso* is made near here. It's called *murcia al vino."*

The cheese was light and creamy, smooth with nothing harsh or offensive about it. I nodded my approval.

"It's a goat cheese," she added almost as an afterthought.

I stopped chewing and wrinkled my nose.

She rolled her eyes. "Don't do that. You liked it when you thought it'd come from a cow. Why change your mind?"

"I don't know. It's not what I'm used to, so it's not what I expected."

"But why not embrace something new?"

"I guess I should," I admitted.

The waiter arrived with a plate of what looked like fried onion rings, only they weren't all rings. Some of them were oddly shaped, but how bad could something deep-fried really be? I tried a bite while she watched closely. The corners of her mouth quirked upward slightly.

The food certainly wasn't onion or any vegetable. It tasted a little bit like fish, but chewy instead of flaky. It wasn't immediately pleasant like the cheese, but still not unsatisfying.

"Te gusta?" she asked.

"I think so," I said, trying a bite dipped in some garlic butter. The taste grew on me.

"It is an acquired taste," she said. "It's called *calamares*."

"Which means?"

Her expression turned mischievous. "Squid."

I coughed and sputtered before I could stop myself, but recovered quickly. "All right, I can handle it." I took another bite. It wasn't bad when you got past the image of a slimy little octopus. "I see your *calamares*, and I embrace them."

"Bien." She applauded lightly, making me feel so good I would've eaten anything for her.

"When you visit me I'll find something truly crazy for you to eat, like chicken lips or pig tongue."

"I'd like that," she said, her voice turning serious. "I haven't been to America since my father died. I'd like to go back to Chicago."

My heart could've exploded of out my chest. "Seriously?

I'm going to school two hours from Chicago, at Illinois State University. Do you think you might really visit?"

She tried to downplay her excitement, but I could tell she liked the idea. "I don't know what the future holds for me, but I will need to visit America if I want to build a connection between España and Los Estados Unidos for tour groups."

I hoped I'd be a deciding factor, but I didn't care if business motivated her instead, as long as I got to see her. Before I could say so the waiter arrived with a cast-iron skillet. He lifted the lid, and a burst of steam wafted into the already humid heat of the evening. When the cloud cleared, I saw chicken nestled in a bed of yellow rice with red peppers and peas. "God, that smells good."

"Sí, arroz con pollo."

"Chicken and rice?" I teased. "No cat guts or frog parts?"

She laughed. "No, it's simple but perfect Spanish cooking."

I took a bite and wasn't surprised in any way. The dish tasted every bit as delicious as it smelled. Clear flavors mixed with exotic but not overpowering seasoning. "Wow, it's great."

"I'm glad you like it," she said happily. We ate quietly for a few minutes, savoring the food and our surroundings before resuming conversation.

"On the bus, you said you still had goals. What are they?" I asked.

"The big plan is to own a tour company someday. Nothing too large or far reaching, but one that runs tours for Americans through Spain. I want to design the tours myself and coordinate them with guides who specialize in different areas like art, or food, or music."

"What's stopping you? You'd be great."

"I have much more to learn," she said modestly.

"Like what? You know everything about Spain and you clearly love it."

"Gracias, but I need a stronger background in running a

tourism business. I need connections in America and credibility to attract investors," she explained. "At the university I studied Spain's history and culture to become a good guide. Now I must learn other sides of the business."

"Will you go back to school?"

"Eventually. I want to find a program in tourism or travel that focuses on running a business."

"Do they have those in Madrid?" I asked, fascinated that type of degree existed. I'd only considered things like math, science, or history, the stuff you studied in high school. Art history and tourism weren't options I'd heard of. No wonder I didn't know what I wanted to study, I didn't even know what my choices were.

"There's a few programs in Spain, but they're more popular in America."

"Why don't you move there?" I asked, my excitement getting the better of me. "Your father was American. It should be easy for you to get the paperwork approved."

"It's not about paperwork, Ren," she said softly.

"What then?"

"You said it yourself. I love this country. It wouldn't be easy for me to leave it for years at a time."

"Even if you had a good reason?"

She took my hand again, from across the table, this time intertwining our fingers. "I'm not saying I couldn't ever do it, or that I don't want to, but I won't rush into anything. Even with the right motivation, these types of commitments take time, and now isn't the time."

"I understand," I said, even though my heart ached.

"Do you, *nena*?"

I smiled at the endearment. "I do. I don't know what I want to do with my future at all. I can't blame you for not wanting to make a decision too fast."

"You have time." She squeezed my hand. "We both do."

"Time," I said, trying to convince myself more than her. "We've got time."

"Tiempo!" she exclaimed. *"Qué hora es?"*

I checked my watch. "After seven o'clock."

"Dios mío, we've been gone for almost six hours. We have to meet Jesús at eight."

"Camarero," I called quickly, *"la cuenta, por favor."*

"You see what I mean?" She laughed. *"Perfecto."*

I'd spoken Spanish without fear of fumbling. "It was, wasn't it?"

"Sí," she said, reaching for the check, but I snatched it up quickly.

"I asked you out." I prayed she wouldn't fight me. I wanted to have the experience of buying dinner for an amazing woman.

"Gracias," she said graciously, letting me feel like I'd done this first-date thing right.

❖

We got off the subway and headed quickly toward the hotel. "What time is it now?" Lina asked.

"Seven thirty."

"Oh no," she groaned. "We'll never be showered and changed in time."

"I'm sorry I kept you out late."

She stopped and took my hands, turning me to face her. "Don't be sorry. I wouldn't trade this afternoon for anything. Tardiness is a small price to pay for the memories we made today."

I was relieved she felt the way I did. "Come on, we'll make it," I said as I broke into a jog.

She stayed with me up the block, fingers intertwined and laughter echoing down the narrow street behind us. We ran into the hotel grounds, through the garden, and around the pool, chasing and pulling each other along like giddy children, playful and lighthearted. We raced around the final corner and saw the others exiting their room.

"Are you guys just getting home?" Caroline asked.

"We went to get dinner after the tour," she said in her professional tone. "Have you eaten?"

"We ordered tapas by the pool," Hannah said as if that were the most exotic sentence she'd ever spoken.

"We had a great afternoon," Andi added.

"Bien." She seemed relieved they didn't feel neglected in our absence. "Are you ready to dance?"

"Absolutely," Caroline answered.

"All right, I'll change and meet you out front," she said.

I grabbed some clothes. "I'll use their shower to save time."

"Thank you, Ren."

I shrugged. "It's no big deal. They're already ready."

"That's not what I meant," she said hesitantly, and I stopped halfway out the door, turning to see she'd paused her frantic preparations. "Thank you for this afternoon."

"El gusto fue mío," I said, then walked out the door before I didn't have the strength to leave her. I closed the door and immediately bumped into Caroline and Andi.

"Hey guys, can I use your shower?"

They stared like they didn't recognize me.

"What?"

"El gusto fue mío?" Caroline asked in a cheesy impression of me.

"It means 'the pleasure was mine,'" I said sheepishly.

"Yeah," Andi said, "in Spanish, and you even conjugated a verb."

"I guess Señora taught me more than I realized."

"Or maybe Lina did."

"Maybe," I said casually. "Can we go to your room? I need to shower."

They opened their door, and I slipped into the bathroom quickly. They wanted details, but how could I tell them what had happened to me over the past few days? Where would I even start? It was easier for them to think me mysterious and wild than for me to admit I was lost in a wonderful tailspin. I needed to play it cool. Unfortunately that wasn't as easy as I expected because Caroline was still waiting for me when I finished showering and changing.

"You're playing with fire," she said when I exited the bathroom.

"I don't know what you're talking about," I lied.

"We're leaving in three days."

That hit me in the chest, causing a sharp ache. "I know."

"I thought you just wanted to have some fun," Caroline said more sympathetically. "What happened in Madrid?"

I looked away. Now wasn't the time for that conversation. There might never be a time for that conversation.

"Something bad?"

I nodded, forcing a smile. "But it's over. I'm okay now."

"I know people make fun of me and Carl. We're goofy about each other. People think I'm crazy to choose the same college as him, but I love him."

"That's great," I said, not sure why we'd changed subjects.

"It is, but sometimes I wish we hadn't met so young. It's hard not to be with him all the time, and it's hard when other people are carefree and your friends can't understand what you're going through," she said, touching my shoulder.

"I get what you're saying."

"I don't think you do," she said, "but you should think about it before you get in too deep with Lina."

I straightened up. "You're making too much out of this, but I'll think about it."

Caroline shook her head. "No, you won't. You're already gone."

"I'm not," I said as seriously as I could. "We're just having fun."

Caroline laughed and headed out the door. "Keep telling yourself that, Jackass."

❖

I joined the others as Jesús pulled into the parking lot with "Goodbye Earl" blasting from every speaker in the bus. My friends groaned, and I probably would've to if I hadn't been distracted by the sounds of footsteps behind us. I turned to see Lina hurry around the corner. She wore a simple yellow sundress with tiny blue flowers along her neckline and the hem. Her hair fell across her shoulders as she slowed, flashing me one of her brilliant smiles. Silly romantic clichés ran through my mind, and I finally understood what they all meant. My knees really did feel weak, and for a second I honestly thought my heart might beat its way out of my chest. She was so beautiful I could hardly stand to look at her, but I couldn't turn away.

Caroline nudged me out of my trance. "Get on the bus."

"Right," I said, trying to ignore the warning expression she gave me, but she was right. With Lina looking like that, I was definitely in way over my head. The real problem now was, I didn't care.

As we rode through the streets of Sevilla I gave into the moment and sang along with the Dixie Chicks.

Hannah laughed. "You're kind of crazy."

"It took you seven days to figure that out?" Andi asked over the music and my singing. "We've known she's crazy for years now."

"And you love that about me," I joked.

"Yes, we do," Andi said, throwing her arm around my shoulder and joining in the song.

Caroline rolled her eyes at us.

"Canta." Andi commanded Caroline to sing along.

"Give into it," I added. "You know you want to."

Caroline couldn't help herself either, and soon everyone on the bus was singing along with the Chicks at the top of their lungs.

We arrived at La Torre del Oro singing and laughing with each other. Lina started to tell us how the tower was a military outpost built in the thirteenth century, but I placed my hand lightly on her arm.

"No tour guide tonight, only *amigas* out for a night on the town."

"A night on *el río*," she corrected, nodding to a boat docked on the river behind us. "It's a floating *discothèque*."

"I love this city," Andi said reverently, and we all headed toward the dock. Loud music thumped through the lower deck from speakers in every corner, and a large dance floor covered the space in between. A table with tapas and coolers full of drinks ran along one railing. Almost everyone on board was a student, and many wore name tags identifying them as being with one tour group or another. Lina said hello to several other guides on our way through the crowd but stayed near our group.

She pointed out the stairs to the upper deck, and we all headed up. It was quieter there with a warm breeze blowing along the river. The sun sank low in the distance, casting an orange glow over the city, which fit the color of the Moorish architecture lining the river.

"It's beautiful," Caroline said. "I wish we could stay here longer."

"Sí," Lina agreed, "but tonight is our only night in Sevilla.

Tomorrow we leave for Málaga and the Costa del Sol, so make the most of your night on the Guadalquivir."

The boat gave two loud blasts of its horn and pushed into the central waterway of one of Spain's oldest cities. Our hair blew in the breeze, and the sounds of a classical guitar with an African drum pulsed into the evening air.

"I could dance until dawn," Andi said, her hips swaying a pulsing salsa below.

"I don't know about dawn, but you can certainly dance until the boat docks at midnight," Lina said. "There're plenty of other Americans here and a few Europeans as well. Go find a lucky guy and see if he can salsa."

"Carl gave me strict instructions not to get cozy with any Spanish boys," Caroline said. "Come on, Hannah. You're my dance partner for tonight."

They left Lina and me standing with our arms folded on the top railing of the boat in the fading light. We didn't have to speak. I felt exhilarated just to be by her side. She was stunning. The light yellow of her dress accentuated her dark complexion. Her black hair stirred lightly in waves and wisps. She affected me on a level much deeper than attraction. Everything about her pulled at me, a siren call resonating throughout my body. This wasn't what I came to Spain seeking, but like so many other things on this trip, just because the experience didn't match my expectations didn't mean it couldn't exceed them.

The music below switched from a techno pulse to one more like a heartbeat followed by a dramatic entrance of guitars and horns. Spanish lyrics wafted up in a deep voice, and a smile tugged the corners of Lina's mouth. Something about the tune struck me as familiar, but I couldn't place it. I didn't know the song, and couldn't understand the lyrics, but when she started to hum along, I remembered where I'd heard it.

"What's the name of this song?"

"It's called 'Sevilla.' It was a big hit for Miguel Bosé. Do you know it?"

"You sang it in the shower this morning."

"I did not." She blushed.

"Yes, you did." I laughed. She was so adorable I could hardly stand it.

She grinned. "Maybe I did. It's always on my mind when I visit this city."

"What do the words mean?"

"They don't translate perfectly, but he's basically singing about the myth and passion of Sevilla."

"Passion?"

"*Sí*. A passion you could fall in love with."

"In love with the city or with someone else?"

"Both."

"Oh," I managed to squeak out, "is Sevilla known for that?"

"Some believe so."

"And you?" I asked, trying to breathe normally while I waited for her answer.

"I've never believed it before, but maybe it's my turn to be pleasantly surprised here."

The sound of my own pulse rushed through my ears, drowning out the end of the song and the start of another. *Did she just say what I think she said?* It wasn't a declaration of love, but it wasn't a denial either. I could fall in love with her—how could I not?—but it was a shocking possibility that she could fall in love with me.

"And this song is by Ana Torroja," she said lightly, like she hadn't just shaken me on some profound level.

"What's it called?" I asked absentmindedly, barely noticing the pop beat and rapid rolling tune.

"'Corazones.'" She took my hand and tugged me down the stairs. "Don't think about it. Dance with me."

How could I argue? I let go and danced to a song called "Hearts" with the woman I was losing mine to.

One song faded into another. We danced with abandon, fast and free at first, then more slowly while I mimicked Lina's salsa steps and rolling hips. She held my hand in hers and spun me around, then laughed when I did the same to her. She smiled sweetly, easing my anxiety when I stepped on her toes, and I returned the favor when she bumped into me. Our moves weren't flawless, but our joy made up for our lapses in style. Moving together with her was easy, relaxed, and yet charged with possibility.

The contrast between our dance and the one I'd shared with a stranger in Madrid was like the difference between the Mediterranean and the Midwest. The only thing they had in common was me, and even that commonality was debatable since I wasn't sure I was even the same person I'd been in the bar. I certainly wasn't the person who'd left home seven days earlier.

The music turned slow, an old Ricky Martin song I remembered bits of from the radio when I was younger. A bunch of people left the dance floor, opting for a drink over the chance to get closer to their dance partners. I wondered briefly if we'd be with them, but Lina didn't let go of my hand. Instead she stepped closer, giving me the invitation to close the gap between us.

I nervously threaded my arm under hers and around her waist. I wanted to hold her so much I worried I'd smother her, but she didn't seem to notice as she swayed in my arms. Her body grazed mine…chests, stomachs, hips, and thighs brushing against each other with each fluid movement. I breathed in the scent of her, desire mixing with her perfume and filling my lungs. I didn't know I could crave something this completely. I wanted to talk to her, dance with her, hold her, touch her, kiss her, and if I didn't I might explode.

Then again, I might explode either way.

She was terrifying in the most wonderful way.

The song ended, and her eyes met mine, her brown irises swirling with emotions even I, for all my inexperience, clearly read.

"I haven't seen the others for a while. We should probably find them," she said as if that were the last thing she wanted to do.

"It's a boat. Where are they going to go?" I didn't want her to pull away again. I didn't want to lose her to her job or whatever excuse she was using to restrain herself. "Let's get some fresh air."

She hesitated, but this time instead of pulling away she nodded in agreement. "Okay."

Back on the upper deck we found a corner of the railing all to ourselves, the complete darkness offering a fragile shroud of privacy from the few others escaping the noise and crowd of the dance floor.

She stared down as the Guadalquivir rippled in our wake, distorting the reflected lights of Sevilla. "Ren, we need to…" she started, then stopped.

I pulled her close to me. "Whatever you're going to say, please don't."

She cupped my cheek in her hand. "You're…you make me… *Cristo*. Ren, I can't even say it, you make me feel so…"

The tension was exquisite. I didn't know whether to laugh or cry, so I closed my eyes and closed the distance. The softness of my lips on hers, or maybe hers on mine, saying what neither one of us were able to.

We parted—only the distance needed for a shared breath—then collided again, this time less timid, lips parting, mouths matching intensity. Lightning flashed through my chest, and I clutched her waist, both steadying myself and pulling her in. She ran her fingers up along my jawline and behind my head, caressing the soft skin at the back of my neck. I was coming undone and being completed simultaneously, unable to process anything other than Lina.

"There you guys are," someone said. "Hannah's in trouble."

Lina pulled away quickly, leaving me shaken and exposed as every part of me cried out to have her back. My mind refused to acknowledge the interruption or the person who caused it, but Lina moved away quickly, and I instinctively followed her.

As my legs moved and air returned to my lungs, the haze that covered me burned away like morning fog. We were going down the stairs, Lina ahead of me and Andi in front of her. As we threaded our way across the dance floor, the urgency I'd felt while kissing Lina transferred into the chase, toward what I wasn't sure. Something about Hannah? Another level of awareness came to me. Hannah was in trouble?

We reached the other end of boat, where Caroline held Hannah's hair while she bent over the railing. What an odd image, one that I couldn't understand, until Hannah stood up and wiped her mouth. She was pale, her skin clammy, her nose running slightly and her eyes watery. We'd clearly missed her throwing up.

"What happened?" Lina asked.

"We were dancing, and she said she wanted to take a break," Caroline said. "We only lost track of her for like half an hour."

"We found her by the coolers," Andi said dejectedly.

"Sangría," Lina whispered. "Hannah, how many glasses did you have?"

"Veintidós," Hannah said.

"Twenty-two?"

"No." Hannah giggled, then recovered as though she realized the situation wasn't funny. "Three or four."

"Okay," Lina sighed. "That's better than twenty-two, but still not good."

"What should we do?" Andi asked.

"Get her some water." Lina pulled out her cell phone. "I need to make a call."

"Don't call my mom," Hannah shouted. "Please, please, please, don't call my mom."

"Relax. I'm calling Jesús. We'll deal with your mom tomorrow."

Lina stepped as far away from the dance floor as she could, trying to be heard over the noise. I didn't know what to do. I wanted to help her and help Hannah, but I didn't know how to do either of those things.

"Hey, Ren," Hannah said, then pointed to the DJ, "is he going to keep playing this Mexican music all night?"

I stared at her, flabbergasted. How was it possible that while I was kissing the woman of my dreams, my Spanish teacher's sweet twelve-year-old daughter was getting lit on Sangría? I wondered briefly if it was possible to fail Spanish class retroactively.

Andi came back with Hannah's water, and Lina said Jesús would pick us up as soon as we docked in half an hour, and we'd go straight back to the hotel. In the meantime we needed to focus on getting Hannah as much water as possible. The mood was somber and resolute. We sat there on a bench, the five of us staring into space, immune to the dance beats and youthful energy pulsing around us. Of all the ways I'd thought this night might end, this wasn't one of them.

❖

Lina withdrew completely on the way back to the hotel. She was understandably focused on Hannah, but it still stung that she hadn't acknowledged me since our kiss. The disconnect hurt. Even the brush of her shoulder against mine would've been welcome, but she kept her distance, diligent, alert, professional. The quiet on the bus ride felt unnatural, and my discomfort grew as we ushered Hannah back to our room. Lina dismissed Caroline and Andi, then closed the door to the bathroom behind her and Hannah, leaving me on the outside. I rested against the wall and cringed when I heard Hannah throw up again. Then the shower turned on, and I wondered if Hannah was getting the cold water treatment I'd gotten a few nights before, only without the whole "come to Jesus" moment.

God, why wasn't someone watching her? She was too young for that crowd, too young to be left alone with us in a foreign country. Why did I keep forgetting that? First I'd been so caught up in myself I'd lost track of her. Then I'd been absorbed in Lina, and we both lost her. I wanted to blame Caroline and Andi since Hannah should've been with them, but that wasn't fair either. They'd been great about caring for Hannah and giving me the space I needed.

I left the room and went to Caroline and Andi's.

"How's she doing?" Caroline asked.

I shrugged, not knowing the answer. "She's in the shower. I came to get her bag."

Andi started packing up Hannah's things. "I can't believe we let this happen. We should've paid better attention to her."

"We all should have, but she's not a baby. She knew what she was drinking."

"She's still pretty young."

I nodded. I was eight years older, and I'd made the same mistake.

"How's Lina? This type of thing will probably bother her a lot." Andi impressed me once again with how much she noticed about people's personalities.

"It probably will," I agreed.

"Don't let her be too hard on herself," Caroline said.

"Or you either," Andi added.

"Okay," I said on my way out the door, then worried I'd agreed to an impossible task.

As I entered our hotel room, the bathroom door opened and Lina stepped out. I held up Hannah's bag. "Here are her clothes."

"Thank you." She took them from me without making eye contact, then closed the door again. The chill was palpable. She clearly didn't want to face me, but I couldn't bring myself to walk out, so I waited.

When they emerged, Hannah's color was returning, but she still didn't look completely herself.

"Hi, Ren," Hannah said with a weak smile.

"How're you doing?"

"I'm sorry. I didn't mean to get drunk."

"I know you didn't." I felt bad for her, especially since I'd been in her position recently. "Get some rest, and it'll be better in the morning."

"Okay."

Lina led her to my bed and got her tucked in, then motioned for me to step out into the courtyard.

"You should stay with Caroline and Andi tonight."

"Lina, please don't."

"Don't what?" she snapped, finally facing me. "Don't do my job?"

"Please don't push me away."

"When you're near me, I don't think clearly."

"That doesn't have to be a bad thing, does it?"

"It was tonight. I showed bad judgment by neglecting the others, and now Hannah's paying for it."

That was hard to argue with, but I couldn't let her go, not after how close we'd been earlier. "No one's sorrier than I am about Hannah, but I don't regret what we did. Please tell me you don't."

"It's not that simple. I love our time together, but this isn't a game. I have a job to do, and I can't do it with you close to me. You make me forget everything else."

As she pulled farther away, the desperation claimed me. I couldn't lose her. I knew she was drawn to me. Every emotion she expressed mirrored mine, but she was walling herself up behind her professionalism again. I had to do something. I couldn't freeze and wait for her resistance to solidify.

She turned to go, and I felt myself sinking. I did the only thing that felt right and reached for her. I caught her hand in mine and pulled her back to me. Our bodies met, followed by our mouths. Her resistance cracked in a flood of heat and hands and tongues. She clung to me, and I gripped her fiercely. We kissed deeply, passionately, both of us consumed with each other. Then the fire turned cold more quickly than it sparked. Lina wrenched herself free, her arms holding me away stiffly.

"Stop it," she ordered, the vehemence in her voice killing any desire to try again.

"You said, I mean, I thought you wanted me."

"You're not listening," she said harshly. "This isn't about what I want. It's about what's right, and if you respect me at all, you'll let me do that."

I stood there, mouth open, heart aching, and head throbbing with the echo of her words. She'd cornered me into an impossible situation. I wanted her so badly I had to let her go. I'm not sure whether I actually nodded or if she took my silence as acquiescence, but she whispered "thank you" and left.

I don't know how long I stood there staring at the door to our room—her room now—as my mind filled with painful questions. How had such a perfect day ended this horribly? How could I fight for someone who begged me not to? How could I let go of the first thing that ever felt right? Couldn't we work through this together? As usual I didn't have the answers, but unlike my previous dilemmas, I wasn't eager to make peace with this one. I didn't want to get back to being myself. Even as my chest ached and my eyes stung with tears, I knew being in turmoil with Lina was better than being at peace without her.

DAY EIGHT

I woke up in a reclining pool chair the next morning. I didn't remember lying down there, but wasn't surprised. I hadn't gone to Caroline and Andi's room since I still wasn't ready to explain anything to them. I didn't know how I would face anyone this morning. How could I tell my friends what happened? Seeing Lina would be even worse after everything that passed between us in the last twenty-four hours. A sharp pang reverberated through my chest at the thought of her. I didn't know what bothered me more, how much I wanted her or how guilty I felt about not respecting her wishes last night.

I glanced at my watch. It was almost eight o'clock, and the others would be up soon. I had to pull myself out of this depression long enough to get ready and get on the bus. Sitting here reliving the night before wouldn't help. I'd have to deal with each situation as it arose.

I crossed the courtyard and stopped midway between the room I'd shared with Lina and the room I was supposed to have slept in the night before. My bags were still in Lina's room, but I wasn't welcome there. I could shower and get ready in Caroline and Andi's room, but they'd know something wasn't right when I showed up wearing the same clothes I'd worn the night before. Nothing about this day would be easy if I couldn't even shower without complications. Deciding avoidance was the easiest path, I opted for breakfast in the hotel lobby over changing my clothes.

An hour later, still rumpled but fed, I'd successfully avoided any awkward "morning after" conversations. I decided to strive for more of the same and boarded the bus before anyone else arrived. Surely someone would bring my stuff, right? I sat down right behind Jesús.

"Good morning," I said, then amended, "Well, it's morning anyway, though not a good one."

He turned to face me with one eyebrow raised, but true to our pattern of conversations, said nothing.

"I made a mess of things last night." I grumbled, "I don't know what to do about it now."

He waited, still watching me expectantly while I tried to figure out what to say next. Clearly, I had plenty of venting to do, but the words wouldn't come. I could tell him any or all of my problems, and he wouldn't judge me, but he couldn't help me either, so what was the point? If I intended to wallow in self-pity, I could do that on my own. The time for any empty confessionals had passed. I wasn't that person anymore.

"You know what, thanks for letting me vent, but whining won't solve any of my problems, and I think I'd better save my energy for real solutions, okay?"

"Okay," he repeated. Or had he agreed with me?

I regarded him suspiciously, until he grinned and patted my head and turned back around.

Unsure of what to make of his response, I moved to the backseat and curled my knees to my chest. Maybe I could get some sleep before anyone else arrived.

No such luck. Caroline and Andi flopped into the seat directly in front of me. "Here's your stuff, Jackass," Caroline said, dropping my bag in my lap.

"Thanks." I grumbled and closed my eyes.

"Do you want to talk about why Hannah brought that to our room this morning?" Andi asked more sincerely.

"Not really."

"Shocking." Caroline snorted.

I heard Hannah and Lina board the bus and couldn't stop myself from glancing up. Hannah looked better than I expected, more tired than anything else. Lina, on the other hand, was a shell of herself. Her eyes were red-rimmed and her smile was flat, as though she could barely even muster the effort to appear chipper. Her eyes passed over the three of us in the back, lingering on me barely long enough to check I was there.

"It's a two-hour ride to Málaga. Everyone try to get some rest." Her voice strained under the veil of professionalism. Then she took the front seat on the opposite side of the bus like she needed to put as much space between us as possible. My body hurt at the separation, knowing this time I wouldn't be welcome even if I did have the strength to approach her. She wasn't rejecting me. It was herself she didn't trust, but that sort of intellectual understanding didn't keep my heart from feeling shot down.

"Okay," Caroline whispered, turning around in her seat, "what's going on?"

"I said I didn't want to talk about it."

"I don't care." Caroline pushed. "Something's wrong and it's not affecting just you anymore. You haven't said a word to us about anything since Madrid. You disappear, you sulk, you come back in the morning looking like shit. One minute you and Lina can't keep your hands to yourselves, then you won't even acknowledge each other."

"I'm sorry I screwed everything up," I whispered. "I'm not really good at anything. I'm a crappy friend and a terrible lover. What else do you want to know?"

"You've got a two-hour ride with the people who are

supposed to be your best friends," Andi said softly. "Why don't you start at the beginning?"

I could push them away one more time, cementing our roles as barely more than travel companions, or I could embrace them as the friends they were offering to be, the friends I desperately needed right now. I heard Lina's words in my head: *Do you have to do everything for yourself? Ask for help.*

I opened my mouth, not even sure where to start, but the words poured out. I told them about my isolation since coming out, how badly I wanted this trip to change all that, but I'd failed. As Seville faded behind us, I told them everything about Chueca and the woman Lina saved me from. I talked about the time I'd spent with her and how it'd finally felt right. I talked about our first date and our kiss and how I thought we might be falling in love. While flat, arid plains rose into lush green mountains, I recounted last night's argument and Lina's request to respect her. I expressed my hurt and frustration about how trying to do what was right for her meant doing what was wrong for me, and how trying to make her happy made me miserable.

A city began to rise around us as my story came to a close. Andi and Caroline listened patiently, only interrupting to ask a question or offer gentle words of support. When I finally stopped talking, they both had tears in their eyes, and Caroline wiped at her nose as though she was trying not to cry.

"God, you really are a jackass," she snipped. "If you'd told us sooner, we would've told you we knew you were full of crap and we loved you anyway."

"Really?"

"I thought being a big talker was part of your sense of humor, so we played along," Andi said. "We wanted to be supportive of you being gay. We didn't mean to add to the pressure."

"I know you didn't," I said. "It's not your fault I wasn't open with you. You couldn't have known how I felt."

"What can we do to help now?" Caroline asked.

"I don't know if there's anything you can do to help with Lina," I said, my melancholy returning.

"She's lucky to have you, and I'll go right up there and tell her so if you want me to," Caroline said.

I smiled and shook my head. "I appreciate it, but that wouldn't do any good. Thanks for letting me talk about it, though. It's better to have it out there, like I'm not carrying it by myself."

"You can talk to us whenever you need to, but you're not going to give up on her, are you?" Andi asked.

"She asked me to stay away, and I care about her too much to risk hurting her more."

"She was scared last night. Maybe she'll come back after she has some time to think."

"Maybe," I said. It was a possibility. Just not one I had a lot of hope for.

❖

It took a long time to get checked into the hotel, and I wasn't sure why. There was only one woman working, and she spent a lot of time laughing and talking excitedly on the phone while we waited in line. This was the smallest hotel we'd stayed in. The lobby was sparse but richly colored with deep woods and wrought-iron accents. The thick, brick-orange, ceramic tiles on the floor belonged uniquely to southern Spain with a distinctly Moorish flare. A little Wi-Fi logo sat on the front of the reception desk, reminding me despite the old-time ambience, we were indeed in a modern hotel. I liked how the warmth of the design featured predominantly while the amenities served more as trimmings. That attitude seemed very Spanish. I wanted to share these observations with Lina, but she'd yet to acknowledge my presence though we'd been standing a few feet from each other for over fifteen minutes.

"What's taking so long?" Hannah whined.

"We're in southern Spain now," Lina said patiently. "This place is less American or even European than others we've visited. Málaga is a big city, but the people here run on their own clocks."

"What is there to see here?" Caroline asked.

"La Playa," she said with a weary grin. "There're castles and bullfights, museums and mansions in the greater Málaga area too, but we're staying above the city center, less than two kilometers from the Mediterranean. Most students can't resist the call of the beach."

"That sounds heavenly," Andi said. "We don't get a chance to lay out on the Mediterranean coast very often."

"It is beautiful," Lina admitted, seeming to relax a little. "I'm going to need a long siesta before I go anywhere, though."

"That's a nap, right?" Hannah asked.

"It's more than that here. Everything shuts down from about two to four o'clock in the afternoon. The busses don't run and local restaurants and stores close. A few bigger places for *turistas* will stay open, but even the cab drivers take a break, so you'll have to travel on foot."

"Why didn't that happen in Barcelona and Madrid?" Andi asked.

"It did to a lesser extent, but those are cities of the world with lots of people from all over, so they've adapted, but in Sevilla and even more so here, we're much more purely Spanish. It's also much hotter here than in Barcelona, and the tropical climate makes it unhealthy to work hard during the hottest part of the day." Then she added, her tone shifting only briefly out of her tour guide mode, "And we're a more relaxed breed here than our neighbors to the north."

The hint of joy in her words sparked a similar joy in me. I relished the quick peek behind her professional façade.

The receptionist finally turned her attention to us, and we were in our rooms in a matter of minutes. I'd stay with Caroline and Andi while Lina stayed with Hannah. How strange that the room assignments I'd been happy about in Barcelona and Madrid now made my chest ache. I accepted that nothing I'd wanted when the trip began was relevant anymore. Only now I had to decide what did matter and what I needed to do about it.

❖

I awoke from my siesta well before four o'clock feeling restless. The urge to move overwhelmed me. I quietly scribbled a quick note to Andi and Caroline saying I'd return before dinner and headed into the streets of Málaga. The busses weren't running, and while I could see the Mediterranean in the distance, I didn't have any intention of walking that far. I wanted to see this town and its people. Lina's town. Lina's people.

I traveled down the narrow one-way street leading away from our hotel. Wandering freely, I picked a new direction at each intersection. The roads dipped steeply in places, all heading toward the sea. The buildings were uneven and close together. Most of the homes and little shops I passed were whitewashed with brightly colored trim. I heard the distant sound of cars, and the occasional far-off voice, but I was the only person moving in my immediate area, which gave the scene a surreal feeling. The sun's burning heat served as a constant reminder why everyone else was inside.

I was alone in a strange city, in a foreign country, without a guide, a map, or even access to public transportation, and yet completely at ease. The rhythm of this trip had become natural to me, the process of constantly learning, exploring, and growing. Every day taught me more about myself. Even though I'd given up on becoming the confident, experienced lesbian of my dreams, I *was* turning into a better version of my real self. I must be better than when I'd arrived, or I wouldn't be able to do what I was doing now. I'd given up on having all the answers, but by embracing my curiosity, I'd built the confidence to explore without fear of failure. I'd let go of my need to impress the people around me and in turn strengthened my connections to everyone on this trip.

The sound of a Spanish guitar wafted from an alley, filtering between apartments, under clotheslines strung with white sheets, and over cobbled steps. I wasn't sure where I was headed, but I felt the city waking up around me. I exited the alley into a small square of stucco and tile storefronts. A metal window cover went up, then a door swung open, while a tent flap was hoisted slowly off the ground, uncovering an awning-shaded market. People moved slowly, unveiling carts of fresh fruits or laying out brightly colored paper fans on display tables. Black lace shawls were hung out for my inspection, and the scent of tea and tobacco spilled into the hot afternoon air.

"Hola," a heavily mustached man said from the doorway of a small cigar store.

"Buenas tardes," I replied with ease.

An old woman with long gray streaks through her black hair smiled from behind her knitting needles. *"Perdida?"*

"No." I wasn't lost, or maybe I was, but I wasn't bothered by it anymore.

I picked up one of the paper fans, opening it carefully to see the scene of ladies and bullfighters printed on the fabric.

"Para ti?"

"Para mi madre." I told the woman it was for my mother. She patted my hand, then shuffled over to another bin and fished around for another fan.

"Aquí está," she said, *here it is.* She held a blue fan with white lace around the top. The scene was of a little village near the sea.

"Gracias," I told her and brandished my wallet. I wasn't sure how much it cost, so I handed her twenty euros, and she gave nearly all of it back to me. Had she miscounted my change?

I held up more money as if to say *I'd pay more*, but she chuckled and shook her head, mumbling *"Americana,"* as if my nationality was an excuse for my lack of understanding.

Realizing the fan was the first souvenir I'd bought for my parents, I searched the shops for more. I came to a *tetería* and stepped inside the cool, dim shop. A bar ran along one wall, and the other held shelves of loose tea.

"Bienvenida," a young man said from behind the bar.

"Gracias," I replied casually while I struggled to translate the descriptions of the tea. My Spanish was increasingly functional, but my vocabulary lacked descriptors, and I couldn't tell much more about the tea other than "sweet" and "dark," the only two words I recognized on the little cards under each variety.

The man asked a question I didn't understand. *"Lo siento."* I apologized for my lack of knowledge of his culture and language.

"No hay ningún problema," he said understandingly and motioned for me to sit on one of the bar stools. He set out several cups, small like shot glasses but thick like coffee mugs, then took a kettle from a nearby burner and a small mesh strainer from a hook. He poured from the kettle to one of my cups so the loose tea leaves caught in the strainer and before he whisked them away.

I lifted the cup to my lips and tasted the tea, musky and rich with a strong aroma. *"Bueno,"* I said.

"Africa," he answered. I found his response odd until he pointed at a map hanging on the wall, his finger tapping a spot in northern Africa. He then pointed back to the tea in my hand.

"Oh." I nodded. The tea came from Africa. I glanced at the map again, noticing the little strip of water separating our location from the northern tip of a whole other continent. I hadn't realized I was so close to Africa. There's so much about this world I never paid attention to.

He poured another cup of tea through the strainer. I tasted

this one, dark and full, but not bitter. *"Té Paquistaní,"* my host said, pointing to Pakistan on the map.

I loved this game, a world tour through teas. My host and I couldn't speak the same language, and yet we were speaking through a shared experience. He poured another drink. This one smelled sweeter, familiar. I lifted it slowly, inhaling deeply before drinking. There were oranges in this tea. I saw a flash of images, Lina surrounded by orange trees, their smell thick in the air, and her striking beauty under the golden sunlight streaming through their leaves.

"De dónde es?" Where's it from? I asked, remembering my Spanish as though my vocabulary was tied to my memory of Lina.

"Aquí," he said, pointing to the region just north and west of our location on the map, along the route we traveled from Sevilla that morning.

"Quiero éste." I told him I wanted this one, then remembered my manners and added, *"Por favor."*

He smiled and pointed to the boxes on the shelf. I bought all five cartons he had in stock. I wanted to take this feeling home with me.

Back in the streets I moved quickly in the direction of our hotel. I couldn't wait to tell Lina about my experiences in her city. She'd understand the connections I felt to this place. She'd feel them too. She'd be proud of me for opening my mind and trying something new without worrying I'd look foolish. My grin widened. My Spanish, though far from perfect, was enough to carry me through the market. I couldn't wait to tell her about my adventure.

I turned a corner and saw Lina on one of our hotel's small balconies, her chin resting on her hand like some Latina Juliet. I froze, unable to do anything but stare at her.

She looked down and I started to raise my hand in an

exuberant wave but stopped. Her expression was more than pensive. It was sad. My chest ached as she gave me a halfhearted smile, then quickly turned back inside.

She didn't want to see me. She didn't want to talk to me. She'd asked me to stay away and let her do her job. But wasn't the type of experience I just had exactly what she loved about her job? Did me falling for her mean I could no longer share Spain with her? Why couldn't I at least be near her even if I couldn't be *with* her? There had to be a better option than the all-or-nothing choice we'd made.

A note from Caroline and Andi said they'd taken the bus to the beach so I flopped onto the bed, painfully alone. I wanted to go back to some other point in the trip, like last night before Hannah got drunk, or the night before when we'd all gone out together. I wanted Lina to be happy, even if I wasn't the one sparking her happiness. I wanted to listen to her speak animatedly about the places and the people we passed even if we weren't on a private tour. I wanted her in my arms, but I'd settle for seeing her smile.

I sat up quickly. This situation was like many others on this trip when I needed to take a chance. When I stewed in my own depression or sulked for the sake of my ego, I missed out. If Lina did reject me again, I'd be no worse off. However, if I could reach out to her under her terms, we'd have a chance to share a few more experiences before I left. Time wasn't my ally, and every minute I spent away from her or trying to force our relationship into some model I held in my mind was one minute we'd never get back.

I jogged down the hall and knocked on her door. She opened it and smiled politely. "Hello, Ren. What do you need?"

"I, well, I wanted..." Hannah sat on the bed behind her. I hadn't thought this through, and I didn't even know what I wanted to ask, but I guess that was the point. "Would you like to go to dinner?"

"I told you, I need to focus on my job," she said, her voice low.

"You have to eat, Hannah has to eat, and coincidentally so do I. Since you know the area, maybe you could show us a good place and we can all eat together."

"I'm getting hungry," Hannah called, giving me a conspiratorial smile behind Lina's back. Including Hannah hadn't been part of my original plan, but now it seemed perfect. I hadn't been good enough to her on this trip. Plus her presence might make Lina more comfortable.

She seemed skeptical, and I couldn't condemn her hesitance, especially if her heart was pounding in her chest the way mine was. Going back to being friends wouldn't be easy, but it was better than nothing. "Please, we won't get ahead of ourselves, just three friends out to dinner in a beautiful city."

She glanced at Hannah, then back at me. She finally smiled, a slow but genuine warmth infusing her expression, and said, "Just dinner."

❖

Lina led us through the streets of Málaga like only a native could. We weaved around stores and churches. Occasionally through a break in the buildings we'd have a clear view down to the sea, causing us all to pause and soak in the beauty. We probably walked a mile, but it hardly felt like it with Lina pointing out the sights, both famous and personal. She showed us the church where her parents married and a park Picasso frequented as a child. We passed the university where many of her friends studied, and from an overlook she pointed out the city's bullfighting ring. Slowly her joy returned, and genuine excitement replaced her shell of professionalism. Her delight was clear as we drew ever closer to the sea.

Finally, she turned off the main street onto a smaller one

lined with restaurants and bars with each patio blending into the next. She chose one and we seated ourselves, the setting more informal than any other restaurant we'd visited, including the McDonald's in Barcelona. The entire place wasn't much bigger than our hotel room. The only visible employee stood inside the door to the bar, too engrossed in a soccer game to notice us until a commercial break.

"Hola, hola, hola," he called out cheerfully.

"Buenas tardes." She returned the greeting, choosing "good afternoon" instead of "good evening," causing me to remember her comment about people in Málaga running by their own sense of time. At seven o'clock the restaurants around us only held a smattering of people. Then again, the whole town napped until four o'clock, so it probably wasn't late to them.

The waiter brought three glasses and a big pitcher to our table. "Sangrías?"

"No." We all answered in unison, then burst out laughing.

"Bueno." The waiter laughed along even without understanding the joke. *"Agua?"*

"Sí." Water was the safest option.

Lina unfolded her menu and pointed out some of her favorite local dishes. Anchovies soaked in garlic and oil, crispy fried shrimp, gazpacho, cured pork, and garlic soup. The waiter returned with our waters and took our order. Perhaps the proximity of the Mediterranean, which we were now close enough to smell, weighed on our decisions because we all chose seafood.

Lina warned us with the soccer game on we might wait quite a while for our food. Soccer—or *fútbol*—was a passion in all of Spain, and Málaga had a city team local residents were crazy about. I wasn't in a hurry. It was wonderful to spend some time with Lina just relaxing. There were moments I wanted to slip my arm around her waist or reach for her hand, but my longing was tempered by the joy of being around her.

Hannah seemed better too. She showed no lasting signs of

trauma, and other than our strong rejection of the sangría, we hadn't mentioned last night. We'd all been properly horrified and remorseful about the whole experience. Now it was time to let go. I wondered if we'd be able to let go of what'd passed between Lina and me as easily. Somehow the span of emotions we'd covered didn't seem as easy to forget as a hangover.

"Are you excited to see your mom tomorrow?" Lina asked Hannah.

"Yes, I can't wait to give her a big hug and tell her everything we've seen on this trip," Hannah said. "Can I go to the airport with you to get her?"

"Sí, claro," she assured her. "We'll have to get up early. Her flight comes in at eight o'clock."

"I'm glad she'll get to spend a day in Málaga," I said, once again feeling guilty we all experienced this trip without her. She'd worked hard to plan everything and prepare us.

"She'll still be weak, but maybe you can spend the time on the beach. It doesn't take much energy to sunbathe, and she'll probably need to work on her tan after ten days in a hospital."

"I can't imagine Señora with a tan."

"Yeah," Hannah agreed, "we'll have to find her an umbrella to sit under."

"I'm sure you can do that. What about you, Ren? How will you spend your day?"

I wanted to say "with you," but just shrugged. "I did some exploring this afternoon and had a good time. I may do that again."

"What did you find?" Hannah asked.

"I stumbled on an open market, and an old woman picked out a beautiful Spanish fan for me to give to my mom. Then I went into a Moorish *tetería*, and the man there let me sample a bunch of teas from all over the world. I ended up buying some to take home."

"Some tea?"

"Yeah, it's all loose. You have to brew it in a pot and then pour it through a strainer, but it smells like orange blossoms, and it comes from between Sevilla and Granada. The store owner showed me the spot on the map."

"You did all that by yourself?" Hannah asked. "That's crazy."

"Yeah," I admitted, "but I had an amazing time. No one spoke English, and everything I saw and tasted seemed magical. I was totally out of my comfort zone, and at the same time more comfortable than I've been back at home. It was one of those experiences that makes you realize how much there is to learn and see and do here."

"It sounds like Spain worked its way into your blood," Lina said, her smile broader than I'd seen all day.

"I think so."

"Good," she said resolutely, "then you'll always return to her."

My throat tightened with emotion, beautiful and overwhelming emotion for this place, these people, and the woman who'd showed them to me.

Yes.

I would always return to her.

❖

Our waiter brought our food and then stayed with us. I gave Lina a bemused smile as he took the fourth chair at our table and introduced himself as Tomás, not only our waiter but also the owner of the restaurant. He informed us Málaga won the soccer game and he was happy to have new friends to celebrate with. Apparently having the good taste to eat at his restaurant on such a wonderful evening qualified us as friends. I thought about the lengths I'd gone to hide from my own friends until this morning and was awestruck once again at the openness of Spanish people. Their way of life had soaked into my consciousness, but I still had so much to learn from them.

"De dónde sois?" He asked where we were from.

Lina answered she was from Málaga, then looked at us, obviously not letting us off the hook when it came to understanding and answering in Spanish.

"Los Estados Unidos," I told him, then added, "Illinois."

His eyes grew wide. "Chi-caw-go?"

"No." I shook my head. We weren't from Chicago. That was a common misunderstanding even in the United States.

"Corn?" he asked in English.

Hannah and I both laughed. *"Sí."* We came from a place where they grew corn, miles and miles of corn.

While we ate, Tomás told us of his own visits to the United States as a teenager, his cousin in Florida, and a girl he knew in New York. He shifted between halting, broken, but joyful English and excited, rambling Spanish, and without thinking about it, I did the same as Hannah and I told him of our trip through Spain, the cities we'd visited, and the things we'd seen. He was especially interested in the food we'd eaten. We talked of tapas and paellas, fresh fruits and bread drizzled in olive oil while Lina listened quietly, an expression of pride occasionally flickering across her beautiful features.

A few more customers drifted into the patio, and Tomás ignored them. It was unnerving at first to see the owner of the establishment, his livelihood resting on his customers, give sole consideration to only a few of them, but his undivided attention made me feel special, as though his interest in us went deeper than the money he'd make from our check.

"Jamón," he said, suddenly slapping a hand on the table. "I'll give you my best jamón."

"Ham?" I asked, confused.

"*Sí,*" he said. "You must have some before you leave. I'll share mine with you Americanas to welcome you to my country."

"*Gracias.*" Lina answered before either Hannah or I had a chance to say anything.

"*Bien.*" Tomás jumped up and headed for the kitchen.

"I'm full," Hannah protested.

"He offered to give freely of his best *jamón*. It's a grand and generous gesture. You cannot turn him down."

Hannah still appeared skeptical and barely hid her distaste when Tomás returned with three plates piled high with thinly sliced, deep red ham. He beamed with pride and informed us he'd cured it himself for eighteen months.

"*Gracias, Tomás,*" Lina gushed, and I followed her lead. Hannah was less enthusiastic, but to her credit she did thank him. We all took a bite in front of him, grinning like fools to show our appreciation. He clapped his hands and bowed lightly, clearly pleased with our reaction, then motioned for us to keep eating while he finally went to acknowledge his other customers.

As soon as he headed inside, Hannah spat the ham back onto her plate. "Oh my God, that's awful."

I managed to swallow my bite but didn't disagree. The ham tasted like chewy salt.

"It is a little oversalted," Lina admitted but ate another bite.

"A little?" Hannah pushed her plate away. "I couldn't eat it if I was starving."

"It is supposed to be salty," Lina explained. "It is Serrano ham, and it's a delicacy in Spain, but this is a little overdone."

"Why are you eating it?" Hannah asked horrified.

"It was a gift given with openness and love. It's ungracious to refuse."

When she put it that way, I didn't see any other option, so

I took another bite as well. This time it was less of a shock, the saltiness of the meat tempered by the sweetness of the smile she gave me.

I returned the smile and kept eating. This wasn't about the ham. I was accepting everything Spain had to offer. Grace and generosity were on the table, and I intended take in every last bit. Lina smiled wider, the unspoken understanding returning between us as we matched each other bite for bite until we'd cleared our plates.

Hannah looked at us like we'd both lost our minds. "If you like it so much, eat mine too."

"No," we both said, then laughed.

"We did our part, now do yours," I said. "Don't be rude."

"I don't care if it is rude," Hannah said. "I can't eat it."

Apparently Hannah was still too young or too stubborn for some of the lessons I'd learned on this trip. Lina's shoulders slumped and her smile faded. I felt desperate to hold onto the joy of our connection, so I laid down a swift ultimatum. "Eat it or wear it, Hannah."

"What?"

"Eat the ham or find a way to sneak it out of here without letting Tomás see. Your pockets, your purse, whatever. Just get it off your plate."

"Gross, I can't put bad ham in my pockets."

I pointed to the little purse she'd hooked over the back of her chair. It wasn't much bigger than a cell phone or a large wallet, but it would probably hold all the ham. "It's new," Hannah whined. "I got it in Madrid."

"Eat it or wear it."

Hannah looked to Lina as if for help, but she remained quiet, her lips pursed as if trying not to giggle.

"Fine." Hannah pouted and emptied the purse, setting a handful of Euros, her hotel key, and some lip gloss on the table.

She sighed dramatically and began to stuff handfuls of the ham into her purse while Lina and I watched, amused beyond words. The more she shoved in, the funnier the situation got, and by the time she'd finished, the sides of the little purse bulged from the full load of Serrano ham. Even Hannah was having a hard time sulking. She closed the little gold clasp just as Tomás emerged from the kitchen.

"Os gusta?" he asked hopefully.

"Sí," we all agreed, our smiles bright and genuine. Despite the fact none of us enjoyed the ham, we'd greatly enjoyed disposing of it, and Tomás wasn't aware of the difference. He smiled proudly as we paid our check, thanked him profusely, and waved good-bye, then left with a purse full of salty shaved ham.

As soon as we turned a corner, all three of us burst out laughing. Hannah found the nearest trash can and dug strips of ham out of her purse. The scene was absurdly comical, after almost twenty-four hours of turmoil, and none of us could contain ourselves. It felt so good to laugh again that we didn't try to stop. We laughed so hard tears rolled from our eyes, and we stumbled into each other on the sidewalk.

"Hannah, the ham smuggler," Lina said, sending us into giggle-fits again. The echoes of our laughter followed us all the way to *la playa*.

Caroline and Andi called to us from a seaside restaurant they were leaving. We all talked about our adventures as we strolled along the Costa Del Sol. We kicked off our shoes, sinking our toes into the warm, dark sand, the crash of the surf blending easily with our joyful exuberance.

"This is beautiful," Hannah whispered.

"Wait until you see it in the morning when the sun rises out of the sea," Lina said.

I tried to picture that, but the thought was too beautiful for even my imagination. The sun sank low now, but it would be light out until after ten. Being in Málaga made for magically long days, and I was grateful for every second Lina and I spent near each other. The sunbathers and surfers had retired for the evening, but we passed couples walking hand in hand, tourists with cameras raised, and the occasional painter trying to capture the scene on canvas.

In the distance a group of people stood together in the sand, all of them focused on three figures toward the front of the cluster. As we got closer, I saw they weren't dressed for the beach, but rather for a formal event. The couple at the front both wore white linen pants and flowing tops. The guests wore everything from suits and skirts to slacks and jeans. It wasn't until we were a few yards away that I realized both of the people up front and two-thirds of the celebrants were women.

"It's a lesbian wedding," I said reverently.

"Sí," Lina said, *"muy bonita."*

"You can do that here?" Hannah asked.

"Por supuesto, it's been legal for years."

"I thought the whole country was Catholic," Andi said.

"The church is the church, the state is the state, and love is love," Lina said matter-of-factly. "In Spain you can have all three at once."

I couldn't move. I'd heard stories about gay weddings, even seen pictures from places like Massachusetts and San Francisco, but I'd never been to a gay or lesbian wedding or even known anyone who had. I watched intently as the women slipped rings onto each other's fingers and recited their vows while staring into each other's eyes. They looked so much in love, and the people around them radiated joy and approval. We all stopped, transfixed by the sight.

A longing, a need, a wish washed over me. This was what I'd been searching for when I came here. This is what I'd looked for down the side streets of Barcelona and the bars of Chueca. This was what I'd brushed up against in the restaurant in Sevilla and while cruising the waters of the Guadalquivir. This was the image I'd been striving toward, but I hadn't known how to formulate it until this moment. Friends, family, love, and joy mingled together and celebrated en masse. What a beautiful concept.

I felt Lina beside me, the subtle brush of her hand against mine, the scent of her perfume on the sea breeze. "What do you think?" she whispered.

"Do you want that?" I asked, my chest tight with emotion.

"Sí," she answered, *"y tú?"*

"Sí, I just realized that's exactly what I want."

Quietly she took my hand in hers, and we stood joined together in the moment while we watched two women joined in matrimony.

❖

When darkness fell completely, we took a city bus back to our hotel. Lina sat beside me, our reconnection unspoken and untested, but hopeful. The tension gone from her shoulders and the spark back in her eyes, she smiled easily and laughed lightly as the conversations floated around us.

"What are you going to do tomorrow?" she asked Caroline and Andi.

"We want to shop and see if we can spot Antonio Banderas," Caroline said.

"He is the world's most famous Malagueño. You might see him and Melanie Griffith en la calle Larios. That's the fancy shopping area of the city."

"Yay," Andi said, obviously thrilled by the idea, "and then we can go back to *la playa* after our siesta."

"Maybe me and mom will go to the beach with you," Hannah said.

"That'd be funny."

"Why?" Hannah and I asked in unison.

"The beaches are topless," Caroline explained, and we all laughed.

"What will you do?" Lina asked me.

"I'm not sure, but the beach just started to sound more appealing."

Lina gave me a playful shove. Her easy way of touching was picking up again. Was that a Spanish habit or something unique to her personality?

"I don't have any plans," I continued more honestly. "I'll see what the day holds when the time comes."

"You sound more like a Spaniard every day."

"I *feel* more like a Spaniard every day."

The bus stopped a block from our hotel, and we trudged up the hill together. Below us the lights of the city shined all the way to the darkness of the sea. Salsa music wafted into the night from a nearby club, and the salt air hung heavy around us.

Inside the hotel we all said good night in the hallway between our rooms, then I turned one way to follow Caroline and Andi while Lina turned in the other direction with Hannah. I wanted to go with her, but I was willing to wait, happy for the second chance I'd had with her this evening. Being close to her on her terms was infinitely better than being distant on mine. Before I closed the door to our room, I glanced down the hall one more time. Lina stood watching me. She smiled sweetly, wistfully, and I returned the expression.

"Buenas noches," I said softly.

"Hasta mañana," she replied, then closed the door.

I fell asleep thinking of the promise in Lina's parting words: *I will see you tomorrow.*

DAY NINE

Caroline, Andi, and I were waiting in the lobby when Señora walked in. She appeared smaller and more frail than usual. Her skin was still sickly pale, and she seemed to have lost weight, if that was even possible. Still, she smiled brightly and hugged us all. "I've missed you all," she said cheerfully as we sat down to breakfast in the hotel restaurant. Lina hesitated off to the side of our group, her role now cloudier in this situation where we didn't need a tour guide, translator, or chaperone. I wondered how different our interactions would've been if Señora had been around. Would Lina have accompanied us to dinners? Who would she have sat with on the bus or talked to during down time? We certainly wouldn't have shared a room. Those professional barriers would've made the trip a lot easier for her, but less fulfilling for me. I couldn't imagine Spain without Lina, and I didn't want her to fade into the background now.

I pulled out the chair beside me and nodded for Lina to take the seat. She smiled at the welcome and patted my shoulder lightly as she sat down.

"We've missed you too," Caroline said. "We've got a lot to tell you about."

"I want to hear all of it," Señora said.

I doubted she'd ever hear all of it, and a look of conspiratorial agreement passed quickly among us before the official stories of our trip began to spill out.

We paused only long enough to order our meal, omelets, fresh fruits, and coffees. Words slipped freely from our mouths in easy if not always grammatically correct Spanish, and Señora gushed her approval. "Your Spanish has improved beyond my wildest expectations. Lina, how did you do it?"

Lina blushed. "I didn't do anything. They always managed well when they needed to. They must've had a good teacher."

Señora smiled. "Necessity brought out the best in them." Was it necessity that brought about the changes in me, or was it inspiration? Feeling Lina's presence beside me, I suspected it was the latter.

We all ate and laughed and caught up for almost two hours. The restaurant staff, in grand Andalusian fashion, never hurried us as we recounted adventures on Las Ramblas, swordfights in Toledo, the heat and beauty of Sevilla, and the markets of Málaga. Señora listened raptly, asking frequent questions about things we saw and what we enjoyed the most. She was sufficiently pleased we'd all had appropriate amounts of education and fun.

"All my worrying has been for nothing," she finally said. "You've obviously had a wonderful guide."

Lina blushed again and tried to wave off the compliment, but we all joined in the praise.

"Lina taught us all about the food and the culture, and she knows all the best shopping spots," Caroline said.

"And I don't think I asked her a single question she didn't know the answer to," Andi added.

"She made me fall in love with her country," I said seriously and wanted to add that she taught me to love, period, but that was too much for a breakfast conversation.

"She's the best tour guide ever," Hannah said, "even if she did make me put ham in my new purse."

Everyone laughed, and then we had to share that story with

Señora too. By the time we were done, she seemed happy but worn out. "Maybe your Señora should get settled into her room and lie down for a little bit," Lina suggested. It was funny that she was calling Señora Wallace just Señora too now, as though that was her name.

"Come on, Mom," Hannah said. "We're going to be roomies again and give Lina a night to herself."

"We're going to go to calle Larios," Caroline said. "Time to shop and do some Antonio Banderas hunting."

"Melanie Griffith, meet your competition," Andi said, trying to strike a sexy pose. "Want to come with us, Hannah?"

"Go ahead. I'm going to rest until lunch," Señora told Hannah, who hugged her mom and headed off with the girls.

"It's hard to watch them go off into a strange city in a foreign country," Señora said to Lina. "I wouldn't have thought they were capable of that a few weeks ago, but they seem more like young women than girls anymore."

"They're the most rewarding group I've ever had," Lina agreed.

"What are you plans today, Ren?" Señora asked.

"I'm going to go where the day leads me," I said. "It's a new trick I picked up in Spain."

"It is very Spanish," Señora agreed, "and right now the day is leading me toward a nap."

Lina offered to show Señora to her hotel room, then move her stuff into a new room of her own. I watched them go, wanting to follow Lina but understanding I hadn't been given that kind of invitation. As much as I wanted to be near her, I wanted to give her respect more. She deserved time and space to define our relationship in whatever terms she wanted, but it still wasn't easy.

I slipped outside onto the hotel patio and looked across the city all the way down to the sea. It was warming up rapidly as the sun sparkled off the water and radiated up the hillside. I should get moving. It was my last day in Spain, and I wanted to see much more of it. My brain was telling me to go as quickly as possible, to exert every bit of energy I had imprinting images, sounds, smells, and tastes into my memory so I could call them up for comfort long after returning home. It made sense to cram everything I could into these last few hours, but every time I thought about getting up, I was overwhelmed with the sense that I should stay still. I was learning to listen to that inner voice, the one that came from somewhere deeper than my mind, some place calmer and more secure. Maybe I was developing that instinct or intuition I'd hoped for early in the trip, or maybe I was becoming more Spanish, learning to abandon a conventional sense of time and take up a more natural rhythm. Either way, I relaxed into my patio chair, content in the moment.

Lina exited the hotel in a hurry, then stopped abruptly when she saw me. "I thought you would've gone exploring by now."

"I thought so too," I admitted.

Lina's smile was more radiant than the Mediterranean sun. "I'm glad you're still here."

"Me too."

"Would you like to go with me?"

She didn't say where, and it didn't matter. "Yes."

❖

I followed her to a little blue Peugeot in the parking lot. "This is my car, Azul," she said.

"You named your car?"

"Of course."

I fell a little harder for her.

We drove higher into the mountains, with a Spanish pop station playing softly on the radio and the windows rolled down. The warmth of the day grew but wasn't unpleasant with the breeze. The streets got narrower, and most of them were one-way. The houses we passed were more like continuous buildings linked together for an entire block, all whitewashed with ceramic-tiled roofs and vividly painted doorways. Everything shone bright and clean under the endless Andalusian sky.

"I can't believe you grew up here," I said.

"I'm sure I'd feel the same way if I visited your home," Lina said.

"I'd like you to visit, but it's not this impressive. This place is all so foreign. I'm from a pretty standard, mid-America, small town."

"That would seem foreign to me."

"I suppose." It made sense to be impressed with something because it was different, but there was more to my reaction than that. This place was special to me.

We turned off a small square and into a communal parking lot. I followed Lina without asking where we were headed, simply happy to be along for the journey. We walked uphill between three- and four-story white buildings. An old woman stopped hanging her wash out on the patio long enough to wave to Lina.

"Buenos días," Lina said in return.

"Hola, Lina," called a young boy in shorts and a soccer shirt as he jogged past us.

"Hola, Julio," she replied happily.

"Everyone knows you here."

"I grew up here."

"Here? In this neighborhood?"

"Right here, in this house." She pointed to a blue door.

I couldn't believe I was standing in front of her home. It was personal, so unrelated to her role as tour guide, but deeply connected to her as a person. I was excited and nervous at the same time. Lina didn't pause for my reverence. She opened the door and walked through, leaving me to either follow or stay frozen in the street.

I crossed the threshold timidly and glanced around. The

inside walls were as white as the outside, making the space feel bigger than it was. The doorways were painted the same bold cerulean blue as the door. A small cylinder fireplace curved out of one corner of the room, and the only furniture was a small couch and a rustic coffee table. Two paths led toward a stairway and a small kitchen, both a pristine white. Pictures hung along the wall on either side of the stairs. Lina as a girl, small and skinny in a school uniform, but with the same bright smile that drew me to her now. Lina as a teenager on the beach at sunset, in the stage between woman and girl, her deep brown eyes swirling with promise. Lina, in a city with a man who was clearly her father, his arm hugging her shoulders tightly and his expression barely containing his pride in her.

"Mamá," she called cheerfully. *"Dónde estás?"*

"Lina," a woman called and footsteps fell rapidly on the stairs. First a pair of arms reached out from beyond my view. Then a compact woman followed, connecting with Lina in a massive hug. The embrace went on, both women squeezing tightly as if they hadn't seen one another in years instead of less than two weeks. I stood back, feeling as though I should look away from such unrestrained emotion, but my curiosity was too strong to be averted. This was Lina's mother. *Dear God, she's brought me home to meet her mother.* The thought overwhelmed me even as I tried not to read too much into it.

"Mamá," Lina said when she finally stepped back, *"esta es Ren."*

"Ren?" her mother asked, studying me curiously. I didn't blame her. Lina offered no explanation as to who I was or why she'd brought me with her.

"Hola," I said, vaguely remembering there was a formal tense in Spanish, a way to address people to show greater respect, but the ability to conjugate it failed me. *"Soy una turista."*

"No," Lina corrected, *"una amiga."*

So I wasn't a tourist, but a friend? "Friend" wasn't the title

I hoped for, but it was better than I'd been yesterday morning. While I hoped I was still moving up in status, friendship certainly covered part of what I wanted to share with Lina.

"Una amiga?" Her mother's eyebrows shot up. *"Una amiga Americana?"*

"Sí," Lina said, a slight blush rising in her cheeks.

Her mother looked me up and down a couple of times as if sizing me up and giving me the time to do the same to her. She wasn't as old as I expected, probably in her late forties. She was short, not much over five feet tall, but still a little intimidating with the way she probed me with her deep brown eyes. They were darker than Lina's soft brown ones, but the same shape. Mother and daughter had the same mouth too. What did she notice about me? I squared my shoulders, waiting for the verdict. She stretched out her arms and pulled me into a hug. *"Bienvenida, amiga Ren."*

I returned the hug slightly, casting a questioning glance at Lina over her mother's shoulders. What did I miss? Surely something got lost in translation. Did "friend" mean something else here?

"Cálmate," Lina said, and her mother let go of me but continued to grin as she bustled into the kitchen.

"Hablas español?" Lina's mother called.

"Un poquito," I replied, secretly proud of the "little bit" of Spanish I now spoke.

"We can speak English," she said. "Lina gets to speak English at work, but she's never brought anyone home for me to practice with."

Her mother pulled massive amounts of food from the fridge, and I wondered if her comment was really about her desire to practice her language skills or her way of letting me know I was the first person Lina'd ever brought home. I liked her already.

"I'm happy to be here," I said. "You have a beautiful home, Señora Montero."

"Please, call me Carmen," she said as she heated a pan on the stove. It was early for lunch, but her cooking seemed instinctive, almost compulsive. "Lina, why don't you show her around?"

Lina, who'd been quietly watching me interact with her mother, motioned for me to follow her upstairs. There were two bedrooms on the second floor. "This one is *mi madre's*," she said as we went by. I glanced in to see only a double bed on one wall and a dresser on the other with a crucifix hanging above it.

"This is my room." She opened a door and went inside. The small space, like the rest of the house, was clean, white, and tidy, with only a twin bed, a dresser, and a small desk, but it bore her personality in a myriad of little ways. A college diploma hung over the desk, along with several art prints, including one of El Greco's I recognized from El Prado. A set of photographs atop the dresser caught my attention, and I inspected them more closely.

"This is your dad?" I asked, pointing to the same man I'd seen in the picture downstairs. He looked younger in this one. He sat alone on a beach, his dark hair long, shaggy, and windblown.

"*Sí*, it was taken before I was born, during his first summer in Spain."

I wanted to ask more but was unsure how much she'd want to share. "That's when he met your mom?"

She smiled. "Love at first sight, he used to say. Mamá tells it differently. She says she didn't like him at first. He was cocky and arrogant, but also persistent, and over time he proved himself to her."

The description sounded familiar. Lina probably would've described me as cocky and arrogant early in the trip. How many Americans had a similar story unfold during their time in Spain? "How'd he win her over?"

"He never wavered in his devotion. He focused on her and did whatever he needed to do to be near her. She told me once he loved her from the first moment, while her love for him started small but grew with each passing day," she said, clearly marveling at the contrast. "She still loves him. That's why she never remarried. She doesn't even date."

"That must be lonely for her. She's still young."

"It is, and she is. That's why I stay here when I'm between tours."

"And one of the reasons you haven't left for the United States," I finished.

"Yes."

My heart ached, our situation more hopeless than ever. I'd get on a plane tomorrow morning, and Lina would stay here where she belonged. I started to understand what Caroline meant about the blessing and the curse of finding love so young.

She must've sensed the gravity of my thoughts because she took my hand lightly, giving it a little squeeze. "Come on. I'll show you my favorite spot."

She led me up another flight of stairs and through another blue door to a rooftop terrace. Deep orange tiles lined a patio holding a small table and a set of canvas chairs. A low hammock rocked in the breeze along one side, and a distressed wooden bench lined the other. A low wall rimmed in terra-cotta shingles surrounded the platform, providing little barrier to the stunning views beyond. In one direction, the town continued to climb farther up the mountain behind us, bright white buildings interspersed between patches of lush green. The other way, Málaga spread out below, a swatch of vibrant city, white, bright, and clamoring all the way to the sea. The farthest reaches of my sight disappeared along the glimmering blue and green horizon of the Mediterranean.

"It's breathtaking," I said in awe. "I've seen so many amazing things in this country you'd think I'd be immune by now, but this view is the most beautiful one yet."

She held my hand tighter. "I agree."

❖

"We should eat on the roof," Lina said when we went back down to the kitchen. "It's a beautiful day, and the food makes it too hot in the kitchen."

"I'd love that," I said as I continued to watch Carmen cook. She'd sautéed chicken in a mix of spices and then added peppers, rice, and wine. Now the whole mixture bubbled into steam that carried the delicious scent through the house on a wave of warmth. Periodically Carmen would stir the rice or taste the sauce, then toss in another pinch of garlic or saffron before she covered the cast-iron pan again and checked the bread she'd started baking before we arrived.

Carmen got Lina caught up on neighborhood gossip. Someone married, someone had the flu, someone moved to Madrid. Lina told her about her most recent tour, how Señora got sick, and how Hannah got drunk on the boat. Thankfully, she left out the part where she'd pulled me out of the gay bar. Carmen asked about my home, my parents, and what I liked best about Spain. The conversation flowed easily in the tiny kitchen. It actually worried me how comfortable I felt in this little mountainside *casa*, where foreign sights, smells, and tastes abounded. How could I feel at ease here when I never had at home? Would my peace of mind travel home with me tomorrow or would it stay in Spain? Could it still be home if I didn't feel at home there? Could this place still be a foreign country now that it felt so familiar?

"We should set the table," Carmen said, stretching to reach some glasses in the top cabinet.

"Here, let me." I stood and plucked three of them easily.

"Gracias, Ren." Carmen's broad smile reminded me of Lina's, so beautiful, warm, and unrestrained. She was what Lina would look like in twenty-five years. The thought both pleased and disconcerted me because it meant someday Lina would still be captivating, but also probably in a seaside Spanish kitchen. Where would I be?

"I'll carry these upstairs." I took the glasses and some plates, eager to get away from the depressing topic of my uncertain future.

"We'll be up in a minute," Carmen called.

I laid out the dishes on the glass-top table, arranging each simple place setting carefully, then turned to enjoy the view once more. Standing here on this beautiful, sunny day, admiring an amazing view, and preparing to share a meal with the most captivating woman I'd ever met, the edges of perfection were close enough to grab. I wanted to hold on as long as possible, but I wasn't sure how.

I started back down the stairs, wondering if Lina and her mother needed help carrying things up, but when I reached the landing on the second floor, I heard their conversation slip back into Spanish. They spoke rapidly, maybe even heatedly.

I didn't mean to eavesdrop, at least not at first. My listening was purely an academic exercise at first as I tried to follow the language in the quick native form I'd heard but not actually had spoken to me. I picked out words I knew. From Lina I caught the phrases "she's young," then "very smart." From Carmen I understood "she's handsome" and "blue eyes." Lina agreed to something, then added "too stubborn." I picked up the bulk of the conversation in this vocabulary-quiz style. Then I heard my name and everything changed. Had they been talking about me the whole time?

Lina repeated the word "young" again. Was I being written off for my age? Carmen quickly pointed out Lina was young too and deserved the chance to act her age. Then Carmen added I was good-looking. I loved Carmen. Lina responded she was focused on work, and I thought Carmen said she wasn't completely focused on work, or she wouldn't have brought me here. Good point, and I silently thanked her for making it.

Lina sighed heavily and said, *"Ren es Americana."*

I had nothing to decode there. I lived several thousand miles away, not in the country Lina loved, not near her mother, and not where she wanted to build her future. Carmen conceded that point, and hopelessness consumed me. Then she spoke again, this time softly, with more compassion in her voice. *"Hija mía, tu padre nació en America pero tenía un corazón español."*

I steadied myself against the wall as the meaning of the words came to me, not merely the literal translation, but the real meaning. Carmen had said Lina's father had been an American, but he'd had a Spanish heart. A Spanish heart. The poetry of the phrase was worth a passing notice, but it lodged somewhere deep inside me. Was that why I felt an attachment to this place? Was Spain my heart's home? Or was Lina my heart's home? Could the two be separated? Lina was Spain to me, and Spain was Lina. What did it mean for us together? She sounded conflicted, not like someone whose mind was made up. Did she need some sort of reassurance about me or *from* me?

I went back upstairs quietly and sat at the table, trying to act casual as they came up carrying a pitcher of ice water, a basket of bread, and Carmen's amazing food creation in the hot iron pan. I jumped up quickly and pulled a chair out of the way so she could set the dish directly on the table.

Carmen patted my cheek. "Such manners on this one, Lina. We might have to keep her in España."

Lina rolled her eyes at her mother's transparent compliment, but Carmen forged on as she sat down and spooned out heaps of lunch, which turned out to be a local version of *arroz con pollo*. "What are your plans for the future, Ren?"

"I've been accepted to Illinois State University in the fall," I said between bites of rice with chicken, peppers, and peas.

"What will you study?"

"Ren has time to decide these things." Lina cut in, probably remembering my previous unease at the subject.

"I don't know for sure, but after this trip I may study Spanish and art history, or maybe tourism. I've found a lot of new interests here. I want to explore them when I start school in the fall." I knew the news would please Carmen, but I watched Lina instead. She didn't smile the deep exuberant smile I'd hoped for. Instead, her forehead creased. What was she trying to hold in?

"Qué bien," Carmen gushed. "So you might like to come back to España, then?"

I nodded, my eyes never leaving Lina's. "I'd like that, if she'll have me."

This time the corners of Lina's mouth twitched upward, and I sensed her tension slowly easing. "And what would you do here?"

"I have a friend who wants to start her own touring company with specialized guides to Spain. I hope someday she'll have a job for an American with an eye for the Spanish masters."

Carmen gasped, obviously realizing I'd painted myself into Lina's dreams, but neither one of us focused on her presence any longer.

"What if this friend isn't ready yet?" Lina asked.

I sat back, the answer coming to me with a clarity I'd never experienced before "I'll wait as long as it takes."

❖

Carmen refused my offer to do the dishes, complimenting me again on my manners and taking one last chance to point out my helpfulness to Lina before she left us alone on the rooftop.

"You know my mother has fallen in love with you," she said.

"I'll take all the love I can get, but she's not the Montero I hoped to spark that reaction in."

She shook her head. "Sometimes you're too charming for your own good."

"But not charming enough for you?"

"Ren," she said, stepping closer, "you know how I feel

about you. It's not that you aren't charming enough. You're too charming for me."

"How's it possible to be too charming?"

"It's more than that. Don't you see? You're not only too charming, but too young, too smart, too beautiful, with too bright a future ahead of you. You're too much. You burn much too brightly to last." She pleaded with me to understand. "You're going home a new woman. You'll always remember this time, our time together, but soon that's all I will be: a nice memory."

"You've been right about everything," I said as I took her hand in mine, "until now. You're wrong about this. For the first time in my life, I'm where I need to be. I'll never forget this feeling, and I'll do whatever I have to do to get back to it."

She turned away. Standing near the edge of the patio, she braced her arms on the wall and breathed a heavy sigh. I heard her mutter something. Maybe she was praying or simply talking to herself, but she stood up with a smile on her face.

"Fine," she said resolutely.

"Fine?"

"Let's enjoy our last day in the sun."

"I'm not talking about today." I started to say I wanted more than that, but she gently hushed me.

"The future will bring what it will. I can't stop that. What choice do I have?" she asked, leading me to the hammock. "I can't resist you."

"Do you want to?" I asked, fearing the answer but still needing to hear it.

"*Dios perdóname*, I don't."

I kissed her, knowing everything I needed to know in that moment. We were together. It was enough for now. She felt perfect on my lips, both of us surrendering to our own desires. She wrapped her arms around me and guided me down onto the hammock until we lay side by side. Kissing deeply, we took our time exploring each other's mouths, and I marveled at the way she fit against me. When we kissed, she swept away my doubts about everything. I had no worries about whether I was doing things right, no fear of rejection, no turmoil about tomorrow. I had only the incredible rightness of two people finding their way home.

We spent hours in the hammock on the roof of her little house in the hills above Málaga. We kissed and cuddled, talked and laughed, then kissed some more. We told stories of our childhoods, talked about our families, compared favorite foods, listed favorite bands, warned each other about our pet peeves. The barriers between us now demolished, she opened up more about her dreams, and I added my own to them.

She lay with her head on my chest, her body cradled in my arms while we talked of her culture and mine. We shared ideas and made broad plans for hypothetical futures, all the time careful not to break the spell by getting too specific or alluding to our inevitable time apart. She traced light circles on my arm, and I ran my fingers through her long, dark hair. We eventually dozed off into the siesta wrapped in each other's arms.

❖

We awoke to the sounds of the town beginning to stir on the streets below us. I would've been content to live in that hammock forever, but after more kissing, Lina pushed me out onto my feet and led me back downstairs.

We said good-bye to Carmen. She kissed me on both cheeks in the European tradition, then added one on my forehead, which seemed like a universal mom thing to do. "You'll come back here," she said matter-of-factly.

I promised I would.

She accepted this with another hug and then stood outside her pretty blue door waving to us until we'd walked out of view.

Lina drove through the countryside and back into Málaga

along the coast, the waves of the Mediterranean crashing along the shore. We ended up back in the heart of the city and abandoned the car in a public lot. I'd quickly come to prefer walking to driving, as though I couldn't stand to be cooped up and needed to feel, hear, smell, and taste everything I could. Lina led me past street vendors and through open markets like the ones I'd visited the night before.

"Let's pick out some souvenirs for your family and some dinner for us," she said with childlike exuberance. I trailed happily wherever she went, in and out of shops and through cobbled streets.

"I'll show you some of Spain's finest products," she said, tugging on my hand.

I tugged back, pulling her into my embrace. "I've already got Spain's finest right here."

"You see what I mean? You're too much." She laughed and rolled her eyes dramatically, but she kissed me anyway.

"A few days ago that would've been the kind of thing I'd obsess about."

"What?"

"I said something personal, something heartfelt, the kind of thing that could get me rejected or laughed at."

"I did laugh, but not at you."

"I know, but it probably wouldn't have mattered then. I was busy trying to prove myself."

"And now?"

"It's different now." I shrugged. "I'm different now."

"How so?"

"I always had an image in my mind of who I should be and what I needed to do to be that person. I didn't allow any room for uncertainty or exploration. I had to have all the answers all the time."

"You don't feel that way anymore?" she asked, still weaving between vendor stalls, albeit more slowly, stopping occasionally to touch my shoulder or brush against my side. Her little gestures soothed and encouraged me.

"I don't think I've let go of that mentality completely, but it doesn't paralyze me anymore." I thought for a moment. "I guess I have a better sense of what matters, and I'm open to any path that'll lead me in that direction. I'm learning to enjoy the questions, not just the answers. Does that make sense?"

"Spain has changed you."

"Spain played a role, but I think it was more important to see Spain through your eyes. You taught me to look at everything differently, even myself."

"I didn't teach you anything you didn't already know."

"Maybe you gave me the freedom to look at myself in a new way. You weren't put off by all my defenses. You pushed me to be the real me."

She smiled and tousled my hair. "In case you haven't noticed, I like the real you."

"That's what I mean." I laughed, not fully believing we were having this conversation so lightly. "I like what you see in me, and you've helped me to see those things too."

"That makes me happy."

"Making you happy makes me happy." Actually it made me giddy, but I didn't have time to say so because she pulled me into a shadowed doorway and kissed me again. I braced myself against the wall and kissed her back, but the craving didn't subside. It continued to grow, strengthening like the connection between us. My body hummed with energy, calling out to her, wanting more, needing more, in a way I'd never experienced and couldn't explain. My hands closed on her hips, feeling the soft curves under my fingers. She cupped my face in her hands, and when she did, her shirt rose up, slightly exposing her midriff, giving me my first brush of her bare skin. The effect was dizzying and we moved from sweet to sexy in record pace. I wasn't entirely sure what to do about it, but I wasn't about to stop it either.

"Ahem." Someone nearby did the fake half cough, half throat-clear that must be a worldwide method for getting someone's attention. A woman, probably in her mid-thirties with dark hair and deeply tanned skin, stared at us with an amused expression. *"Perdonarme, pero este es mi piso."*

"What?" I asked, the lusty haze not allowing my translation skills to function properly with Lina's skin still heating the tips of my fingers.

"It's her apartment," Lina mumbled and broke the contact between us by stepping out of the woman's way.

"Lo siento." I apologized, following Lina back toward the market.

The woman grinned. *"Buena suerte, chicas."*

We both giggled. "Did she wish us luck?"

"Yes, she must be familiar with the compulsion to kiss women in doorways. We appreciate all kinds of romance here in Spain."

"I love that about this country."

"I know something else you love about this country," she said in a tone so intimate it almost sent me toward the cover of another doorway.

"Oh yeah?" I asked coyly.

"Sí. You…love…"

I held my breath while she drew out every syllable…

"…our olive oil."

I almost choked on the wind she'd knocked out of me with the end of her sentence, and she laughed. "What, that wasn't what you thought I'd say?"

"No," I admitted but couldn't find the strength to pout with her so happy and beautiful in front of me.

"Well, you should think about it now, because we've got to find some olive oil for dinner tonight and some for you to take home too."

We were off again, in and out of shops, through alleyways,

and under crowded awnings. She loaded our shopping bags with two bottles of olive oil, fresh fruits, a Spanish scarf for my mother, some Manchego cheese, a few books for my father, a Miguel Bosé CD for my own collection, and some freshly baked bread. Finally, she grabbed a black matador's hat off a rack and dropped it lightly on my head.

"What's this for?" I asked.

"Your first day in Spain, when Señora Wallace got sick and I had to leave you on the subway, I could tell you were scared, but you raised your chin in an adorably defiant way. I thought to myself, if this one had been born here, she would've been a bullfighter."

"Did you like that about me?"

"Bullfighters are heroes here, but they often get gored. I'm glad you've chosen another future, but selfishly I hope you apply the same determination in your desire to return to Spain."

I straightened the black velvet and lifted my chin defiantly. "How does it look?"

"*Perfecto.*" Her smile was happy and sad at the same time. "Wear it when you doubt yourself, to remind you of what I see in you."

I nodded, understanding she was preparing me for a time when she wouldn't be around to remind me of those things herself. The realization made my chest hurt, and I quickly pushed it aside. The day was fading, but we had one more night, and I refused to confront the reality of my departure until I had to.

❖

We worked our way back to the car. Lina sped us down the coast and out of the city. The sun hung low over the mountains, casting an orange glow across the waves that crashed along the dark sand shores. She pulled over in a grassy area with a narrow trail along the rocky roadside. I followed her down a sandy path around boulders to the point where the sounds of surf replaced the sounds of highway. The area was far from isolated with homes above us on the hill and hotel cabanas clearly visible down the beach toward the city center, but there was no one else in our immediate area.

We unpacked apples and oranges, unwrapped the bread, drizzled it with oil, and broke off hunks of cheese. I dug my toes into the warm sand and peeled a Valencia orange. "Does it always feel like this?"

"What?" she asked.

"This spot, this city? Does it always feel so comforting?"

"*Sí*, sometimes colder, but even in the winter you feel the warmth of Málaga."

"Do you always come back here between tours?"

"In the summer and during school holidays I get only a few days off between groups, but in the winter I'm here usually every other week. Why?"

"Because I want to imagine you here when I'm in the cold and snow. I want to picture you surrounded by warmth and love," I said, lying back and propping myself up on one elbow to study her.

"What about when I'm traveling?"

"I'll think of you at Sagrada Família in Barcelona, your eyes closed and your face serenely lifted toward the sky. I'll picture you cross-legged in the Plaza del Pilar. I'll imagine you in Madrid, strolling the corridors of El Prado, keeping company with El Greco, and windblown on the hillsides of Toledo. I'll think of you passing under the watchful eyes of Don Juan in Sevilla, but I'll like it best when I know you're behind a blue door of your mountainside home."

Her eyes clouded over, but they appeared to be filled with happy tears. "It is not fair for you to have so many images of me. I haven't seen your home. I don't know how to picture you."

I intertwined her fingers with mine, running my thumb along the soft skin of her wrist. "Don't imagine me where I am, imagine me where I want to be. Here with you."

"Then I'll see you everywhere I go," she said resolutely. "I'll imagine you striding confidently down Las Ramblas and looking up at the crest in Plaza Mayor. I'll hear your laughter as you wield a sword in Toledo. I'll feel you beside me as I walk along La Plaza de España, and no matter what else happens between us, I'll never again fall asleep in my hammock without dreaming of you."

I kissed her, getting lost in the brush of her lips on mine. Despite the talk of happy memories, we kept slipping into the depressing topic of being away from each other. I hated that our first day with nothing standing between us was also our last, but the feel of our bodies together helped ward off the thoughts of our impending separation. I tasted a mix of orange and olive oil on her lips, Spanish flavors mixing with her tongue as it grazed mine. I could kiss her forever and not get enough. I ran my hand down her arm and over the soft curve of her hip, then back up again, each pass making me hungry for more. I shifted my weight and scooted closer to her, my body instinctively seeking more of hers, but as we pressed fully together something tipped between us. Literally. The bottle of oil spilled onto its side, and the liquid pooled on the blanket.

I jumped up, grabbing the bottle and coating my hand with oil. She rolled into the sand laughing heartily. "Nice catch."

"Thanks." I sniffed at the fragrant scent of olive all over my hands. "Now you'll think of this every time you smell the olive groves outside Sevilla."

"*Qué* romantic," she teased before walking with me to the water's edge.

We washed our hands in the salt water side by side. All the while, she gave me a goofy, unreadable grin.

"What?" I asked.

"Now you'll taste like salt and oil. You're practically a marinade."

I laughed and splashed her. She squealed and kicked a spray of water back at me, soaking my shirt. Then she turned to run up the beach, but I caught her around the waist and pulled her back to me. We stumbled backward and were knee-deep in the sea by the time I steadied us. The water swirled against the back of my legs, drenching my shorts, but I held her close, rocking with the rhythm of the waves. We stared at each other, her brown eyes darker than I'd ever seen them. She started to look away, but I cupped her face in my hand and held her gaze.

"Don't hold back. Tell me."

She shook her head. "I can't say it."

"You don't have to, but I'm going to." The emotion was too strong not to name.

"Ren," she started, but didn't seem to have the will to fight it.

"Lina, I love you." Then, because it was so right, I repeated it in Spanish. *"Te amo."*

She nodded. *"Dios ayúdame,* I love you too."

❖

We entered the hotel lobby, soaking wet but holding hands. I was relieved none of my friends were around. I'd have time to explain what had happened later, but right now I had to be alone with Lina. I had no expectations for the night, but I needed to spend it with her. I didn't know how I'd bear it if she sent me away. Our footsteps fell silently through the richly carpeted hallway. Lina paused in the space between our rooms.

Would this be good-bye?

Excruciating seconds ticked by while I waited for her to resolve whatever conflict still lingered within her. Maybe I should say good night, and walk away gracefully, but I couldn't play cool anymore. I burned for her. I wouldn't force my will on to her, no matter how much my body cried out to cling to her, but my heart pounded as I fought the urge to beg her to not let this be the end.

A dizzying wave of relief washed over my anxiety as she kissed me lightly on the mouth, then opened her door and nodded for me to go in ahead of her.

The tidy room welcomed me. Despite being laid out just like mine, this space held so many of her little touches. The top of her suitcase was flipped open, revealing a stack of perfectly folded T-shirts and shorts. A half-full glass of water sat atop the television, and the small desk was strewn with postcards. I wondered who she wrote to. Would we just be pen pals after tomorrow? Could what happened tonight make us something more?

I walked deeper into the room and noticed that only one side of the bedspread was rumpled, the side closest to the still-open sliding glass doors to the balcony. I imagined her lying awake this morning as she watched the sun rise, a soft breeze stirring the curtains and caressing her skin. I ached to be part of that image, arms curled around her, my lips pressed to her shoulder.

"I'll get you some dry clothes," she said, bringing my attention back to the present as she rummaged through her bag for a pair of sweatpants and a plain red T-shirt. "Do you mind if I shower?"

"Go ahead," I said, suddenly nervous and a little shy. We'd spent two other nights in the same room, but now that I'd held her in my arms and felt her lips against mine, everything carried a heightened sense of possibility.

I peeled off my wet pants and damp shirt, then put on the clothes she'd left out for me. They smelled like her wonderful mix of shampoo and orange blossoms, and I breathed the soothing scent deeply. I craved everything about her. What would I do tomorrow? I'd finally found everything I'd come to

Spain searching for. How would I ever be able to leave? I'd lived without her for twenty years, but then again, I hadn't known what I was missing.

I stepped onto the balcony and stared into the night sky. The crescent moon hung low in the sky above the sea, its silver light shimmering across the Mediterranean. I was pulled to this place, like the distant moon drew each wave to the shore. It was bigger and stronger than I could fully understand, but I felt it, as surely as I could feel the salt air against my skin. It didn't seem fair to be given such a brief view of heaven only to have it stolen away. How could I go back to the life I'd led before? Would my memories of this country and the woman I loved be enough to sustain me, or would the pain multiply with each passing day? How much would I change before I could return? Would Lina still feel the same way? Fear welled up inside me. So many unknowns. I clenched my jaw to stifle the urge to scream into the night sky, my mind crazy with questions. I'd have to face the answers soon.

I heard her come up behind me. She wrapped her arms around my waist and rested her head on my shoulder. "What're you thinking, *nena*?"

I exhaled slowly, listening to the sounds of the sea, wishing they could drown the voice of reason from my head.

"I'm afraid," I whispered, my chest constricting as I surrendered to the wave of sadness we'd held at bay until now.

"Afraid? Why?"

"I'm afraid of leaving this place, of leaving you." But I feared it was more than simply missing her. "I'm afraid of who I am without you," I said, low. "And I'm afraid I won't ever feel this way again." I trembled in her arms, the reality of our inevitable separation overwhelming me. My throat tightened and my ribs suddenly felt too small to contain my heart. "Mostly I'm terrified I'll never see you again."

"Listen to me." She turned me around in her arms. "You're

a strong, smart, beautiful woman. You'll be fine, more than fine. You'll thrive—"

"I didn't before I met you. I bumbled through, and I don't want to go back to that. With you I'm secure and steady, like I'm where I need to be. I don't want to lose that." My voice cracked under the magnitude of the transformation she'd inspired in me. "I don't want to lose you."

"*Cálmate, mi amor,*" she whispered, running her fingers through my hair and cupping the back of my head. "You can't lose me. I can't promise we'll always be near each other, but you're in my heart all the way. We're part of each other now. That won't ever change."

I stared into her eyes, even as tears clouded my own. I wanted to shake her, or clutch her to me so tightly, something, anything to make her feel the immensity of the love I had for her. "No, you aren't part of my heart. You have the whole thing. *Mi corazón que con el tuyo se pierde.*"

She kissed me the way we'd kissed each other all day, passionately, searchingly, but this time our collision held an urgency, a hunger even I, with all my inexperience, could tell would lead us past previously unspoken boundaries. My heart twisted, and in its breaking, opened up a path for us to reach further into each other. Our passion both transcended and fueled the physical. My heart beat for her, every breath I took filled me with her, and still every part of me ached for more. The connection would have been too much to stand, like looking into the face of the sun, but in her I was safe, strong.

I was home.

My body moved against hers, fingers, mouth, skin. Each labored breath carried her scent, soothing and exciting. Her touch anchored me to everything that mattered, to the feeling we were exactly where we should be. Right here. Right now. Warmth became heat. The kiss directed us off the balcony and toward the bed. Clutching at clothes, the kiss broken in shared breaths,

I struggled for words to express desire, need, and uncertainty. I stroked her face and ran my fingers through her long, dark hair. I was desperate to hold her, to touch her everywhere, to feel her against me, but I trembled, in too much awe to claim something so beautiful as my own. Her perfection humbled me. I had no skill or even grace to offer her, only an innate sense that my body knew its way to hers. My hands closed on her hips, instinct taking hold of me as I took hold of her. I couldn't have explained how I knew, or even what I knew. If not for the pure, unadulterated love in her endless brown eyes, I might have wilted in my unworthiness, but she gave me the strength to acknowledge my weakness. "I want to be…I don't…I mean I've never…"

"It's all right," she whispered, guiding me down beside her. "Let's learn each other together."

As our clothes fell to the floor, so did my hesitancy. I sought her body, marveling at the stunning contrast of skin against skin, the imprinting touch of flesh meeting its mirror. Each time she responded to my contact, opening and offering more of herself, I grew more purposeful. My body overrode any remaining hints of insecurity and I trembled again. Not from nerves this time, but from excitement. I shook in the face of her beauty, the desire to do right for her—for us—overwhelmed me. We were becoming an "us," urgently, beautifully, if not always gracefully.

"I want…I need," I ran my hands along the length of her body, "Lina."

"Yes." She arched up into my touch.

She pulled me down into a searing kiss. The fire consumed me and drove me forward. My mind may not have known the way to her, but my heart and my body did, and I surrendered fully to them. Patience and understanding interwove with incendiary desire, building, cresting, consuming us completely, then crashing only to be rekindled as the cycle renewed again.

"I can't get enough," I said, reaching for her again.

She responded with her mouth on my neck. "God, Ren." Her

breath fell hot against my skin, but the words were lost in the rush of my own pulse roaring in my ears.

Rolling her over, reaching now without hesitation, I reveled in the rhythm of her body beneath mine. I stared at her, amazed at the masterpiece laid out under me. "Did you know it would feel like this?" My voice shook.

"The way you look at me, the way you touch me, your passion?" She cupped my neck with her hand and pulled me closer until our eyes met, flashing with the instantaneous recognition of what we both craved. "I knew you could consume me."

She took my mouth with hers. Parted lips, tangled legs, open hearts. I found the best parts of myself in her, longed to hold on to them, and her, with a ferocity that would have frightened me under other circumstances. Breathless, I pulled back, studied her. "I think...somehow, I knew it too."

She reached up with one finger and traced the side of my face. "I love you, Ren."

Her words slammed into me, and I closed my eyes for a moment to absorb their impact. If I'd needed anything else this much it would've frightened me, but with Lina beside me, against me, in me, there was no room for fear.

"I love you too." I kissed her again, tasting tears. Mine or hers? It didn't matter anymore. I luxuriated in the incredible rightness of this moment and the woman who'd inspired it.

We had one night to explore, awaken, and learn every part of each other's bodies. We spent every minute making memories, the kind that would sustain a lifelong connection.

DAY TEN

Fringes of sunlight streaked pink across the archway to the balcony as we lay in each other's arms and a tangle of sheets.

"What're you thinking?" Lina asked, her head resting on my chest.

"I finally understand Goya."

She arched her perfectly curved eyebrows. "What about him?"

"Why he wouldn't paint over the *Maja Desnuda*," I said, taking in the length of Lina's body, love and lust mingling into a powerful emotion that filled my chest. "I wouldn't cover you up for all the money in the world."

She kissed me soulfully, and I marveled at the need she still stirred in me, even after a full night of trying to quench the craving. I would've given in to the desire again if she hadn't pulled away. "If you won't cover me up, then I'll have to do it, or we won't ever make it out of this bed."

"I'd love to never leave this bed."

"But then we would miss the sunrise." She playfully pushed me to my feet.

I didn't see how any sunrise could compare to my current view, but I'd deny her nothing. I reluctantly dressed and joined her on the balcony. She rested her elbows on the railing and propped her chin in her hands. I encircled her with my arms, nuzzling her neck and inhaling deeply to capture her citrus scent mingled with the subtle smell of salt in the predawn air.

The uppermost edge of the sun peeked into view, a sliver of orange sending rays of color across the shimmering surface of the sea. Blues and greens were sliced open by a pink almost too bright to take in, and yet as it spread, tinting everything in its glow, it magnified the natural hues of everything it touched. Foamy whitecaps turned fluorescent as they rose and broke and slipped back into turquoise swells rolling into smoothness as they rushed toward shore. The sun crept over the horizon, the pink sky deepening to flaming orange and spreading through the darkness, burning away the night. The outer edges of its reach inched steadily across the shore and into the town. Shadows slipped away, revealing white buildings cast in tangerine warmth. The city came to life in full color before my eyes.

Lina turned and buried her face in my chest, clutching me tightly to her.

"What is it?" I asked, shaken. "What's wrong?"

"I've never hated something so beautiful before," she said.

"Lina?" I asked, not understanding her words.

"I hate this sunrise. Because it's coming to take you away from me."

Realization pulled a gasp from my throat as the pain of her words stabbed through me.

I was leaving.

The bottom of the sun cleared the water now. It had to be almost seven o'clock.

Any minute one of the others would come searching for us, shattering the illusion of timelessness we'd clung to. I wasn't ready for this to end. I wasn't ready to leave. I wasn't ready for any of this.

Oh God, what've we done?

She was in every part of me. Losing her now would be like

losing a limb. She'd tried to warn me, tried to hold back, tried to save us both from the pain coursing through me, but it was too late now. We'd crossed a line we couldn't uncross, said words we couldn't unsay, learned things we couldn't unlearn, and now I had to leave her, leave us, both alone and hurting.

"I can't do it," I said. "I can't leave you."

"Ren. You have to go home."

"This is my home. This is where I'm supposed to be. My place is with you." Desperation welled up, like a tremor rattling my core.

"Your friends, your family—"

"They'll understand. I'll make them understand," I argued, the tightness around my heart making it impossible to draw a full breath. "I'll tell them I love you. I'll shout it from every rooftop in Málaga. I'll buy a ring and get down on my knee right here."

I started to kneel in front of her, but she grabbed my shoulders and stood me up. "You can't."

"Why not?" I heard the hysteria crack my voice, but felt helpless to control it. "I want to marry you on the beach. I want the world to know how much I love you."

"I love you too." She cupped my face in her hands. "And that's why you have to go."

I searched her deep brown eyes for peace, for comfort, for understanding, and I found them all, but I still couldn't summon any of the resolve I saw in her.

"I don't understand." I tried to turn away but she hooked a finger under my chin and drew my gaze back to her.

"Love isn't about grand gestures, *amor*. It's remaining steadfast and strong for each other even when things aren't perfect." She paused, softened. "Can you do that?"

I watched a tear trail down her cheek. Her heart was breaking like mine, but she stood strong for me. She deserved the same in return. I wanted to be steady and confident for her, to reassure her, to soothe her, to protect her. I nodded, my throat tightening with the emotion I struggled to force down. This pain would be mine to carry, even if it crushed me. The words came out rough and staccato against my raw nerves. "I'll go. But I'll work every day to get back to you."

"We'll carve our own paths back to each other. Don't abandon your own in favor of mine. Two hearts that fit together will always find each other."

The sentiment offered a cold comfort. All the pain I'd suffered under doubt and insecurities couldn't touch the anguish I felt about the one thing I now knew with absolute certainty: We were meant to be together. I didn't want to wait for fate or God or the universe to reveal some master plan. I wanted to be with her now, and if not now, then as soon as possible. But if she needed time, consistency, or steadfast devotion, that's what I'd give. "I promise you, Lina, no matter what path I take or how long I'm gone, my heart will always be here with you."

❖

I stood in front of customs at the Málaga international airport and watched my friends hug Lina good-bye. Señora thanked her for taking good care of us, and Lina said she'd never been sadder to see a tour end.

She hugged Hannah. "You have my e-mail address, *amiga*. I expect you to use it."

"I will," Hannah said. "I'll send you the pictures I took on the trip."

"Gracias," Lina said, "and send me some of your home too."

Caroline and Andi jumped forward and squeezed Lina between them. They'd giggled incessantly all morning in an attempt to hide their sadness at leaving.

"Next summer it's your turn to come visit America," Caroline said.

"I may do that," she said seriously. "I haven't been in years, but you've given me new reasons to visit my father's homeland."

"You have one reason in particular," Andi said glancing at me, "and we both approve very much."

"Thank you." Lina's tears filled her eyes again. "You're good friends. She's lucky to have you."

My throat thickened as I listened to the exchange. I may have had the most drastic turnaround during the last ten days, but each of us was changed by our own experiences in some way. Señora said we seemed older. Maybe some experiences aged you more than entire years did. We were becoming who we were meant to be. Caroline and Andi had become amazing friends to me, and now I could also see they were extraordinary women on the brink of bright futures. Hannah went from being an average American kid to showing so much potential for strength and humor, a stellar mix for any teenager. We'd each become a more refined version of ourselves.

When we'd put off our departure as long as we dared, Señora nudged us toward the security line. I lingered at her side, my breathing labored and my heartbeat erratic at the prospect of leaving her. Señora looked back and forth between us. Maybe it was the fact that I was wearing yesterday's clothes, or perhaps my bloodshot eyes gave me away. Then again, it could've been the way Lina and I couldn't stop staring at each other, like either one of us might fall apart at any moment. Señora shook her head and said, "I don't want to know what's happened here. Just tell me if I have to worry about boarding the plane without you, Ren."

"No, ma'am," I said solemnly. "I know what I have to do."

She nodded skeptically but turned to get in line.

Lina held my hand in hers and whispered, "You're an amazing woman, Ren. Please tell me you won't forget that when you leave here."

I studied her lips, the subtle line of her cheekbones, the curve of her eyelashes, trying to imprint everything about her into my memory. I would need these details to sustain me in the long months ahead. It would just be months, and not years, or longer. The panic threatened to over take me. "Why does it sound like you're saying good-bye for good?"

"You know that's not what I want, not after what we've shared. I want to be with you so bad it hurts."

"I feel the same way." My voice cracked, but I managed to hold myself together and look into her endless brown eyes. "I love you."

"I know you do, and I love you too, that's why it would kill me to see you shortchange yourself for me."

"I don't understand."

"As hard as it is let you go, it would be harder to see you forfeit or rush through some of the best years of your life. You're learning who you are and what you're going to become." She sighed. "Don't take any shortcuts on my behalf. That'll only lead to regrets and resentment."

"No." I kissed her, running my fingers through her dark hair. I wanted to disappear into the feel of her against, my lips, my fingers, into the scent of her that filled me with each breath. "I'd never resent you."

"I rushed through my college years, I passed up on friends, and I missed out on valuable opportunities. I don't want you to do the same, especially not because of me."

"I don't know what you're asking. You don't want me to come back to you?" I winced, the emotional agony of that idea so strong it carried a very physical pain.

"I'm asking you to follow your own path."

"My path will lead me back to you." God, why couldn't she see that I wouldn't survive without her?

"Maybe, *amor*." She smiled sadly. "Promise you won't forget the time we've had."

"Never." I touched my forehead to hers and looked into

her dark eyes one more time. "I'll never forget anything you've taught me, and I'll never forget you."

We were kissing again without restraint, love and passion mingling with desperation and anguish, her tears salty on my lips as we breathed the last of our shared breaths. Then by some unspoken agreement we parted, releasing each other, as suddenly and completely as we'd come together.

"I love you," she said softly.

"Te amo," I whispered, then turned slowly away, forcing myself to take one heavy step, then another, a deep breath, then another step. My hands trembled and tears blurred my vision, but I managed to fumble for my passport and tickets. My lungs burned and my chest constricted painfully, but I didn't look back. I didn't want her to see my despair, and I wouldn't be able to survive if I saw the same agony in her beautiful eyes. We both needed me to be strong, and while I wasn't strong enough to face her pain, I was able to bear my own long enough to escape her view. It wasn't until I was through customs and on the plane that I allowed myself to collapse into my seat. With Caroline on one side and Andi on the other, I hung my head in my hands and sobbed.

I cried for myself, for Lina, for the parts of me I'd left on a foreign shore where I belonged, and for the parts of me that had to carry on in a country that no longer felt like home to me. What a cruel turn of fate. I'd come to Spain wanting to find myself, to find my place in the world, and succeeded on every count. But in doing so I'd lost my heart.

JANUARY

I stared at the view of Toledo, the waters of the Tajo cascading darkly over century-old boulders. I luxuriated in the warm breeze that rustled the grassy slopes surrounding the old city walls and breathed the scent of impending rain. The weight of history enveloped me, soothing my restless soul. A soothing presence whispered *"cálmate,"* and Lina sat beside me. I felt her even without looking for her. I belonged here.

A gentle hand on my shoulder drew my attention from the print of El Greco's famous painting. I blinked and looked around my Intermediate Spanish classroom, as if my mind and body refused to process the vast disconnect between my daydream and my reality. In my heart I'd actually been on a hillside in Spain instead of staring at the picture. Lina had told us all that day in Toledo that *View of Toledo* would likely come to symbolize the country we'd visited six months earlier, and as always, she was right. It transported me back there every time I saw it. The habit was comforting but not always productive, especially during class.

My fellow students stared expectantly at me, clearly waiting for an answer to a question I hadn't heard. Señora Perón gave me an amused smile. She had gone through this with me last semester too. *"Siempre en Toledo, Ren?"*

I wanted to mutter no, my heart wasn't in Toledo, it was

in Málaga. But Toledo was as close as I could get right now. Instead, I whispered an apology.

"Está bien. Por favor, lea la página cien."

I quickly flipped to page one hundred in the text and read a passage in Spanish. I found comfort in the language. Right now I took solace wherever I could. I had a part-time job in a tapas restaurant across town, attended showings of Spanish films at the college art-house theater, and listened to the Spanish music CD Lina had bought for me. When those little ties to Spain failed to fulfill me, Caroline, Andi, and I would road-trip to each other's colleges and spend hours going through pictures or reminiscing about Spain. Their friendship amazed me. Every time I opened up to them, they surrounded me with love and support. In turn I'd become a better friend to them too, learning to see them not as giggly, blond, straight girls, but as real, dynamic women with wicked senses of humor. Yet another development I had to thank Lina for.

Lina.

I hadn't heard from her for two weeks, and I longed for any semblance of connection. At first we'd talked every day until she went back on the road, but then she e-mailed every couple of days and we spoke on the phone between her trips. We sent pictures to each other, and when she was gone, I even heard from Carmen a couple of times. When school started and Lina got more time off between tours, we both bought webcams for our computers. On one hand, it was amazing to see each other, but on the other it hurt not to be able to hold her, or to feel close one minute then sharply alone when I turned off the computer.

I'd wanted to visit Spain over Christmas, but we'd decided against it. I didn't have the money for short trips across the Atlantic if I had any hope of spending the whole summer there. Besides, Christmas vacation was a big time for travel, and she had tours almost the whole time. We'd barely gotten to talk to each other. I'd tried to be understanding, but she should've been back in touch by now. We were halfway through the first week of my new semester, and I'd expected to hear from her. My e-mails had gone unanswered for the last week and when I'd called, Carmen sounded guarded, saying something had come up and Lina would be busy a while longer. I tried to have faith, but this was the longest we'd gone without talking. Had she grown tired of all the work necessary to remain connected? Had she decided I wasn't the one for her or that maybe her path led her toward someone else?

No, I'd come to know her so well. I would've noticed if she was holding something from me. My mind wandered to our last conversation on the webcam when we'd talked about our plans for winter break. She hesitated once and changed the subject, but that could have been anything. She'd probably been thinking about my Christmas present, a poster of a Spanish bullfighter wearing full matador regalia. I loved the gift, but as the days passed I worried there was more behind her silence.

I tried to draw strength from everything she'd ever said to me. I clung to any detail associated with Spain. I listened closely to the subtle lisp in Professor Perón's delivery, the gentle roll of an *R*, or the thick grain of El Greco's brushstrokes. There wasn't much to cling to, but I refused to let go and mentally steeled myself for another long semester.

The students around me began to pack up their things, and Señora Perón reiterated the reading assignment for next class period, which I scribbled hastily on my notebook.

"Ren, stay after class, *por favor*," the professor said. I would've loved the easy way she slipped between English and Spanish if I weren't about to get in trouble.

I waited at my desk until all the other students left the room, and Señora Perón sat down next to me. I apologized again. *"Lo siento."*

"You're a good student, Ren," she started. She was probably no more than thirty, a PhD candidate from Bilbao with short black hair and light mocha eyes. "Your grammar and spelling need work, but your vocabulary is excellent, and you speak like a native. Your American accent is nonexistent at times, and I've never had a student roll her *R*s with more gusto."

"Gracias," I said, extremely happy a native thought I spoke well. I couldn't wait to tell Lina.

"I know you want to study in Spain your senior year," she continued.

"I want that more than anything."

"Your language skills make you a good candidate, but you've got to get more involved here."

"I really am sorry," I reiterated sincerely. I didn't want to do anything to jeopardize my chances of going to school in Spain. "I don't mean to daydream. I promise I'll pay better attention."

"I know you have a lot weighing on your mind and on your heart," she said sympathetically. Over the course of last semester, she'd heard a little bit about why I wanted to study in Spain. "You have a lot of opportunities for growth here too, and I'm not talking about your classes."

"What do you mean?" I'd gone to a few meetings of the Gay/Straight Alliance during the first semester, and I'd made a few friends. I hadn't exactly been Ms. Social, but I hadn't been a hermit either. Though I did find it ironic I'd gained the experience to be more confident around girls and wasn't interested in meeting them anymore.

"We have a Spanish club, a cinema group, a mentoring program to pair younger students with grad students. Extracurricular activities look good on your foreign study applications, but they also make college more enjoyable."

"I'll think about it," I said, not wanting to commit to anything.

"Don't be in such a hurry that you miss out on your real reasons for coming to college in the first place."

She sounded so much like Lina my voice caught in my

throat. I didn't really hang out with my classmates or attend social events, and aside from Professor Perón I hadn't made any connections to help me once I left school. "You're right. Lina's told me the same thing."

She smiled. "She and I would get along well."

"You probably would," I admitted. "There are so many options. How would you suggest I get more involved?"

"Good question." She paused, as if weighing the choices. "We have a grad student who got into town today and could probably use a local to show her the ropes. She had some visa issues because of her dual citizenship status, but she needs to get acclimated to campus so she can start her teaching assistantship tomorrow."

"I'd love to meet her."

"Great," she said. "She's filling out paperwork in the department office. Can you head down there now?"

"Why not?" I wasn't eager to sit alone in my dorm room waiting for Lina to call. This might not be the ideal way to spend an afternoon, but it was better than being lonely. Besides, I took comfort in knowing Lina would approve of me getting involved in something other than my classes.

❖

I walked through Stevenson Hall, pushing through the foot traffic in the congested corridor. A mix of frat boys with backpacks and the College Democrats' bake sale blocked my view of the Foreign Languages department. While I waited for a path to clear, I looked longingly at the study abroad map and pamphlets on the department bulletin board. I'd already memorized the program requirements and knew I wouldn't be eligible for another year, but I liked to have a visual reminder of what I was working toward. Not that I needed a map to visualize my goals. All I had to do was close my eyes to see Lina's figure, dark waves of hair blowing in the breeze, brown eyes filled with love, a bright smile that made my heartbeat quicken and my hands tremble with excitement. I could even hear the echo of her easy laughter and smell the faintest hint of her citrus scent. She felt close, even with an ocean between us.

I opened my eyes and tried to shake the visual from my mind, willing myself back to reality. The visions of the beach faded around Lina, the light shifted from golden sun to harsh fluorescent, institutional cold tile replaced the warm sand, and the translucent turquoise ocean transformed into a receptionist counter, but Lina remained planted in my vision. I blinked and shook my head again, but I didn't lose the sight of her standing a few feet in front of me. Maybe I needed to visit the University Counseling Center instead of the Foreign Languages department, because I clearly saw the woman of my dreams staring back at me.

The Lina I saw now wore jeans and a heavy jacket, not the summer clothes I always pictured her in. Her smile was every bit as bright and her eyes as captivating as I always imagined, but her hair was longer than I remembered and her skin not quite as sun-kissed. My heart thundered in my chest. This wasn't the Lina of Spanish summers, it was Lina in a Midwestern winter.

She was here.

We were in each other's arms before I could process anything further. Oblivious to our surroundings we clung to each other, our bodies pressed tightly together. Wrapped in her arms, each breath I took carried a mix of laughter and tears, my emotions too overwhelming to be fully expressed. I ran my hands over her hips, up her arms, still trying to convince myself she was really here. Her presence made me dizzy, but she held me so tightly I had no fear of falling.

"What're you…I mean, how did you…?" I laughed. "I love you."

"I love you too." She touched my face like she was doing

the same kind of reality check I was. I'd imagined this moment a million times over the past six months, but in my mind I'd always gone to her in Spain, and I'd perfectly planned what I wanted to say. Now, here in the middle of the office with a crowd of confused onlookers, all I could do was kiss her.

"*Dios*, I didn't get here fast enough." Señora Perón laughed behind us.

"You knew about this?" I asked, breaking the kiss but not looking away from Lina.

"*Sí*. It was hard to keep from sending you up here when I saw you staring sadly at *View of Toledo*, but if I had, Lina would never have finished her paperwork, and the last thing any of us need is for her to get deported." Señora Perón smiled at us both. "And we don't want either of you reported for indecent exposure, so why don't you move this reunion out of the office until you both have to be back for classes tomorrow."

I took Lina's hand and led her through the maze of people in the hall. "You're really staying here?"

"I've got my paperwork approved to study here for two years."

My heart pounded with the desire to bury myself in her embrace and never let go of her again, but my mind wouldn't let me believe anything so wonderful could be real. "I thought it wasn't about the paperwork."

"It's not. I finally found a good reason to try to make my dreams a reality."

"Oh yeah?" We left the building and walked out to the snow-covered quad, but I didn't feel the cold with her beside me.

"*Sí*. I found someone who wants to share the experience with me."

I stopped and turned to face her. "What about taking our own paths?"

"Our paths brought us together in Spain, and when you stopped trying to fight who you really were, you realized you belonged with me." She delivered the recap with one of those knee-weakening smiles. "When you left, I told myself I had a responsibility to my mom, to my job, and to my country, but the more I thought about your transformation, the more I realized I needed one of my own."

"I wouldn't change a single thing about you."

"You're sweet, but when I thought about all the walls I'd put up to protect myself and my career, I understood the only time I'd honestly followed my heart was during the last day and night I spent with you."

Tears stung my eyes but I blinked them away, unwilling to miss a second of this beautiful moment. She loved me. She belonged with me. The joy was almost too much to stand. I was completely lost in her. There would be time later to focus on the details. Right now I couldn't process anything beyond the perfection of being with her. "This is the last thing I expected to happen today."

"I hope it's a pleasant surprise," she said, nervousness creeping into her voice.

I took her face in my hands and pulled her so close only the space of a breath separated us. Then I kissed her, unhurried and unhindered, and she returned the kiss in kind. There were no more questions, no more fear of time or distance, only the peace of being exactly where we both needed to be.

"It's the best because you reminded me it's often the things we expect that disappoint us most, while the surprises in life are the most fulfilling."

About the Author

Rachel Spangler never set out to be an award-winning author. She was just so poor and so easily bored during her college years that she had to come up with creative ways to entertain herself, and her first novel, *Learning Curve*, was born out of one such attempt. She was sincerely surprised when it was accepted for publication and even more shocked when it won a Golden Crown Literary Award for Debut Author. She also won a Goldie for her second novel, *Trails Merge*. Since writing is more fun than a real job, and so much cheaper than therapy, Rachel continued to type away, leading to the publication of *The Long Way Home*, *LoveLife*, and *Spanish Heart*. She plans to continue writing as long as anyone, anywhere will keep reading.

Rachel and her partner, Susan, are raising their young son in western New York, where during the winter they all make the most of the lake effect snow on local ski slopes, a hobby that inspired her second novel, *Trails Merge*. In summer they love to travel and watch their beloved St. Louis Cardinals. Regardless of the season, Rachel always makes time for a good romance, whether she's reading it, writing it, or living it.

Visit Rachel online at www.RachelSpangler.com as well as on Facebook.

Books Available From Bold Strokes Books

Ladyfish by Andrea Bramhall. Finn's escape to the Florida Keys leads her straight into the arms of scuba diving instructor Oz as she fights for her freedom, their blossoming love…and her life! (978-1-60282-747-9)

Spanish Heart by Rachel Spangler. While on a mission to find herself in Spain, Ren Molson runs the risk of losing her heart to her tour guide, Lina Montero. (978-1-60282-748-6)

Love Match by Ali Vali. When Parker "Kong" King, the number one tennis player in the world, meets commercial pilot Captain Sydney Parish, sparks fly—but not from attraction. They have the summer to see if they have a love match. (978-1-60282-749-3)

One Touch by L.T. Marie. A romance writer and a travel agent come together at their high school reunion, only to find out that the memory of that one touch never fades. (978-1-60282-750-9)

Night Shadows: Queer Horror edited by Greg Herren and J.M. Redmann. Night Shadows features delightfully wicked stories by some of the biggest names in queer publishing. (978-1-60282-751-6)

Secret Societies by William Holden. An outcast hustler, his unlikely "mother," his faithless lovers, and his religious persecutors—all in 1726. (978-1-60282-752-3)

The Raid by Lee Lynch. Before Stonewall, having a drink with friends or your girl could mean jail. Would these women and men still have family, a job, a place to live after…The Raid. (978-1-60282-753-0)

The You Know Who Girls by Annameekee Hesik. As they begin freshman year, Abbey Brooks and her best friend, Kate, pinkie swear they'll keep away from the lesbians in Gila High, but Abbey already suspects she's one of those you-know-who girls herself and slowly learns who her true friends really are. (978-1-60282-754-7)

Wyatt: Doc Holliday's Account of an Intimate Friendship by Dale Chase. Erotica writer Dale Chase takes the remarkable friendship between Wyatt Earp, upright lawman, and Doc Holliday, Southern gentlemen turned gambler and killer, to an entirely new level: hot! (978-1-60282-755-4)

Month of Sundays by Yolanda Wallace. Love doesn't always happen overnight; sometimes it takes a month of Sundays. (978-1-60282-739-4)

Jacob's War by C.P. Rowlands. ATF Special Agent Allison Jacob's task force is in the middle of an all-out war, from the streets to the boardrooms of America. Small business owner Katie Blackburn is the latest victim who accidentally breaks it wide open, but she may break AJ's heart at the same time. (978-1-60282-740-0)

The Pyramid Waltz by Barbara Ann Wright. Princess Katya Nar Umbriel wants a perfect romance, but her Fiendish nature and duties to the crown mean she can never tell the truth—until she meets Starbride, a woman who gets to the heart of every secret, even if it will be the death of her. (978-1-60282-741-7)

The Secret of Othello by Sam Cameron. Florida teen detectives Steven and Denny risk their lives to search for a sunken NASA satellite-but under the waves, no one can hear you scream... (978-1-60282-742-4)

Andy Squared by Jennifer Lavoie. Andrew never thought anyone could come between him and his twin sister, Andrea...until Ryder rode into town. (978-1-60282-743-1)

Finding Bluefield by Elan Barnehama. Set in the backdrop of Virginia and New York and spanning the years 1960–1982, *Finding Bluefield* chronicles the lives of Nicky Stewart, Barbara Philips, and their son, Paul, as they struggle to define themselves as a family. (978-1-60282-744-8)

The Jetsetters by David-Matthew Barnes. As rock band the Jetsetters skyrocket from obscurity to superstardom, Justin Holt, a lonely barista, and Diego Delgado, the band's guitarist, fight with everything they have to stay together, despite the chaos and fame. (978-1-60282-745-5)

Strange Bedfellows by Rob Byrnes. Partners in life and crime, Grant Lambert and Chase LaMarca are hired to make a politician's compromising photo disappear, but what should be an easy job quickly spins out of control. (978-1-60282-746-2)

Dreaming of Her by Maggie Morton. Isa has begun to dream of the most amazing woman—a woman named Lilith with a gorgeous face, an amazing body, and the ability to turn Isa on like no other. But Lilith is just a dream...isn't she? (978-1-60282-847-6)

Speed Demons by Gun Brooke. When NASCAR star Evangeline Marshall returns to the race track after a close brush with death, will famous photographer Blythe Pierce document her triumph and reciprocate her love—or will they succumb to their respective demons and fail? (978-1-60282-678-6)

Summoning Shadows: A Rosso Lussuria Vampire Novel by Winter Pennington. The Rosso Lussuria vampires face enemies both old and new, and to prevail they must call on even more strange alliances, unite as a clan, and draw on every weapon within their reach—but with a clan of vampires, that's easier said than done. (978-1-60282-679-3)

Sometime Yesterday by Yvonne Heidt. When Natalie Chambers learns her Victorian house is haunted by a pair of lovers and a Dark Man, can she and her lover Van Easton solve the mystery that will set the ghosts free and banish the evil presence in the house? Or will they have to run to survive as well? (978-1-60282-680-9)

Into the Flames by Mel Bossa. In order to save one of his patients, psychiatrist Jamie Scarborough will have to confront his own monsters— including those he unknowingly helped create. (978-1-60282-681-6)

Coming Attractions: Author's Edition by Bobbi Marolt. For Helen Townsend, chasing turns to caring, and caring turns to loving, but will love take five steps back and turn to leaving? (978-1-60282-732-5)

OMGqueer, edited by Radclyffe and Katherine E. Lynch. Through stories imagined and told by youth across America, this anthology provides a snapshot of queerness at the dawn of the new millennium. (978-1-60282-682-3)

Oath of Honor by Radclyffe. A First Responders novel. First do no harm…First Physician of the United States Wes Masters discovers that being the president's doctor demands more than brains and personal sacrifice—especially when politics is the order of the day. (978-1-60282-671-7)

A Question of Ghosts by Cate Culpepper. Becca Healy hopes Dr. Joanne Call can help her learn if her mother really committed suicide—but she's not sure she can handle her mother's ghost, a decades-old mystery, and lusting after the difficult Dr. Call without some serious chocolate consumption. (978-1-60282-672-4)

The Night Off by Meghan O'Brien. When Emily Parker pays for a taboo role-playing fantasy encounter from the Xtreme Scenarios escort agency, she expects to surrender control—but never imagines losing her heart to dangerous butch Nat Swayne. (978-1-60282-673-1)

Sara by Greg Herren. A mysterious and beautiful new student at Southern Heights High School stirs things up when students start dying. (978-1-60282-674-8)

Fontana by Joshua Martino. Fame, obsession, and vengeance collide in a novel that asks: What if America's greatest hero was gay? (978-1-60282-675-5)

Lemon Reef by Robin Silverman. What would you risk for the memory of your first love? When Jenna Ross learns her high school love Del Soto died on Lemon Reef, she refuses to accept the medical examiner's report of a death from natural causes and risks everything to find the truth. (978-1-60282-676-2)

The Dirty Diner: Gay Erotica on the Menu, edited by Jerry L. Wheeler. Gay erotica set in restaurants, featuring food, sex, and men—could you really ask for anything more? (978-1-60282-677-9)